LOOPY

A Novel of Golf And Ireland

Dan Binchy

Thomas Dunne Books
St. Martin's Griffin ✵ New York

THOMAS DUNNE BOOKS.
An imprint of St. Martin's Press.

www.stmartins.com

Design by Phil Mazzone

Library of Congress Cataloging-in-Publication Data

Binchy, Dan.
    Loopy / Dan Binchy.
        p. cm.
    ISBN 0-312-24257-3 (hc)
    ISBN 0-312-35201-8 (pbk)
    EAN 978-0-312-35201-1
    1. Golfers—Fiction. 2. Young men—Fiction. 3. City and town life—
Fiction. 4. Ireland—Fiction. I. Title.

PR6052.I7726 L66 2005
823'.914—dc22   2004051433

First St. Martin's Griffin Edition: April 2006

10 9 8 7 6 5 4 3 2 1

PRAISE FOR THE WORKS OF DAN BINCHY

The Last Resort

"Even if he weren't my cousin, I would love this book!"

—Maeve Binchy

"An endearing and entertaining combination of warmth and wit."

—*Booklist*

"From hunt balls to whiskey stills, Binchy takes Luke and the reader to the heart of Erin in this warm and amusing mixture. Lots of wit, characters, and charm here."

—*Library Journal*

"Laugh-out-loud funny. The description of the decrepit golf course . . . is alone worth the price of the book."

—*The Houston Post*

The Neon Madonna

"Dan Binchy's first novel is terrifically funny. *The Neon Madonna* is a hilarious read."

—*The Washington Post Book World*

"A first-rate comic novel."

—*Kirkus Reviews*

"Binchy's first novel promises that the worldly Father Jerry could easily become the lead character of a series."

—*Booklist*

"Dan Binchy delivers a charming first novel."

—*Tampa Tribune-Times*

ALSO BY DAN BINCHY

The Neon Madonna

The Last Resort

Fireballs

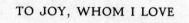

TO JOY, WHOM I LOVE

LOOPY

CHAPTER ONE

Set deep in a bay of shingle and rock, the village of Trabane stood tiny and unprotected from the elements. Even at the height of summer, out of a clear blue sky sudden rain squalls would send parents and children alike scampering for shelter in the sand dunes that protected the village from the mighty Atlantic Ocean. Even now a gale rattled the slates of the schoolhouse roof hard enough to disturb Larry Lynch from his daydreams at the back of the classroom.

Trabane Boys National School had been built in 1848, and apart from electricity and running water, little had changed since then. The gray walls of carved granite looked as forbidding now as they must have when the first scholars traipsed past them to take their places in one of the three classrooms separated only by thin wooden partitions. Larry had tilted his chair backward until it rested against one of these, making it easier to catnap and also to overhear what was going on in the adjoining classroom.

If this were not distraction enough, to his left a window looked out on the road, and if he craned his neck, he could just catch a glimpse of the flagpole. It stood outside the golf club, and a pennant stuck out from the pole, stiff as cardboard. The wind that stiffened it had started somewhere in mid-Atlantic and gathered strength until it struck the sand dunes. Across the road, the twin spindles of the goalposts bent gracefully against the howling gale. Drowsily he wondered if the training session would still go ahead despite the weather. It was going to be a waste of time in a wind like this.

The flag flying outside the golf club indicated that their weekend competitions were going ahead, whatever the weather. Suddenly his reverie was interrupted.

"What did I just say, Lynch?"

Larry turned pink with embarrassment. Patrick O'Hara was the vice principal of Trabane National School and someone not to be trifled with. Of late his moods had become more changeable. He had a temper to be feared and now Larry was about to bear the full brunt of it.

"I dunno, sir."

"*I dunno, sir.*" O'Hara's mimicry was spot-on. He had caught the boy's rural accent to perfection but with an added sting that boded ill for its owner. "How in the name of all that's holy do you expect to graduate if you keep on looking out the window and not listening to one bloody word I say?"

Larry sang dumb. Anything he might say would only make matters worse. As for going on to university, the thought never even crossed his mind. He prayed hard that O'Hara would not go on about the grand family he had come from and how he would have a lot to live up to. A siren buzzed. He had been saved by the bell.

"Right, off home with the lot of you." A pause, then, "Stay back, Lynch. I want a word with you."

Larry groaned inwardly. If he left now and ran all the way to the hurling field, he would just make the practice on time. The rest of the team had long since graduated from school, making him by far the youngest of fifteen players. Should the practice be canceled, he could still get in three hours of shelf-stacking before the supermarket closed on the stroke of six o'clock.

"Have you anything fixed for this afternoon?"

A bolt from the blue but far better than the dressing down he was expecting. He saw that O'Hara was now taking quick gulps from a soda bottle.

"There's training for the hurling team at three o'clock, sir. If they cancel it on account of the wind, I promised Mr. Norbert I'd stack his shelves till closing time."

"When's that?"

"Six o'clock, sir."

"Too late for me so, I'm afraid."

Larry waited for some explanation. When none came, he ventured, "Too late for what, sir, if you don't mind my asking?"

Suddenly O'Hara looked older. As he drained the bottle, he grimaced as if in pain before wiping his mouth with the back of his hand. "Nothing much. I just thought you might like to earn some money caddying for me rather than wasting your time and energy on that silly, brutal game."

"How do you mean, sir?"

"Hurling's as bad as ice hockey in America, worse if you ask me!" O'Hara muttered.

Larry was not going to get into an argument over the merits of his beloved game. Both of them knew that it had been the national game for centuries past. In ancient times warring tribes fought with clubs shaped like hurley sticks, but nowadays the warfare was better organized— teams of fifteen doing battle on a field the size of a football pitch. The players wore no protective padding, and helmets were optional. Larry declined to wear one because it gave him a headache. For now, he decided it was wiser to let O'Hara's unfair comment pass. Instead he observed quietly, "Well, at least, sir, it's played on solid ground, not ice."

O'Hara merely grunted, before mumbling as much to himself as to Larry, "Y'see, I need someone to carry my bag around the golf course these days. I find I can't quite manage the full eighteen holes on my own. No matter, there'll be other times."

He dismissed Larry with a tired wave of the hand toward the open door. On his way out, Larry stopped and turned back to face the teacher. O'Hara was unscrewing the top of another bottle of soda.

"Sir, I'd really like to carry your bag anytime. It's just that I'd given my word to Mr. Norbert that I'd practice taking seventies this afternoon. He said he'd pay me just the same as if I was stacking the shelves."

Larry had been immensely proud of this. The supermarket owner was not renowned for his generosity—quite the opposite. It showed how much Norbert thought of him as a hurler that he would actually pay him for striking a leather sliotair the size of a tennis ball between two posts seventy yards away. His speciality was the taking of frees. From seventy yards out, he could send the hard leather ball between those posts with an ease that belied his years. In a real match every strike that he converted was worth a point for his team. It was a rare skill that required constant practice.

This time O'Hara's grunt was followed by an unmistakable hiccup. "I declare to God the GAA's going professional at long last. Paying their players to practice, no less. Well, that beats the bloody band."

With that he put the bottle back in his battered attaché case and got to his feet with some difficulty. Larry knew that Lucozade was an energy drink more suited to athletes and sportsmen than frail and elderly schoolteachers. Still, O'Hara looked tired.

The wind had turned into a howling gale that was suddenly spitting out hailstones. They stung Larry's face as he leaned forward into the storm. Everyone he passed on his way to the hurling practice roundly cursed the weather. Norbert was waiting for him, snug in his car, and gazing out forlornly on a deserted pitch. He was a large man with what little hair he had carefully arranged in strands to cover a bald pate. Some of these broke free of their moorings and flapped in windblown disarray as Larry opened the car door. Oblivious to how ridiculous he looked, Norbert shouted to make himself heard above the gale.

"Get in. . . . Shitty weather for April, huh."

It was a statement, not a question, yet Larry thought it better to make some response as he settled into the soft leather seat.

"Sure is, Mr. Norbert. Is the practice off?"

"Is the pope a Catholic? You can be damn sure it is. You wouldn't put a dog out in that." He gestured at the hailstones ricocheting off the windscreen and forming an intricate pattern of white lace on the bonnet of the elderly BMW. Norbert started the car and switched on the wipers. "Still, a late spring is just what you want, am I right?"

Larry was mystified. "How do you mean?"

"What I mean is that 'twill give you a chance to sell the hay your father left behind him."

Larry nodded but didn't say anything. The hay was a family matter and had nothing to do with Norbert—or anyone else. There had not been a word from his father since he'd left without telling anyone but the family, and Larry hated him for that. His mother, Brona, was pale with worry, and she had warned him not to discuss his father with anyone. She said, and he agreed with her, that it was their own business and no one else's. When asked about his father, he said he had gone to England in search of work. It was something more and more men from the town were doing of late. It had started with the Creamery, now it was the Maltings that were laying off workers. Three more men were let go last month, and there were whisperings of still more jobs to be lost once the barley harvest was in and dried on the vast wooden floors of the Maltings.

To change the subject, Larry asked Norbert, "Do you still want me to fill the shelves for you this evening?"

"Yes, of course. You can look after the shop for an hour or so. I have deliveries to make in the van. Does your mother want anything? I'll be passing that way."

"I'd say she could use a cylinder of gas. Oh . . . and a loaf of bread, if you don't mind. Will I pay you for that now?"

"Don't bother. I'll take it out of your wages on Friday."

The big plastic sign read NORBERT'S SUPER STORE. Once a small, comfortable cinema, it had been transformed into a supermarket—if only in name. It had just three checkouts, and at least one of the cash registers was usually out of order. The trolleys, too, had seen better days and tended to lurch sideways in an alarming manner. The carpark at the rear of the store was too cramped, and in one corner a rusting incinerator smoldered day and night with burning rubbish. Norbert was as deaf to the complaints of his neighbors as he was to the awful smells coming from it. The public health inspector had warned Norbert that he could be prosecuted if the complaints persisted. Two Stand tickets for the County Final had removed any immediate threat of legal action, but the problem remained.

The shop was empty of customers as Larry pulled on the brown coat with SPAR embroidered over the left breast. He noticed that Maire was wearing a white nylon shop coat that was almost transparent over a very short skirt. Perched on a high stool behind a cash register and showing rather more leg than she needed to, she was checking through a sample basket of groceries. She paused with a finger raised dramatically before stabbing a key with venom.

"Oh, *shite*," her anguished cry greeted him just as he finished buttoning the shop coat. "I'll never get the hang of this shagging thing!" She turned to him in exasperation. "Do you know anything about these things?" She gestured helplessly at the keyboard.

He shook his head his head. "'Fraid not. Anyway, I'm no good at sums."

"That's the whole point, you eejit. You don't have to be any good at sums. All you do is push the stuff across this little window here and it automatically scans in the price. Except that it shaggin' well isn't doing it now for some reason."

He looked closely at the scanner that he had seen Norbert operate with such ease. He told himself that if someone like Norbert could work it, it had to be pretty straightforward.

"Try wiping the window thing. It looks as if something spilled on it."

She tried—and it worked.

"Do you know what you are, Larry Lynch? You're a genius, a shaggin' genius. I thought I'd never get the bloody thing to work, and old Norbert would be leaning over me, breathing down my neck, and saying, 'Maire dear, why don't you try pressing this little button here?' To be fair, he never laid a hand on me, though I don't like the way he looks at me sometimes."

Larry thought to himself that Norbert was going to have plenty to look at when he got back. That miniskirt was almost up to her backside.

"Hard to blame him in a way. You've smashing legs!"

Maire did her best to sound demure, though she couldn't quite bring it off. "Glad you like them. They'll be at the dance on Sunday night, if you're interested."

"You mean the ceili?"

"Will I see you there, so?"

She had no way of knowing that Larry would have preferred to be anywhere else on earth. There was to be no escape, however, as the ceili was run by the GAA on the night of the match between Trabane and their longtime rivals, Lisbeg. Norbert was in charge, and the posters that plastered every telephone pole and shop window in the village promised that both teams would attend—a supposed magnet to all the young and not-so-young girls for miles around. Larry feared the dancing much more than the match itself. The flailing hurleys of Lisbeg worried him less than parading his dismal dancing skills before the likes of Maire and her friends.

He tried to put a brave face on it. "Of course you'll see me there. I wouldn't miss it for the world. I'm not much of a dancer, though."

"A dance isn't all about dancing, y'know!" she replied lightly, looking him straight in the eye as if daring him to contradict her, as the buzzer on the door announced the arrival of a customer. A middle-aged man in his fifties whom Larry recognized as the new owner of The Old Rectory was shrugging hailstones off his raincoat as he pushed through the glass door. Since the Protestant church had closed down, the vicar's residence had remained empty. Windows were broken and slates were missing from the roof. The once-manicured lawns were now kept in check only by the grazing of sheep, and the shrubbery had long since run riot. The avenue was virtually impassable with the rhododendrons on either side now almost meeting across the pot-holed tarmacadam. Its decline mirrored that of the town of Trabane.

Even good houses were hard to sell. The Creamery had laid off eighteen workers with rumors of more job losses to follow unless business picked up. With the Maltings shedding jobs at the end of every month and fewer tourists around than last year, even Foley's, the only pub in the village, was rumored to be in trouble. More empty wage packets made for fewer drinkers. All the more surprising then that a small, dapper Englishman had chosen to make Trabane his home. The Old Rectory had been on the market for ages when Edward Linhurst had bought it, and he had worked miracles on the place in quick time. Even the most skeptical could not fail to be impressed as what had once been little more than a derelict ruin quickly blossomed into the finest property for miles around. Even Seamus Norbert, who had hoped to pick it up for next to nothing if only he could think of something profitable to do with it, could not hide his admiration. He had said to Larry as they'd passed it on the delivery run around the outskirts of Trabane, "What Linhurst has done with that house is nothing short of a miracle, though what brought him to a place like Trabane is a mystery. The bloody man must have money to burn, that's all I can say." With a sigh, the supermarketeer added, as much to himself as to Larry, "I wish to God he'd push some of it my way."

Now Edward Linhurst appeared to be about to do just that. He was deep in conversation with Maire, and she appeared to be getting flustered for some reason. Larry could not help overhearing snatches of the exchange.

"Sorry, sir, but the boss is out just at the moment. I'll have to ask Larry, he might know if we have it."

A moment later he was summoned. "Larry, come here will'ya. This gentleman is looking for his relish. Do you know anything about it?"

Larry thought for a moment. The only relish he knew of was from Yorkshire. He plucked a bottle of YR sauce off a nearby shelf and offered it to Linhurst. "Is that what you wanted, sir?"

Linhurst pursed his lips to hide his amusement. To laugh would have been unforgivable. He should have realized that Patum Peperium, better known as Gentlemen's Relish, might not feature on Norbert's shelves. Nevertheless he was very partial to it smeared across his morning toast. The tartness of anchovy paste with its hint of lemon was just the thing to kick-start his day. That morning he had used up the last of the jars he had brought from London. In what now seemed a moment of madness, he had resolved to seek it out in Norbert's supermarket. His predicament now was how to decline the bottle of YR, a sauce he particularly loathed, without offending either the girl on the checkout or the gangly youth in the long brown coat. It must have been at least forty years since he had seen a "shop" coat like that.

"Er, no, thank you very much. That's not quite what I wanted. Could I have an *Irish Times* instead?"

As he was leaving, he turned back to the girl. "Oops, I nearly forgot. I have to get cigarettes for my daughter. Trouble is, I don't smoke, but I vaguely remember what the packet looks like. It's white with a small, red square. Does that make any sense?"

Here Maire was on firmer ground. "Sounds like Silk Cut to me. Silk Cut Red, in fact."

She plucked a packet from the shelf above the cash register. Norbert believed in keeping cigarettes well away from shoplifters. Maire inquired politely, "Do you think her packet looked like that?"

Linhurst hesitated, then murmured uncertainly, "Ye-e-s, I think so. To be honest, they all look pretty much the same to me, but I think those are the ones."

"One packet, then?" Maire was anxious to resume honing her checkout skills before Norbert returned.

"Better make it a carton. Actually, make it two cartons, if you don't mind."

He paid by a platinum Visa card, the first one Maire had seen.

Foley's Bar was next door to The Trabane Malting Company. Both had opened their doors within a month of each other over a hundred years ago, and neither had changed much since. The pub was lucky in that it had a captive market, being the only one in the village, whereas the Maltings had to compete in a wider market. This it had managed to do until a few years back, when the demand by the distillers of Irish whiskey for malted barley dropped off noticeably. So noticeably in fact that all further investment by the owners ceased, and jobs were being shed regularly. First the seasonal workers were let go, then last year the first of the full-time employees were dropped from the payroll.

The drinkers at the counter were discussing this when O'Hara, the schoolteacher, intervened.

"Sure, if the English hadn't had to pay back all that money to America after the last war, things might be different round here."

His listeners looked mystified but unimpressed. No one questioned O'Hara's assertion, however, because of his famous short temper.

After another long silence, O'Hara held up his glass of whiskey and tapped it knowingly. "All because of this, lads, all because of this innocent drop of malt!"

The others remained silent as the grave, taking sips from their creamy pints of Guinness as they pondered this. After what seemed like an eternity, one of them was moved to ask, "How so?"

"They'd no money to pay America, y'see, so they sent them gallons and gallons of their very best Scotch whiskys, that's how so!"

This was greeted by another, longer silence. No one wanted to look a fool in front of his fellow drinkers, but eventually curiosity overcame one of them.

"What's that got to do with the Maltings going belly-up? Sure, all that war-repayments stuff was years ago, wasn't it?"

O'Hara nodded as if in agreement. "It was a while back, sure enough, but with all that Scotch floating around America, the Yanks got a liking for it and that put the kibosh on our own Irish whiskey." He shook his head sorrowfully at the thought of it, but some were yet to be convinced.

"How come it took so long?"

O'Hara pricked up his ears—as if he had seen one of his pupils giggling at the back of the classroom. It sounded as if his wisdom was being doubted.

"Jaysus," he exploded in exasperation, "I'm not saying America woke up one bloody morning and said, 'Right, no more Irish whiskey!' No, nothing like that. Much more gradual. Scotch became *trendy*, y'see. The youngsters found it smoother to drink than this stuff."

Again he tapped his glass as if to emphasize his point. Then he drained it in one mighty gulp, without flinching. Smacking his lips in satisfaction, he added, "And where America leads, the rest of the bloody world follows. Especially where being trendy and up-to-date is concerned. You only have to think of hamburgers and Coca bloody Cola and you'll get what I mean. It's the same with Scotch. Blander with much less flavor than this stuff." He glared at his empty glass before signaling for another and ended, "But that's what they want nowadays. Smooth and safe, not sharp and strong like"—he paused dramatically before adding a tiny amount of water to the golden double measure of Irish whiskey and taking a swallow from it that reduced its level by more than half—"like this. I'll tell you this and I'll tell you no more, there's more nature in one ball of malt like this one than there's in a hogshead of the best bloody stuff that Scotland ever made!"

The bar sank into an impressed silence, wondering at the fickleness of their fellow drinkers worldwide and its disastrous effect on the huge but dilapidated stone building next door that was The Trabane Malting Company. Then the talk turned to Sean Lynch and his sudden departure for England. This was a topic not just for the regulars at Foley's Bar but for many of the townspeople. They wondered how the Lynch family were getting along without Sean. Did the family talk about him a lot—or not at all? Did Brona and the children long for the day when he would return or were they glad to see the back of him? Most agreed that the family was the better for his leaving.

The truth was that Brona had asked herself day and night since Sean had left how she might react if he ever did come back. After the first shock of his leaving, she had gradually come to where she secretly prayed that he would stay away forever. The family was getting along far better without him. There were no more explosions of rage. No more doors slamming or tears shed by the young ones as they were hustled out of harm's way. While Sean had never actually hit her, his arm had been raised to do so more than once. Her son was working and the girls were doing better at school. She was starting to go out more, meeting friends she hadn't seen in ages. Of course, as in any small community, some whispered behind their hands that Brona Lynch couldn't hold on to her husband. But for every one of them, ten more knew that she was well rid of him.

Father Spillane had been a great help: "God's will, Brona. Maybe

Sean will make a better fit of things across the water. That's often the way of things, you know. A change of scenery might do him the power of good. In the meantime, aren't you all getting along fine?"

No recriminations, no talk of a woman's place being in the home or a wife being subject to her husband, as some of the older clergy might have told her. Instead he encouraged her to play a more active part in the community now that she was free to do so. For the first time since she had walked down the aisle with Sean Lynch, she had a life of her own. While she wondered to herself, *Would I give all this up if he came back?*

Sean also wondered if he should return to Trabane as he trudged the streets of Birmingham in search of a job, any job that would pay enough for him to send something, however meager, back home to his wife.

B rona drew back the curtain and looked out into the yard to see who was blowing the horn. Hailstones were bouncing off the cobblestones and the hens had taken shelter inside the open door of the barn. She hoped they wouldn't lay among the bales of hay that filled the barn. It would take the children half the day to find the eggs if they did.

Brona would have recognized the white van even without NORBERT'S SUPER STORE—FOR QUALITY AND VALUE painted on its side. She waved at the face behind the windscreen wipers to signal him to come in. Norbert climbed out of the van with obvious reluctance and hunched his shoulders against the driving hail. Instead of making straight for the door of the farmhouse, he went around to the back of the van and lifted out a bright yellow gas cylinder. Looped over his elbow was a plastic shopping bag. Before opening the front door, Brona had time to reflect yet again that as his was the only supermarket for miles around, the van's sign's claim was difficult to refute. Yet whenever she shopped in the city, everything seemed to be much less than what Norbert charged. She told herself to be fair as she watched Norbert putting down the cylinder with a gasp of relief. After all, city stores did not deliver to the back of beyond, much less give employment to her eldest son in bad times like these.

"Will it be all right there, missus, or will I connect it up for you? I've a loaf of bread in the bag. Larry said he thought you might want it."

"Great, the gas is fine where it is, Seamus. Would you like a cup of tea in your hand? I know you're in a hurry," she lied easily, "Larry tells me you are run off your feet."

"The boy's right. I have hardly time to draw a breath. Still and all, 'twould be worse if I was idle, I suppose. There's enough of them idle around the town as it is."

He might have expounded further on the virtues of honest toil had not Brona forestalled him, "What do I owe you, Seamus?"

"Nothing, missus. Not a red cent. Larry said to take it out of his wages at the end of the week. You have a grand lad in him and no mistake. I only wish to God he'd pack in the school and come to work for me full-time. I'd give him all the time off he wants for the hurling. If we had a few more like him, we'd beat those Lisbeg shaggers out the gate. We might even win the county championship!"

This topic she was not keen to discuss. Only last week Pat O'Hara had taken the trouble to drive out the four miles to her farmhouse when he knew Larry would safely be out of the way stacking shelves in the supermarket. O'Hara's mission had been to persuade her to keep Larry on at school until he had graduated: "With that piece of paper in his pocket, there'll be no stopping him!"

She hadn't the heart to tell the schoolteacher that it was all she could do to keep Larry at school until the end of this term. Graduation was completely out of the question now that her husband had taken the boat for England—leaving a mountain of debt and four children behind him.

She had been alarmed that the schoolteacher had reeked of whiskey so early in the afternoon, something the mints he sucked on failed to hide. Having extracted a half-promise from her that she would at least talk to Larry about it, he left. He did not, she noticed, make any reference to her absent husband. Now here was Seamus Norbert trying his level best to get Larry to quit school in favor of hurling and a job. It might not be much of a job that he was offering, but anything was worth considering at a time when the talk was of little but recession and hard times.

After much agonizing, Brona had decided that she would leave it up to Larry himself to decide. She had more than enough to do in running the farm and looking after the young ones without having to decide the future of her eldest child. Though still a month short of seventeen years old, Larry had a good head on his shoulders. And a brave heart, too. She smiled as she remembered how he had stood up for her when her husband had ranted and roared about there being no food in the house. Where others might have cowered with fright, Larry had stood up to him with clenched fists: "If you gave Ma half of what you give to the bookies every day of the week, we'd have all the food we could eat."

Of course the boy was right, but Sean, she supposed halfheartedly, had done his best. Backing horses was the only luxury he allowed himself, even if it was an increasingly expensive one since they had let him go at the Creamery. He had tried to get work around Trabane but without success. The work just wasn't there for anyone. It wasn't until after he had left that she'd found out he had borrowed money from his friends. The last straw was the letter out of the blue from Leo Martin, the bank manager. It had arrived that very morning and she had had to sit down after reading it. Little wonder then that she found hurling a safer topic than Larry's future to discuss with Norbert, who showed no signs of leaving despite his claims to be run off his feet. She tried to sound concerned as she asked, "Will they beat Lisbeg this time?"

"I certainly hope so. Lisbeg have beaten us for the past three years, though we should have won it out last year. Only for that blind bastard of a referee—in pardon to you, missus—sending two of our best men off in the first half, we'd have beaten them fair and square."

"It's being played in Lisbeg this year, isn't it?"

"Indeed it is and that's no help, I can tell you. Their supporters are the biggest bunch of savages I've ever laid eyes on. I'd say half of them would eat their young without salt if they got the chance. How they managed to steal that factory from under our noses is something I will never understand till the day I die."

Brona laughed ruefully. A call center with sixty jobs that would handle subscription lists and renewals for several international magazines had been promised to Trabane before the last election, but it had gone to Lisbeg in the heel of the hunt. As for Norbert, he was a fanatic where the GAA and hurling were concerned and could see no further than Trabane Gaels. Brona regarded the Gaelic Athletic Association as just another sporting organization, neither better nor worse than the others, and hurling just a game the same as any other. Not that she would speak such heresy to someone like Norbert. Instead she chided him ever so gently, "Are you forgetting that my husband comes from Lisbeg?"

Norbert could have kicked himself for the oversight. Of course Sean Lynch was born and reared in Lisbeg. That could explain a lot, he decided. Sean, the useless bastard, would bet his last shilling on two flies going up a wall, and look where it had got him.

"Indeed I was, missus. I was forgetting he was born and bred in Lisbeg." A pause, then: "Any word from him yet?"

Brona didn't answer, and Norbert, fearing that he had overstepped himself, hurriedly changed the subject.

"That's a fine lot of hay you have outside in the barn. Should be worth a few bob, I'd say." Hurrying across the cobblestones from his van to the farmhouse, he had seen the hay barn full of bales. They could be worth a lot if this unseasonable weather continued. Farmers who had expected to leave their cattle out on grass by the end of March were still feeding them dwindling winter fodder indoors. Bales of hay that were selling for less than a pound before Christmas were now fetching nearly four pounds each—if they could be got. The

Lynchs might yet sort out their money problems if only they could get rid of what was stacked in the barn before the end of the month.

Brona shook her dead distractedly. "You're right, I suppose. But it's only worth something if we can get rid of it. Someone called a few days ago and offered me two pounds a bale for the lot of it. I refused him. Do you think I was right or wrong?"

"You were dead right. It's worth twice that at the very least. Delivered, of course."

"That's the trouble, you see. We've no one to deliver it. Larry's too young yet to take the tractor out on the road, and it would cost a fortune to hire a lorry, never mind the driver and a helper."

They both lapsed into silence. By prolonging it, Brona hoped that it might encourage him to leave. Sure enough, after a minute or two Norbert shifted uneasily from one foot to another before announcing that he must be going. His parting words were "Good luck with the hay. If there's anyone with a lorry and driver going cheap, I'll let you know. Try to persuade that son of yours to pack in the school, he's only wasting his time at the books."

After he'd accelerated briskly out of the yard and was gone, Brona made herself a fresh pot of tea and took the letter from the bank down off the mantelpiece. It did not improve with a second reading.

Class was over for another day and Larry was putting his books back in his schoolbag when O'Hara crooked a finger at him. He walked up to the schoolteacher's desk as the rest of the class disappeared, pushing and shoving each other, out the door.

"I'm asking you again, do you want to caddy for me or not?"

Larry wanted to say no. He couldn't care less about golf and the kind of people who played it. Anytime he passed by the course, it was dotted with small groups dressed up like eejits who dug holes in the short grass as they tried to hit a small white ball. It seemed a pointless game even for those with nothing better to do. However, Pat O'Hara knew that the supermarket closed for a half day on Thursdays, so Larry could not use that as an excuse. The money, however small, he reflected, would be welcome.

"Of course I do, Mr. O'Hara. Whenever you say."

The teacher put away the Lucozade bottle and dabbed at his lips with the corner of a spotted handkerchief before answering.

"I have a game arranged in half an hour. I'll pay you two pounds to carry my bag. On the way round, I'll tell you what to do, but the main thing is to watch where my ball goes and mark where it lands. The other thing is to shut up. Golfers are easily upset, and talking or standing too near them while they are trying to play a shot is a hanging offense. Now put your schoolbag in the car—I'll drop you home after we're finished."

They drove past the large sign that read TRABANE GOLF CLUB— VISITORS WELCOME and down the short drive that led to the parking lot at the back of the clubhouse. This was a long, rambling building in need of a fresh coat of paint. Larry had never been inside the clubhouse before. Sometimes he would sneak onto the course to look for golf balls as the sun went down. He was usually chased off by the greenkeeper, who did not welcome competition in selling used balls to golfers too cheap to pay for new ones.

The changing room was worlds apart from the corrugated-iron lean-to used by the Trabane Gaels. It had a carpet, wall-to-wall clothes lockers, and hot showers with individual cubicles. The hurlers had to make do with a communal outdoor water trough to wash off the mud.

O'Hara, having changed into a pair of shoes with spiked soles, opened a wooden locker with his name on it and took out a bag of clubs. He hung his jacket on a hook beside the locker, pulled a heavy pullover over his head, and a had quick pee in the nearby toilet before announcing, "We're about ready. The priest wasn't sure if he could make it. We'll give him five minutes more, and if he doesn't show up, we'll head off on our own."

They went out to the first tee, where O'Hara embarked on a series of loosening-up exercises. Larry had difficulty in keeping a straight face at the ridiculous contortions of someone who had ten minutes earlier been expounding on the theorems of Euclid. O'Hara abandoned his gyrations in favor of swishing a golf club at a daisy in much the same way as Larry swung a hurley stick. The way the hands gripped the club looked the same to Larry even if the actual swing was different, being much slower and, in O'Hara's case, more labored. Hitting the ball with a hurley came naturally to Larry, but the teacher seemed to be putting as much concentration into his practice swing as he did in solving a theorem on the blackboard.

When the priest failed to appear, they set off on their own. O'Hara stood poised over the ball for what seemed an eternity. Suddenly, without warning, he unleashed a sudden, vicious swipe at the tiny white sphere perched daintily on a small wooden peg, as if hoping to catch it unawares.

"Did you see that?"

Larry nodded, though he didn't think much of what he had seen. Thus far golf seemed to consist of complicated gyrations that resulted in sending a small white ball to God knows where.

"What I mean is, did you see where it *landed*?"

O'Hara's face was still flushed with the effort as Larry, taken aback by the sharpness of the questioning, could only stammer, "I—I—I think it went over there."

He pointed toward a sand dune to the left of a long green pathway ending at a distant flag fluttering in the breeze. Looping the strap of the bag over his shoulder, he was surprised at its heaviness. He set off at a trot, keeping his eye glued on the spot where the ball had disappeared into the side of the sand dune. It was easier to find than he had imagined. As O'Hara was still some distance away, he picked it out of the thick grass and waved it above his head.

"Here it is, sir. I found it!"

As he struggled up the steep incline, O'Hara complained, "I should have warned you before we started. You see, you're not supposed to move the ball. In future, just find the bloody thing, but don't touch it."

This did not make sense. "How am I to know if it's your ball so? Couldn't it be someone else's?"

By now O'Hara had joined him on the flank of the sand dune, but he was much too breathless to reply there and then. When he eventually got his breath back, a note of exasperation was in his voice.

"By any chance, did you see what kind of golf ball I was playing?"

Larry shook his head. He felt that to answer "small and white" would only make matters worse.

"I was playing a Dunlop Maxfli. I suppose you didn't get its number either?"

This time Larry merely shrugged his shoulders. He had expected praise for finding O'Hara's ball in the long dune grass, instead of which he was getting a lecture.

"Well, luckily I did! It was a number two. So if that ball you found is a Maxfli number two, we'll put it back where it was and we can carry on. Always, of course, assuming I can dig the damn thing out of that grass." Only the top half of the ball was visible. O'Hara moved it with his index finger as gently as if it were a live grenade until he could identify it properly. Then he eased it back to its original position, deep in the grass. It was obvious, even to Larry, he had not given himself any advantage whatsoever.

"Good man yourself! That's my ball all right. Now all I have to do is to hit it onto the green."

O'Hara selected a weird-looking club from the bag and made several practice swishes before drawing a mighty, slashing blow on the partially hidden ball. It flew upward and landed about halfway to the green. O'Hara seemed pleased, so Larry risked a "Good shot, sir."

"Yes, it was, wasn't it? Didn't really think I'd get it out of there so cleanly. Now all I have to do is to pop it up onto the green and sink the putt."

The way he said it made it sound as if doing so would be the easiest thing in the world. It proved to be nothing of the sort. The next shot would indeed have landed on the green had it not taken a sharp deflection off a small mound and skidded sideways into a deep bunker. Larry could not be certain, but he thought he heard a strangled expletive of impressive obscenity. O'Hara selected a different club from the bag and descended into the deep, sand-filled hole beside the green. There followed a lot of scuffling about in the sand before the ball climbed high in the air and landed on the green. After some time it was joined there by a furious O'Hara.

"That bunker is a bloody disgrace. Full of pebbles. A man could spend the rest of his life down there trying to get out of it. I won't be long in giving the groundsman a piece of my mind. Give me the putter like a good man."

Larry knew about putters. It was the shortest club in the bag with a face as flat and as smooth as that of a hurley stick. He plucked it from the bag and handed it to O'Hara, who took three strokes with it before the ball finally disappeared into the hole. As they walked off the green and made for the next tee, O'Hara explained, "I'll give myself a seven there and that's being kind. If I hadn't hit it off the fairway, I would have probably made a four, and that is the par for that hole. Does any of this make any sense to you?"

Larry shook his head and grinned. "Not really, sir."

"Fair enough, I'm probably making the whole business of golf sound too complicated. It's not that bad, once you know the basics. A bit like geometry and Mr. Euclid, eh?"

Again Larry forced a grin. As far as he was concerned, geometry and golf were much the same. One was as boring and complicated as the other. O'Hara was speaking again.

"The next hole is a wide-open one. Why don't you try to play a bit. Might help you understand why I play this game. Anyway, there's no one around to see you. Normally you have to be a member, but who is to know?"

O'Hara selected a wooden club and smacked the ball down the fairway. Then he handed the same club to Larry and teed a ball up on a wooden peg, saying, "Now try to hit it like I did."

Larry missed it completely. He was about to launch another furious attack on the tiny white ball when O'Hara intervened.

"Hold it right there a second, young man. Grip the club as if you're shaking hands with it, then give it the same hit as if you were using a hurley. Keep your head still and don't look up after you've hit the bloody ball. And for God's sake, swing *easy*!"

Larry did as he was told. There was a solid click as club met ball. Remembering not to look up, he had no idea where the ball had gone. O'Hara was watching its progress with amazement. He uttered three words Larry had never heard him use before.

"Jaysus Christ Almighty!"

CHAPTER TWO

The weather seemed to change from minute to minute on the winding road to Lisbeg. A giant patchwork quilt stretched out before them toward the distant hills, its tiny green squares stitched together with gray stone walls. On the other side of the road lay the ocean, slate gray today with white sea horses prancing across its foam-flecked waves.

One moment the wind would chase away the clouds, sending their giant shadows scurrying across the landscape only to drown in the vast Atlantic. The waves trapped shards of light, causing their crests to sparkle like a scattering of diamonds in the afternoon sun. The next moment a dark thundercloud, shot through with rain and hail, loomed overhead, painting land and sea a dull, battleship gray.

Now the hailstones beat a tattoo on the roof, and the lone wiper struggled to keep the windscreen clear, as the driver, Mick Corkery, slowed his bus down outside Lisbeg.

"There it is, Mick," growled Seamus Norbert, "plain as the nose on your face!"

A billboard advertising the new call center with its promise of sixty new jobs for Lisbeg stood proudly in the middle of a green field.

"Not much doing there yet."

"That's not the point, Mick." Norbert shook his head furiously as he explained patiently, as if to a backward child, "That call center was as good as promised to Trabane last year and no more about it!"

A voice from the back of the bus interrupted, "I heard Lisbeg gave them the site for nothing and that's what clinched it."

Norbert shrugged his shoulders and abruptly changed the subject. Now his voice rose and strengthened as he got up from his seat in the front and turned around to address the Trabane team and substitutes seated behind him.

"Now, men, we all know why we're here. I want every single one of you to go out on that pitch and play your heart out. There is not one of you here that needs reminding Lisbeg Rovers have got the better of us for the past few years. Okay, so we were robbed by that blind bastard of a referee last year, just as we were robbed of that call center we have just passed. What's past is past and there's damn all we can do about it. But the game today is the most important one any of you have ever played up to this. You're playing not just for the honor and glory of Trabane Gaels." A ragged cheer from somewhere near the back was silenced by Norbert's scowl. "It's going to take more than a few shouts to beat the Rovers on their home ground. We need to come out fighting and be prepared to spill every drop of blood in our bodies so that we can bring the cup back to Trabane."

The bus slowed to make the turn into the hurling pitch. The slender goalposts at either end of the muddy pitch swayed in the gale as Larry retied the laces of his boots. The team had already changed before they got on the bus in Trabane. The last time they had played in Lisbeg, during the short walk from the dilapidated changing rooms to the pitch, they had been pelted with not merely abuse but assorted missiles. Their center forward was bleeding from a cut on the side of his head even before the game began, the result of a well-aimed coin.

This time the bus, on Norbert's instructions, had driven almost onto the pitch so that his team did not have to run the gauntlet of Lisbeg supporters. Just before he left his seat, Larry crossed himself, then ran out onto the pitch to a mixture of cheers and catcalls.

Though the hail that had peppered the bus earlier on had stopped, an icy wind cut through players and spectators alike. It was a hard-fought battle, frequently interrupted by stoppages for injuries. The Lisbeg team was bigger, which gave them an advantage of four points when the whistle blew to end the first half. This deficit seemed not to trouble Norbert as he urged his team to stick to their game plan.

"Keep on playing the ball out to the wings every chance you get. That way you'll run the legs off their backs. Most of 'em are too big to stand the pace in the mud right to the end. Mark my words, they'll run out of steam very soon, and that's when ye'll get the better of them."

For once, Norbert had read the game correctly. The Lisbeg team started to flag noticeably in the last quarter as the hail slanted across the pitch, pricking exposed flesh like steel knitting needles. As they tired, some of the Lisbeg players resorted to fouling their opposite number in an effort to stop the lighter and faster Trabane team from passing them with the ball. Larry counted himself lucky to avoid serious injury from the flailing hurleys and crunching shoulder charges that became ever more frequent as the final whistle approached.

Over the noise of the wind screaming in off the Atlantic, Larry heard the shrill blast of the referee's whistle. First he thought it was to indicate that the game was over, but instead it signaled a seventy in the dying seconds of the roughest, dirtiest match of his young life. Now, all of a sudden, the outcome of Lisbeg Rovers versus Trabane Gaels depended on him alone. With the scores level, his arms and legs were aching from the pounding he had got all through the match from his opposite number, a stocky sheep farmer almost twice his age. Seamus Norbert was rushing backward and forward along the sideline, screeching like a dervish. His cap had blown off his head, again throwing his strands of hair into total disarray.

A mocking voice from deep within the Lisbeg crowd screamed,

"For Jaysus' sakes, will ya take a look at baldy running over to his pet boy to tell him what to do!"

Larry wasn't sure what this "pet boy" thing meant, but instinctively he didn't like it. He had little time to brood on it, however, for Norbert was screaming in his ear, "There's nothing left on the clock. The ref'll blow full time after you've hit. Go for the point and be sure to aim to the left a bit to allow for the wind. We're depending on you!"

As Larry placed the ball on a tuft of grass for a cleaner contact between it and the hurley stick, he tried hard to ignore the wind and rain. He knew he must be positive and focus instead on the hours of practice he had put in, often in weather as bad as this, for just this moment. Plucking a sodden leather ball off the wet ground with a hurley, flicking it upward as though tossing a pancake before striking it in midair, was difficult enough. In taking the free there would normally have been two options. He could aim to drop the sliotair in front of the Lisbeg goalmouth and hope that one of the Trabane forwards would redirect it past the goalkeeper and into the net for a goal and three precious points. This the forwards had signally failed to do all afternoon, hence Norbert's insistence that he go for the winning point with only seconds left. But in this weather it was a tall order. Even when dry, a leather sliotair could not always be relied on to fly straight and true. Having been battered and scuffed for the entire match, and now sodden and slippery as a bar of soap, it would require a superhuman effort and not a little good fortune to send it between those distant posts, barely visible through the driving rain.

The referee, out of breath like the players, was standing close by. "Take it quick, young fella. I'm blowing time in twenty seconds."

Larry readjusted the sliotair on the tuft of grass to make it sit up a fraction more off the muddy ground. He paused and sucked air deep into his lungs as he took dead aim at the red mark on the cross bar, midway between the posts now bending in the vicious crosswind. Trying to keep his head still, he stooped to pick up the ball with the hurley, then tapping it upward much as a tennis player might toss up a

service ball, he swung the hurley back over his shoulder in a slow, looping arc. At the top of his swing, he paused for a fraction of a second
before pulling it downward with both hands and allowing his wrists to
flick the hurley at the dropping ball in a blur of speed. The sound of
polished ash meeting damp leather echoed around the ground as the
sliotair arched skyward. It seemed to hang in the wind for an eternity,
pinned against the gray overcast by the anxious gaze of players and
spectators alike. Larry was confident that he had hit it hard enough,
but had he allowed enough for the wind?

Two white-coated umpires stationed behind the posts watched
closely as the sliotair drifted erratically in the wind far above their
heads. One raised a flag to indicate that the ball had passed between
the posts and that Trabane Gaels had won the match by a single point.
The other hesitated, then, as if in response to the barrage of abuse
and catcalls coming from the Lisbeg section of the crowd, waved his
flag parallel to the ground. This signaled that the ball had gone wide of
its mark.

The referee had to decide now, but before he could, all hell broke
loose. Norbert, marooned on the wrong side of field and separated
from the Trabane supporters by the width of the pitch, was set upon
and flung to the ground. As Larry rushed to his aid, he was felled by a
vicious, slashing blow to the thigh from the hurley of the sheep
farmer. Larry fell instantly, and the last thing he remembered before
losing consciousness was the referee, ignoring the protests of both
camps, signaling that the match had been abandoned with only seconds left on the clock before the final whistle.

The decision pleased no one, yet it averted an almost certain riot.
Tempers eventually cooled as the crowds made their way out onto the
road. Norbert got back to his feet and called for a water bottle—which
he emptied over Larry's head and neck. When Larry came to, Norbert
asked him how he felt.

"I think my leg is broke."

He was lifted gingerly into the back of someone's car and rushed to the local doctor. He examined the injured, thought nothing was broken, but made an appointment to have it x-rayed the following Wednesday just in case. He gave Larry a painkilling injection, strapped up the thigh, and told him to rest it as much as possible before escorting him to the door of Corkery's bus. Norbert paid the doctor, then helped Larry along the narrow aisle to the seat at the very back. It was the only seat long enough for him to lie down on, as if in bed.

The players' disappointment was almost as pervasive as the smell of damp, sweating bodies. Their hurried departure from the pitch meant that they had not changed out of their wet playing gear.

"The bloody ball was between the posts for sure and certain," Norbert assured his charges, now muddied, bruised, and bristling with resentment. As the steam rose from them, forcing the driver to clear the mist from inside the windscreen with the sleeve of his coat, whispered plans were being made to give the Lisbeg players a warm reception at the ceili.

"We'll appeal to the County Board of the GAA, of course!" Then, turning to Larry, huddled in the seat next to him, Norbert added in a voice so low that no one else could hear, "For all the good 'twill do us! Now, listen to me, young man, no matter what that nurse said, rest or no shagging rest, you had better turn up for the ceili tonight. I promised that the teams would be there, and Seamus Norbert is a man of his word!"

Larry protested in vain. In Trabane he climbed gingerly out of the bus and into Norbert's car. When Brona saw her son, supported by Norbert, limping across the cobblestone yard, she felt as though her worst nightmares had come true. Larry was crippled for life, she told herself, leaving her—and her alone—to run the farm. Norbert tried to reassure her in a torrent of words, each one stumbling over the next.

"Only a small bit of a bruise, missus. Nothing at all to worry about. He'll be right as rain in a day or two. That's what the doctor said, missus. Isn't it true for me?"

For a brief moment Norbert scowled fiercely at Larry, as if daring him to contradict what he had blurted out, before pressing on doggedly, "Sure, like I said, he'll be right as rain in a day or two. 'Twas well worth it, I promise you, missus, if only to see the look on the faces of them Lisbeg supporters. Savages, every single one of them. We'd have won only for that blind bastard, in pardon to you, missus, of an umpire. As it was, the ref abandoned the game, may he roast in hell for all eternity."

Ignoring the outburst, Brona had eyes only for her son and the strapping on his leg. When she asked him if he could walk on his own, he managed to hobble from the door to a chair beside the fire without falling over.

"I'm okay, Ma. It's only a bang of a hurley. Like Mr. Norbert says, it'll be fine in a day or two. I've got to go to hospital though."

Brona, still in shock, now felt as though she had been stabbed through the heart. "Oh, mother of Jesus, what for?"

Norbert thought to intervene but Brona silenced him with a glare.

"Larry, I'm asking *you*! Why do you have to go to hospital?"

"Dunno really. The doctor said it must be x-rayed. That's all he said. Then he strapped it up and told me to rest it."

Norbert again tried to cut in, this time with more success. "I was kind of hoping he could make it to the ceili tonight, missus. 'Twould look bad if he didn't show up."

They both knew that one of the main attractions of the ceili had always been the presence of those who had played their hearts out earlier in the day. Being injured was no excuse for not showing up—quite the opposite in fact. Scars of battle quickly became badges of honor that drew admiring glances from the girls and pints of foaming stout from supporters who could afford it.

Brona still thought to ask Norbert for whom exactly it would look bad, but decided against it. After all, he seemed to have the boy's best interests at heart, despite the injury. Hadn't he given him a job after school in the supermarket and wasn't he mad keen to take him on full-time the quicker the better. The Maltings were leaving more men go at the end of the month if the rumors racing through the village were true.

The Maltings had employed the men of Trabane and its hinterland for as long as anyone could remember. Drying barley was labor-intensive for the grain had to be raked level, then turned constantly on vast pine floors over a long period. Later it would be bagged and loaded onto trucks for delivery to the parent distillery. Of late, demand for the product had fallen to a point where outright closure was in the cards. To make things even worse, there were rumors of the bank downsizing, if not actually closing. She wondered if this would make any difference to her own situation. Judging from the tone of Leo Martin's letter, she thought probably not.

They chatted for a while until, despite Brona's misgivings, it was agreed that Norbert would collect Larry and drive him home again after the ceili.

That night Larry was feeling much better, though still unable to walk properly—much less dance. News of the debacle in Lisbeg had spread like wildfire. Feelings were running so high among the Trabane supporters that the Lisbeg team wisely declined to put in an appearance at the ceili. The community center where the dance was being held did not have a drinks license. However Foley's pub across the road catered for most needs until closing time, which on Sundays was a strictly observed 10 p.m. Larry did not drink but was for once tempted to, if only to ease the throbbing ache in his leg. He was perched uncomfortably on a stool when Maire sidled up to him.

"Are you badly hurt?"

"Not really. Just a bruise."

"They told me you have to go to the hospital. Ma says you'd want to be in the whole of your health going in there if you want to come out alive!"

"Ah, it's all right. I have to go there for an X-ray, that's all."

"By the look of you, you won't be doing much dancing tonight."

As it was a statement rather than a question, Larry did not feel obliged to answer. Maire pressed on, "Tell me, honestly, is it hurt bad?"

"Bad enough I'd say."

"Is it true that some sheep-shagger took a flake at you with the butt end of his hurley after you put the free over the bar?"

"I don't know anything about that. I passed out when he hit me. Are you sure the ball went over, though?"

"All of Trabane say so, and that's good enough for me." She could see by the faraway look on his face that that he hadn't heard a word she had said. After what seemed an age to her, she moved a bit closer and whispered, "You were miles away there—what were you thinking about?"

"Ah, nothing, nothing at all."

"Nothing my arse!" she snorted. "Are you going to tell me or do I have to drag it out of you?"

He tried to hold her angry gaze for a moment, then looked away, reddening with embarrassment but still silent as a tomb. He made as if to say something, then changed his mind again.

"Maire . . ." Again he hesitated, afraid that she would laugh at him, before blurting out, "You know the old fort at the end of the main street? Well, I go there now and again whenever I need a bit of energy."

"How do you mean *energy*?"

"I dunno really. My Da told me he used to do it when he was my age. Anytime he felt tired or fed up, he'd sit in the middle of the old fort and somehow he'd feel the better for it. I only tried it a few times, but it seemed to work okay for me, too. I forgot all about going there before the match and look what happened!"

Maire was about to laugh out loud when she realized that he was serious. Trying hard not to giggle, she asked innocently, "Do you think it might do any good to go there now?"

The noise from the band was ear-shattering, and some of his team-mates were beginning to show the effects of frequent trips to Foley's pub. Someone who'd witnessed the attack was about to tell him how he'd exacted revenge on the sheep farmer in the general melee that had developed after Larry had passed out from the pain. In the circumstances, despite having to limp the short distance to the fort, it was far better than having to endure the drunken recollections of a complete stranger.

As for Maire, she looked sexy as she jigged and reeled with an easy fluidity. Others must have thought the same because she was hardly ever off the floor as men queued up to dance with her. By now he almost felt grateful for his injury. First, it had saved him from making an exhibition of himself on the dance floor, and now it was giving him the chance to take Maire outside. The moon was still high in the dark sky as they approached the fort. They made their way in through the small gap in the briar-covered earthworks made by cattle that sought shelter. At this time of year, however, the cattle were still in their wintering sheds, so they had the fort to themselves.

"What do you do exactly—when you come here on your own, I mean?"

"Well—and you must give me your word of honor that you won't tell a soul about this—I stand about here"—he was standing in the middle of the fort, surrounded by stone slabs that looked in the moonlight like giant gravestones—"and I just feel the force. I know it sounds crazy but I swear I can feel it even now."

She got up from the flat rock where she had been sitting and stood close to him. Her body felt soft and warm as she pressed close to him, her chin resting on his shoulder. He could not find the words to tell her how marvelous she looked in the soft glow of the moon. Nor could he pluck up the courage to tell her how much his body ached for hers. Suddenly she put her arms around his neck and kissed him full on the lips. It seemed to last an eternity, and while it did, he felt a stirring in his body, a force that had nothing to do with the fort or its strange powers.

After an age she broke free and whispered mischievously, "What does it feel like now—the force I mean?"

He grabbed at her as she pretended to move away from him and buried his mouth in her neck, reeling from the heady scent of her body and the softness of her hair. As he tried to steady himself, he put weight on his left leg and fell heavily. As he did, he jarred his thigh on the ground. He yelped, "Oh, Christ, Maire, it's bloody agony!"

She was kneeling beside him, her hand on his as he clutched his thigh, squeezing it hard to drive away the red-hot needles that were lancing into it. Suddenly they were kissing again, this time with even greater ferocity. Her hand was still on his thigh but moving slowly upward until he thought every fiber in his body was about to explode. Her soft breast inside the blouse was rubbing against his cheek. Fearing rejection, he nonetheless found the courage to slip his free hand inside her blouse and fondled the nipple, suddenly grown hard as a berry. Emboldened by his success, he moved his other hand along her inner thigh. The ache of wanting her was almost unbearable, but then she moved his hand away gently but with an undeniable firmness.

"Ah, for God's sake, Larry, give it a miss!"

With that she got to her feet and was about to stalk off when she realized he was having trouble getting to his feet. She offered her hand to pull him up off the grass, but try as she might, she couldn't hide her amusement at his discomfiture.

"Will you look at Romeo now—can't even stand up by himself!"

Annoyed, as much with himself as with her, he ignored the helping hand and struggled painfully to his feet on his own. His ham-fisted attempts at seduction had yielded nothing but embarrassment, and now she seemed to be laughing at him. Worse still, the pain in his leg was almost unbearable as they made their way back to the community center in silence. When they got there, they found Norbert was about to close up for the night.

"I was wondering where the two of you had got to. I thought I'd shut this place up early before the lads got too drunk. As it is, someone will have to take Mikey Kelly home—he's pissed out of his mind. You wouldn't be a darling and do it for me, would you, Maire?"

She nearly had apoplexy. "Bring that tub of lard home in my mother's car, is it? Are you gone clean out of your mind? He'd be sick all over the backseat before we'd gone 'round the first corner. Not to mention his roving hands! No thanks, Mr. Norbert, I've had enough of those for one night." Then, turning toward Larry, she gave him a forced smile for Norbert's benefit. "Good night Larry, I hope your leg gets better."

With that, she was gone. Norbert looked inquiringly at Larry, then thought better of asking whatever he had in mind before shaking his head sadly. "I didn't really think she would drive Mikey Kelly home, but it was worth a try anyway. Now we'll have to drop him off ourselves. Then I'll run you out home."

This time Larry sat up front with Norbert. Stretched out the length of the backseat, the goalkeeper snored loudly. Occasionally he would break off to burp, causing his bulk to shudder ominously. This made Norbert nervous as a kitten.

"Keep an eye on him for Jaysus' sake. If you think he's going to throw up, let me know in good time. I don't know why I'm always the one to drive these bastards home. I never get one bit of thanks for it, I can tell you. Still"—Norbert brightened as he remembered the goalkeeper's spectacular save in the first half—"he's one hell of a great goalie. We'd have lost only for him."

Soon they were at the goalkeeper's home, where his sister and mother would put the burping hero to bed. Later as Norbert dropped off Larry outside the thatched farmhouse he said, "Don't worry about Wednesday. I'll take you to the hospital in the van. We can do a few deliveries on the way."

His mother and the three younger children were long gone to bed as Larry struggled upstairs to his bedroom. Just before he closed his eyes, the memory of what had happened in the fort returned. Flushed with embarrassment, he buried his head in the pillow and prayed for sleep to drive away the pain and the shame.

The thirteenth hole was the most difficult of the eighteen. It required a better than average drive to clear a wide ravine that had a stream meandering through it. The green lay behind the stone wall of a disused graveyard, an arrangement that had caused much comment down the years. The golfer, having successfully negotiated the ravine, was now faced with a testing second shot over the corner of the graveyard and onto an elevated green. Anyone getting a par here had reason to be well satisfied.

The twosome paused on the tee to regroup and take stock. Pat O'Hara announced happily, "I get another shot off you here Tim. Why don't you go for the green?"

Tim Porter brayed happily and snorted, "I think not, old chap. I leave that sort of thing to Joe Delany. Anyway, he had the wind behind him when he did it, or so I am told."

O'Hara turned to his caddy and said, "Larry, I need another drop of Lucozade if I'm to get across that bloody thing."

After taking a swig from the bottle, O'Hara put it back carefully in one of the pockets of his golf bag and watched as Tim Porter swung smoothly at the ball. It soared effortlessly across the ravine and came to a halt in perfect position on the narrow fairway, a short iron from the green. O'Hara asked Larry for the driver and, as he was teeing up the ball, remarked casually, "There was no wind the day Joe drove the green. I know because I was with him. He hit an unmerciful flake of the ball in those days, with a hint of a slice. Just the perfect shape to land the ball short of the green. From there it just trickled onto the front. Never been done before or since. Most of those that tried ended up in the graveyard."

Tim Porter was about half O'Hara's age. Larry had seen him every now and again. His father owned a large estate nearby and a wine-importing business in which Tim worked. A good golfer, he had plenty of time to sharpen his skills as his sales job in the family business was none too demanding.

"No wind, you say. Well, that makes it even more impressive. He wouldn't do it today though, not into a wind right in our faces like this one."

O'Hara hit the ball and was delighted to see it land on the far side of the ravine. "I think that calls for a celebration." Without waiting for anyone to agree with him, he took another deep draft from the Lucozade bottle and suddenly turned to his caddy.

"Would you like to have a go? You don't mind, do you, Tim?"

Tim shrugged. If the schoolteacher wanted his caddy to try to hit it across the ravine, that was his affair. Not that Tim had anything against the lad. Quite the opposite, in fact. Despite being in obvious difficulties with a game leg, he kept up with them and didn't speak unless spoken to.

"Not at all, go right ahead."

Larry teed up a ball and took the driver from O'Hara. He completely missed the golf ball on his first attempt, but before Tim could say anything, O'Hara murmured gently, "Go *on*. Try again. This time, remember what you did the last time and swing *easy*."

This time Larry made a good connection. Clubhead struck ball with a resounding click. Like the seventy he had taken in Sunday's match, the ball seemed to hang in the air forever. The only difference was that this time the sky was blue and the wind was blowing directly into his face. He remembered not to look up as he hit the ball, but when he eventually did, he saw that the two men were following the flight of the ball in stunned silence. Still airborne, it disappeared over the corner of the graveyard.

Tim was first to speak, in a strained voice. "I-I-I'm not absolutely certain, but I think it carried the second wall."

O'Hara took the club from Larry before muttering, as if to himself, "If it did, it's more than likely on the green."

As the trio walked down one side of the ravine and made the steep climb up the other, Tim Porter confided to Larry, "That is the longest drive I have *ever* seen. Quite honestly, I wouldn't have believed it was possible unless I had seen it with my own eyes."

The effort of descending, then moments later climbing back up the steep path leading out of the ravine, reduced all three to silence. Larry felt the weight of the bag for the first time that day, and it caused him to limp even more. If either of the two golfers noticed this, they made no reference to it. Having reached the top and walked along the fairway, they still could not see where Larry's ball had finished because the first of two stone walls that formed the corner of the graveyard cutting into the fairway obscured their view of the green. Tim, ignoring his own ball and O'Hara's effort even farther back toward the tee, strode purposefully to a spot from where he could get a proper look.

He called back to the other two trailing in his wake, "I think I see something on the green, but I'll walk on a bit to get a better look." He strode briskly right up to the front of the green. "He's on all right—about ten feet from the hole!"

This ten feet was, of itself, significant because the flagstick was at least another twenty yards farther back in the green, making Larry's drive even farther than Joe Delany's effort all those years ago. Furthermore today's drive was *into* a stiff breeze—a point not lost on the other two.

After further oohing and aahing, O'Hara lifted the ball off the green and handed it to Larry. "Keep this for the rest of your life because there's only one first time for anything."

Tim protested loudly that Larry should have been allowed to hole the putt, but his playing partner would have none of it, explaining, "Larry doesn't know how to putt yet. Believe it or not, that's only the second time he has ever hit a golf ball. The rest of the game is still ahead of him, including how to putt."

Tim nodded, still thunderstruck by what he had just witnessed.

"Yeah, I suppose you're right if that's the case. Still, it's a new record, duly witnessed by two playing members. Wonder what Joe Delany will say to this?"

O'Hara chuckled. "The first thing he will do, I expect, will be to try to get that loop out of Larry's swing."

Tim was less certain about this. He asked Larry, "Where does that loop at the top of your swing come from?"

"Dunno, sir. I take the frees for the Trabane Gaels, so maybe it's a hurling swing or something."

O'Hara slapped his thigh in excitement. "That's it," he cried, "the bloody GAA have a lot to answer for, by God. That's where the loop comes from all right. They nearly killed the lad last Sunday, by the way."

Again it was Tim's turn to be surprised at the many facets to the young person carrying the schoolteacher's golf bag. "So you're the young fella that got the belt of a hurley just as the referee blew for time. I heard there was nearly a riot afterwards—typical GAA if you ask me. Some of those fellows would get a year in jail if they did on the street what they get away with on the hurling pitch. And what does that fine body of men, the Gaelic Athletic Association, the biggest bloody sporting organization by far in the whole bloody country, do about it? Sweet damn all, that's what! So that's where you got the limp? I was afraid to ask until now in case you had it from birth or something!"

Porter's laugh might have sounded like a donkey braying, but Larry, despite the unfair reference to the GAA, was beginning to like this big, fair-haired man with the posh accent and the double chins.

"That's right, sir. That was me that got hurt at the end. They said at the hospital that I wasn't to even think about playing again until next season. Even then, they'll have to take a look at the leg again before they give me the go-ahead—"

O'Hara cut in, "Hurling's loss is golf's gain. You'll have more time to play golf now that Norbert won't be at you to practice every day of the week."

Larry was not as enthusiastic as the other two about taking up golf. Of course it was gratifying, thrilling even, to see two grown men dancing with excitement at the way he had just hit a golf ball. But that did not change his view one iota: golf was a game for snobs. That's what he had been told for as long as he could remember, and old habits died hard. Admittedly this was only his second time out on the golf course with Mr. O'Hara, but in that time he had never seen anyone of his own age around the place, except for some of the caddies. And they weren't up to much. When not caddying, they could be seen, hanging around the chip shop, smoking cigarettes and making comments about passersby, especially girls. Only yesterday, a group of them had called after him, "Hey, Skippy, how's the leg?" and "You got what was comin' to you from the Lisbeg crowd!"

Though his ears had reddened, he'd walked past them without making eye contact. There were too many of them to take on all at once—but he hadn't forgotten their faces.

The trio finished the round in something of a daze, Larry still being the one least affected by the amazing feat. Instead of heading for the changing room, both men made straight for the professional's shop with the sign reading JOSEPH DELANY, PROFESSIONAL AND PGA-QUALIFIED INSTRUCTOR.

Larry had never been there before. Inside was an impressive array of shiny new golf clubs, bags, shoes, sweaters, and all the other odds and ends associated with the game. Behind a counter a strongly built man in his thirties was doing something complicated to the grip of a club as they entered. He looked up and smiled.

"Good afternoon, gentlemen." He looked questioningly at Larry. "I haven't seen you 'round here before, have I?"

O'Hara made the introductions, adding solemnly, "We have some bad news for you, I'm afraid."

Joe looked startled at O'Hara's mock-serious expression. "What is it? What's the bad news?"

"This young man"—suddenly Pat O'Hara looked much younger.

Larry suddenly realized that this was the first time he had ever seen him look really happy—"has just driven the thirteenth green."

"From the medal tee?" Joe's eyebrows were arched high in surprise.

"From the medal tee, Joe, the same one you hit from yourself all those years ago. What's more, this young lad did it *into* the wind!"

The professional whistled in admiration.

Tim Porter chimed in excitedly with further details. "His ball finished ten feet to the side of the pin—which is, as you know, well back in the green. He must have carried the graveyard on the fly. Anyway, Joe, old boy, your record is gone the way of all flesh!"

Joe's reaction surprised even himself. Wordlessly he grasped the boy's hand, saying, "Well done, young fella! Make my day and tell me that you holed the putt for an eagle?"

Larry was fairly certain that an eagle was better than a birdie. Not being sure, he chose to say nothing.

Again Tim intervened. "Pat picked up his ball there and then. Said the lad hadn't got as far as learning how to putt yet!"

"My God, but that takes the bloody biscuit." Joe was aghast. "Doesn't even know how to putt and he drives the thirteenth—into the wind at that!"

A stunned silence descended on the little group gathered in the pro shop as each pondered the recent miracle, then Joe Delany carefully put aside the club he was working on and took a key down from a nail above his head. As they filed out of the shop, he locked the door behind him. He watched Larry closely as he limped from the shop to the clubhouse, carrying O'Hara's bag over his shoulder.

"Aren't you young Lynch, the lad that takes the frees for the Gaels?"

Larry's chest swelled with pride. That someone who had nothing whatsoever to do with the GAA and the game of hurling should recognize him off the field of play was fame indeed. He gave Joe Delany a wide, toothy grin as he replied proudly, "That's me, sir."

"The same lad that nearly got the leg cut off him last Sunday?"

This time Larry didn't grin, just nodded. The pro shook his head several times, muttering more to himself than anyone else, "What a waste, what a waste!"

He did not elaborate on this. Wordlessly they made for the bar, which was deserted at that time of the evening. Joe went behind the counter and announced, "This one is on me. It isn't every day your record is broken."

By the time the bar began to fill up with golfers, Joe had learned that the drive that had removed him from the club record books was only the second time Larry had ever hit a golf ball in his life, and that the lad had an amazing loop at the top of his backswing. By then Larry had long since gone home. When Brona asked him how he had got on caddying for O'Hara, he replied that he had earned five pounds. Two for carrying the bag and one each from three men in the bar. He didn't mention the long drive at the thirteenth hole because he didn't really understand much about it. Because of this he felt he couldn't even *begin* to properly explain to her what Mr. O'Hara and the Porter person were getting so excited about.

CHAPTER THREE

The injured leg had not improved as quickly as he had hoped. It was not helped by Larry's falling off a load of hay. He had been stacking the bales high up on a trailer when one of them had given way under him and he'd fallen heavily on the cobblestone farmyard. He had had to go back again to the hospital, where they'd strapped it up once more and warned Brona, who had accompanied him this time round, that he should stay far away from tractors and trailers. Mother and son were also told that any further setbacks to his recovery could result in a permanent limp.

The hospital consultant had reluctantly allowed to him continue working in the supermarket and to help out in the golf club bar as long as he didn't overdo it. Spring was when most golfers took their clubs out of the attic after the winter hibernation, and the sudden rush of players on the Trabane links put a strain on Joe Delany's schedule. In return for looking after the pro shop while Joe was on the practice range giving lessons, he promised that he would coach Larry at every opportunity. Unknown to Larry, some members had already been complaining: "What's the point in having a blasted professional if there is a CLOSED sign on his door every time you need him?"

Some lady members attributed Joe's frequent absences to his intensive coaching of Rosa Martin, wife of Leo the bank manager. Rosa was not popular among the other lady members, for her shorts were too skimpy and the tops she wore revealed more than they concealed. Worst of all, she had somehow acquired a generous handicap that enabled her to win more than her fair share of competitions. The men, on the other hand, mostly welcomed her presence on the course and in the bar, feeling that she added a bit of glamour and excitement to their lives.

Whatever the reason, Larry was now spending most of his time either serving behind the counter of the bar or looking after the pro shop. He had left school long before graduating, much to O'Hara's disgust. Falling off the trailer had aggravated his leg injury to the point where the bending and kneeling in stacking Norbert's shelves was becoming a daily agony. To make matters worse, Norbert's attitude had changed when it had become clear that Larry could not play for the Trabane Gaels. Overnight, Larry had become just another employee, and now his work was being criticized as it had not been before. Matters were not improved by Maire using her senior status as checkout operator to order him around, as well as accusing him of spending too much time "with those snobs up at the golf club."

Eventually Joe Delany did get round to giving Larry his first lesson. He pointed to a bucket of balls and handed Larry a driver out of his own bag of clubs. Larry recalled that when he had driven the thirteenth green, the ball had been placed on a small wooden tee that raised it off the ground and made it easier to hit. This time there was no tee, but he thought it better not to ask for one. Instead he made a vicious slash at one of the balls—and missed it completely. Joe Delany said nothing. Nor did he offer to put the next ball up on a tee. Out of the blue O'Hara's words came back to Larry like a mantra learned in the classroom: "Shake hands with the club, head still, and swing *easy!*"

It wasn't easy to do all three things at once, but nonetheless he managed to give the ball a really solid hit. It took off on a low trajec-

tory and was still climbing as it disappeared over a fence at the far end
of the practice range. He thought he heard a strangled oath coming
from behind him but wasn't quite sure. He was about to hit another
ball when Joe grabbed his shoulder.

"Stop right there! Who taught you that swing?"

"No one, sir. That is, Mr. O'Hara told me to do a few things, that's all."

"What were they?"

"A-h-h . . . swing easy, try to keep my head still, and shake hands
with the club."

Joe exhaled through pursed lips, making a sound like a tire deflat-
ing. "Good advice. Now about that loop in your swing. You have just
hit a driver off the ground and sent it out over the back fence. I haven't
seen anyone do that before. Not off a tee, never mind off the deck.
Here"—Joe took a long wooden peg out of his pocket and handed it to
Larry—"tee a ball up on that and hit it."

He did as he was told. This time he didn't hit it as far, but it went
much higher and landed just short of the fence.

Again Joe exhaled noisily. "Try hitting it with this."

He handed Larry an iron club with the number 7 engraved on it. It
looked completely different from the weapon he had just used. It felt
lighter in his hands but it did *look* slightly more like a hurley. This time
no tee peg was offered. Larry swished the club a few times and it felt
very different from the heavier driver he had just been using. He
swung hard at the ball but hit the ground well behind the ball, making
an enormous divot but sending the ball not more than twenty paces.

Joe did not seem in the least perturbed by this. "Have another try,
only this time imagine the ball has an arse—and try to look up it!"

Larry glanced at his mentor to make sure he had heard right. He
had. Joe's expression was one of utter concentration with not a hint of
a smutty joke. Larry tried really hard to do as he was told, even though
it meant craning his neck behind the ball, which felt awkward and uncomfortable. He swung the club more slowly this time and was grati-

fied to see the ball soar skyward, in much the same flight path as the sliotair had taken just before he was felled by the sheep farmer.

Joe grunted with satisfaction. "That's more like it. I'll leave the driver and the seven iron with you. Hit the rest of those balls, then come back to the shop. I've a lesson in a few minutes. Oh, yes, another thing. From now on I'm going to call you Loopy. After that swing of yours—in case you were wondering."

With that Joe disappeared in the direction of the clubhouse. Alone now, Larry stopped hitting golf balls for a moment to get his breath back. Below him lay Trabane in all its glory, a jumble of houses, their windows sparkling with the sun's reflections. The village might have been a glittering pendant hanging from the golden necklace of sandy beach that almost encircled the bay. The Atlantic was calm today, a mirror of deepest blue with scarcely a ripple. Overhead, gulls swooped and shrieked. In the distance a green mail van, tiny as an ant, crawled along the winding road that meandered from Trabane to Lisbeg.

There were many more lessons like that. Joe would loan Larry his own clubs, a bucket of balls, and let him get on with it. Whenever he caddied for O'Hara, he picked up the basics of the short game and got to hit a few putts on the green when O'Hara was certain no club members were watching.

When Tim Porter returned to Trabane after a lengthy visit to the vineyards, he was amazed at the strides Loopy, as everyone now called him, had made at the game. His length off the tee was still phenomenal, but now he could also hit iron shots long and straight. This improvement decided Tim Porter to give Larry an old set of golf clubs he had stopped using. When Joe Delany looked them over, his only comment was that they would do for the time being.

However, there remained the problem of Loopy's membership. Because he was no longer attending school, reduced student rates did not apply to him. It went without saying that the annual subscription of five hundred pounds was out of the question. For the moment O'Hara and Joe Delany agreed things could go on as they were, but both men realized that sooner or later the problem would have to be met head-on. If Loopy was to continue to progress at the game, he would have to play regularly on the golf course, and to do so, he would have to become a paid-up member of Trabane Golf Club.

It was just as well that Loopy was blissfully unaware of the problem for he had others to keep him awake at night. With the arrival of another spring, most of the hay remained unsold. As the weather got better every day, cattle were leaving their winter quarters to graze fields of fresh grass. In the barn, the hay would keep indefinitely, but selling it would provide some much needed cash. Leo Martin again wrote to Brona inquiring when her bank account might "be put on a proper footing" and looking forward to her proposals for "reducing the arrears in the account, which have now assumed alarming levels of indebtedness!"

Leo did so in a determined effort to clear his file of any overdue accounts that might hinder his prospects. The grapevine at Allied Banks of Ireland was humming with rumors that the Trabane outlet was due for the chop, despite the furor caused by the recent closure of the Lisbeg branch.

If that were not bad enough, things were going from bad to worse at the supermarket. Maire's so-called promotion had gone to her head, so much so that whenever Norbert was absent, she would seek out extra jobs for Loopy to do in addition to stacking shelves. These often entailed lifting heavy cartons or climbing up ladders in the storeroom—the very things he had been warned against by the hospital consultant. His pride would not allow him to explain this to her, so relations between them went from bad to worse.

There had been no more trips to the fort, nor did they laugh together as they had done before. He sometimes wondered if her attitude had changed so drastically because he was no longer a rising star of the hurling team. Working with her in the supermarket was a job now—nothing more.

God, he thought, *women are so complicated.*

The schoolteacher Pat O'Hara was another complication. He had
still not abandoned hope that his ex-pupil might go back to school in
the autumn, after a year's absence. "If you don't, you'll live to regret
it, young fella. Can't you see that education is your only way out of a
place like Trabane where there isn't a decent job for man or beast at
the minute? Why don't you come back to school, graduate, and then
the world will be your oyster. With a bit of paper behind you, you'll
be the equal of any man. Stay the way you are and you'll still be stacking shelves when you're my age. And don't think that being able to hit
a golf ball out of sight is going to do you any good when push comes to
shove. Oh, sure, Joe Delany's doing his best for you right now, but a
time will come when there's nothing more he can teach you, and
what'll you do then?"

Loopy did not attempt to answer this. He didn't know, and to tell
the truth, he didn't really care. What the schoolteacher was going on
about was far away in the distant future. Getting rid of the hay in the
barn and improving his golf game were his two immediate objectives
in life. Going back to school again was simply not on the agenda because, apart from any other considerations, the pressure to pay off the
·bank was increasing letter by letter.

Leo Martin, apart from being manager of Allied Banks of Ireland
in Trabane, also held down the position of honorary treasurer to the
Golf Club. Whether it was from a wish to add to the profits of the bar,
the ever-worsening recession, or because of some deeper, personal
reason, he had taken to spending a lot of time there of late. Loopy noticed that when Leo and O'Hara were there at the same time, they sat
as far apart as possible. Tonight, the bar was almost full and both men
had been drinking for much longer than anyone else.

The talk among the members had been of the deepening recession
that had descended on their town, with rumors of job losses and im-
pending closures flitting forward and backward across the bar. The
Maltings were due to shed eight more jobs at the end of the month,
bringing to thirty their job losses for the year—a disaster for a tiny

place like Trabane. To lighten the gloomy atmosphere, someone thought to change the subject by asking Loopy if his golf game was improving and if he was playing much.

Before he could answer, Leo Martin grumbled aloud, "If he's playing on the course, then he shouldn't be. You all know damn well that only members or those who have paid their green fees are allowed to play on this golf course, no matter"—here he paused with glass uplifted and glowered across at O'Hara, who was sitting at a table not far away—"*what* some other members whom I would have expected to set a better example may like to think!"

Pat O'Hara, drunk through he was, caught every syllable—and nuance. "Leo, you really should try not to be such a stuck-up old bollocks. Young Lynch here is shaping up to be the best golfer this place has ever produced by a bloody mile. All he needs is a free run at it without bother from pompous ould eejits like yourself"—a murmur of disapproval greeted this, but it failed to silence the irate schoolteacher—"so if it's the young lad's membership that's troubling you, I here and now propose Laurence Lynch as a full member. Now"— O'Hara glared around the bar with a piercing look that he had perfected in the classroom when seeking out miscreants—"who'll second my proposal?"

There was a long silence. Most of the drinkers would have supported O'Hara, though they would have preferred that his proposal were couched in milder terms. Leo Martin, though widely disliked, was nevertheless a force to be reckoned with in a small community such as Trabane. At the stroke of his pen, one's line of credit could be cut off—or restored—according to his whim. At the best of times, Leo would not have been someone to trifle with, but just now with half the business firms in Trabane struggling to survive, no one in his right mind would deliberately upset him. All the more surprising then when the silence was broken by a voice coming from the open door of the bar.

"I'll second that."

Joe Delany had just come back from the practice ground, though the sun had long since gone down. He had given Rosa Martin a lesson in the short game in which he had stood behind her, then put his hands around her waist and onto the golf club she was already gripping a little too feverishly. As he'd thought to himself on the walk back from the practice ground after she'd departed in a flurry of gravel from the club, the lesson may not have done her golf much good but it had certainly made him feel a whole lot better.

All eyes focused on the professional for a moment, then swung back to the man who had started it all—Leo Martin. He did not react well. It may have been the drink or perhaps his natural disposition. Whatever the cause, his next question was unforgivable.

"Who'll pay his sub," he snarled, "or does anyone here imagine that the bank is going to loan him the money just so that he can play golf?"

This was greeted with a silence even longer than the one that had preceded it. Then an English accent cut through the tense, smoke-filled atmosphere like a knife through butter. Edward Linhurst was on his feet and rummaging in his jacket for a checkbook. "That won't be necessary, Leo old man. I trust a check will be satisfactory?"

If Leo Martin detected the sarcasm in the voice of Trabane's richest resident, he chose to ignore it. Instead he muttered something unintelligible into his pint glass and developed a sudden interest in the beer mat on his table. The roar of conversation resumed as Loopy tried to come to terms with his suddenly having become a full member of Trabane Golf Club.

CHAPTER FOUR

The tournament was held throughout the year, come wind or rain. To win it was the ambition of every member of Trabane Golf Club. Despite being called the Monthly Medal, it did not mean that a real medal was presented. Instead the winner received a voucher from the pro shop, which complied with the rule that amateurs were not to play for prize money. It was played on the last Sunday of every month, and the presentation of the prize was at seven o'clock on the dot. This gave everyone time for a drink beforehand—and afterward, should they be so inclined.

Handicaps define a golfer, the lower the number the better the player. Beginners usually start out with the target of a really low handicap, then get caught up in the complexities of the game and settle for a higher handicap off which they can play with some degree of comfort. Almost a parable of life itself, wherein the pilgrim starts out full of hope until disillusionment arrives on the scene and, sometimes, takes over completely.

Edward Linhurst was different, for disillusionment never stood a chance. His self-confidence—some called it cockiness—guaranteed that. In his younger days he played off a single-figure handicap and could see no good reason why he should not do so again. With plenty of time to concentrate on the game, he had been taking lessons from Joe Delany, who treated him much the same as Loopy. He would give Linhurst a few things to work on at the start of the lesson, then let him get on with it. When a bucket of balls had been hit, Joe would come back to check for any improvement. If not, he would try something else. The method usually worked because most people did better on their own than with the professional looking over their shoulder. Rosa Martin was the exception.

On the driving range after one of these lessons, Edward Linhurst renewed his acquaintance with the young man whose subscription he had paid on the spur of the moment. In the excitement that had followed Linhurst's intervention, Loopy had not had an opportunity to thank his benefactor until now.

"I never got a chance to thank you properly, Mr. Linhurst, for doing what you did. I'll pay you back as I can. Honest I will."

Linhurst was both gratified and nonplussed. He had wondered several times since then what could possibly have sparked such an uncharacteristic intervention. He was not one to draw attention to himself. Quite the opposite, in fact. Those who knew him well regarded him as a shrinking violet—cocky and self-confident, of course, yet someone who shunned the limelight whenever possible. He couldn't blame it on too much drink, either. He had had two, possibly three, gin and tonics before responding to the bank manager's outburst. Nor was he trying to impress anyone. He liked almost everyone in the golf club and found them fun to be with, but by paying Loopy's subscription, he wasn't trying to impress them with his wealth. No one, he reflected, could accuse him of trying to impress *anyone*.

He drove a three-year-old car, his golf equipment was far from new, and he rarely if ever tried to buy a round of drinks out of turn. As for any dislike of Leo, his dealings with the bank manager had, up till then, been run-of-the-mill. The invitation to dinner at Leo's, he supposed, must have been suggested by Leo's superiors as the opening shot in a campaign to get more of his business. Yes, that must have

been it, Linhurst decided, for he had bought The Old Rectory through
Leo's bank and they would have checked out his financial standing as a
matter of routine. The next step would, predictably, have been for
them to encourage Leo to do all in his power to get some of Linhurst's
banking business.

That he was unable to accept Leo's invitation may have caused the
first coolness between them. The invitation had arrived at a particularly chaotic period in the restoration of The Old Rectory. Builders,
plumbers, and electricians were all engaged in a form of guerrilla warfare with each other. Only the landscape gardeners were content
merely to squabble among themselves. That, of course, was on the
rare occasions when they bothered to show up at all.

It was just then that Amy, his only daughter, had announced herself for the weekend. Having done everything she could to effect a
reconciliation between her parents, she now took her mother's side
in everything. When Linhurst told his family that he was retiring, no
one, least of all Amy, believed him. It was dismissed as nothing
more than a midlife crisis brought on by the divorce. When his re-
tirement looked to be lasting longer than expected, Amy had decided to check it out for herself. She could hardly have chosen a
worse moment.

Electricity had just been cut off and the water supply gave up the
ghost shortly after her arrival. The thunderstorm that had caused
these twin disasters had also, almost as an afterthought, stripped half
the slates from the new roof. What annoyed her most of all was that
her father appeared to take these calamities in his stride. He had nothing but praise for everyone and everything in this rathole of a village.
He enthused about how refreshing it was that people remembered his
name in shops and bars and waved to him on the street. He filled his
lungs with fresh air on long walks along the beach, and he had fallen
head over heels in love with the local golf course.

"Pure linksland," he burbled happily, "you couldn't play on better
turf. Just what Saint Andrew's must have been like before the tourists

swarmed all over it. If it were anywhere else, the world would be beating a path to its door. That's how good it is!"

She had to admit that he had never looked better. The deathly pallor of his days doing "something in the city" had gone. There was a spring in his step and a cheerfulness about him that she had never seen before.

Yet in no way could she share his enthusiasm for such a godforsaken spot. She had little doubt that her father would transform the house and grounds into something special—he had already done just that on two previous occasions. The home her mother had acquired as part of the divorce settlement was outstanding even in the London stockbroker belt where splendid residences were two a penny.

It was a pity, she would report to her mother, that they had argued for so much of the weekend. She had arrived overwrought, tense and blaming her father for the family breakup. Her humor was not improved when services taken for granted everywhere else had failed in the case of The Old Rectory. Her father's suggestion that they accept a dinner invitation from the local bank manager was the last straw.

She stamped her foot in exasperation. "I came here to see *you*, Daddy. Now I'm no sooner inside this . . . this . . . *house* and you want me to go out to bloody dinner with complete strangers. Not on your life!"

When Linhurst phoned Leo with his regrets, he got the impression that the bank manager was less than pleased. He was not to know that in Trabane an invitation to dinner from the bank manager was something not to be lightly declined. The weekend, despite its setbacks, had gone sufficiently well for Amy to promise to return in the near future.

Now, good as her word and completely out of the blue, she had arrived by bus that very morning. Linhurst would happily have withdrawn from the tournament that afternoon to be with her, but Amy would not hear of it.

"You go play your silly golf and I'll cook dinner. That way you can see where at least *some* of my school fees went, Father dear!" Then she had set off along the beach, barefoot, with the spaniel gamboling at her heels one moment, then launching himself into a frenzied attack on seagulls that waited until the last moment before taking flight, leaving the dog with nothing more substantial to chew on than a triumphant squawk.

Linhurst pushed the picture of Amy and the dog to the back of his mind as he watched Loopy hitting one golf ball after another with that incredible loop at the top of his swing. The distance the ball was traveling was quite stunning, even if the direction was erratic. All the while he was desperately searching for the right response to the offer of repayment—one that would not offend the lad. Eventually he settled for "Don't worry about the money for now. If you can pay me back, well and good—otherwise not to worry."

Then, to change the subject, he observed, "You're hitting that ball a long, long way."

Loopy would not be deflected so easily. He put the club he was using back in the bag and looked Linhurst straight in the eye as he spoke. "My father left Trabane a while back owing nearly everyone in the town. If I ever get to sell the hay he left behind him, you'll be paid right after the bank. You have my word on that, sir."

"Do you mean Mr. Martin's bank?"

"Yes, sir. My father borrowed money before he took off to England. The bank have been writing letters to my mother ever since."

"What did she say—to the bank, I mean?"

Loopy had never discussed this with anyone before, but this Englishman seemed genuinely interested. "She told Mr. Martin that when the hay was sold, he'd get his money."

"And did he?"

"No. He got two hundred and forty pounds. Then I fell off the trailer and hurt my leg again. The rest of the hay is still in the barn. It will keep forever as long as it under cover and kept dry—that's not the problem."

"What is the problem then?"

"Now that my leg's nearly better, no one seems to want hay."

"Why is that? What causes the drop-off in demand for the hay?"

"Well, y'see, when the fine weather comes, the cattle are left out on grass. Why would anyone pay for hay when the grass is there for free? Anyway, I can't deliver it myself. The doctor told me that if I went near a hurling field or a hay trailer, he'd have the guards on me!"

They both resumed hitting golf balls, then Linhurst stopped in midswing. "What about horses?"

"How do mean, sir?"

"I mean, don't horses eat hay all the year round?"

"Some of them do alright. But not the ones around Trabane."

Now it was Linhurst's turn to sound perplexed. "Are Trabane horses any different from the rest of the world?"

"Ah, no, that's not what I meant at all, sir. The horses that eat hay all year round are racing horses, show jumpers, that class of an animal. There's none of those around here. The horses we have in this part of the country would only be good for foxhunting or the odd point-to-point race. That class of horse is put out on grass for most of the year, just like the cattle."

They finished practicing and walked back to the clubhouse together.

"Are you playing in the tournament this afternoon?"

"I can't, sir. I still haven't got an official handicap, and anyway Mr. Delany says I'm not ready yet. He says I need to sort out my short game—the chipping and putting part of it."

Linhurst nodded. It made sense, he supposed, not to push the lad too far too fast, and yet . . . Linhurst believed that the sooner Loopy got the taste for battle, the tightening of the gut that comes with the pressure of real competition, the sooner he might discover what the future held in store for him. It was one thing to hit perfect shots nine times out of ten on the practice ground but quite a different matter to reproduce them where it counted, in competition.

"Are you caddying for the schoolmaster then?" Linhurst's tone was almost too casual for he already knew the answer.

"No, sir. Mr. O'Hara has had to go to the hospital for a checkup. He won't be playing golf for a while, he thinks."

"Does that mean you are out of a job—as his caddy, I mean?"

Loopy sounded doubtful at first. "I suppose so . . ." He added by way of explanation, "Y'see, Mr. O'Hara hasn't been well in himself this long while."

Linhurst said nothing. It was no secret that the schoolmaster was drinking more than ever since the start of the summer vacation. Up to now the discipline of having to show up sober five mornings a week had placed a curb on his drinking. Once this restraint had been removed, he'd "climbed straight into the whiskey bottle," as Leo Martin had so unkindly put it. Not that Leo himself was a paragon of virtue in that regard.

"Would you caddy for me instead, starting this afternoon? And don't think you have to because of that subscription business or anything like that."

"Nothing I'd like better, sir."

"Good! Would two o'clock suit you?"

"That'll be fine, sir. I go on bar duty at six, but we should be well finished before then."

At two o'clock sharp Edward Linhurst was ready to hit off the first tee, watched by Loopy and Michael Spillane, CC, curate of Trabane parish. The priest's delight at seeing Loopy was genuine.

"Larry Lynch! I never expected to see you here. What does the GAA think of you playing foreign games?" In an aside to Linhurst, the priest explained, "In case you don't know, I'm the patron of the local hurling team, the Trabane Gaels."

"Good for you. Quite an honor, I expect," Linhurst murmured politely, being more interested in getting the round under way than wasting time in what sounded like idle chatter.

"Not *that* much of an honor, to be honest. Every GAA club in the country has its local priest as patron. They do it"—he broke off to run his finger around inside the stiff white collar worn by clergymen and priests in Ireland—"from a mixture of fear and respect for the collar."

The priest turned again to Loopy. "I heard you had left school. Pat O'Hara was giving out like hell about that. Any word from your father?"

"Not a word—or a penny, Father."

The priest pursed his lips, nodding in sympathy. "Try not to worry about it too much. It may be all for the best in the long run. In the meantime I'll say the odd prayer for you."

With that he plucked a club from his bag and hit a solid drive down the middle of the fairway. As he stopped to retrieve his tee, he looked back at his playing partner. "The usual pound, okay? The bishop warned me not to play retired millionaires for big money."

It was a standing joke between them. Linhurst affected a tone of weary resignation. "Okay. Do you want it now or do we have to go through the ritual of eighteen holes before I hand it over to you?" In a stage whisper to Loopy, Linhurst muttered, "This man takes money off me *every* time. He's a seventeen handicap but plays to single figures. Priest or not, I'll never know how he gets away with it."

They strode down the first fairway at a brisk pace, which they maintained right through the round, finishing in well under three hours. The result was a win for Linhurst—as welcome as it was unexpected—because he had played better, far better, than usual. As both men signed their cards before dropping them into the wooden scorebox in the changing room, Linhurst suggested, "A drink, perhaps?"

The priest glanced at his watch. "Just time for one. I'm hearing confessions at half past five. Here's your pound and well done—that was as good as I've seen you play. Maybe you should offer Larry a permanent job as your caddy. He seems to bring the best out of you. By the way, why were you calling him Loopy?"

When it was explained to him, he stared at Loopy in wonderment. "Well, to be honest, I'm not *all* that surprised. I never saw a better striker of the ball on a hurling field." Turning to Linhurst, the priest explained, "Though the last free he took from the sideline nearly got him killed. But that's all over and done with now, thanks be to God." Then brightening, he asked Loopy, "What do you think of this game of golf? Do you still think it's a game for snobs?"

Loopy thought for a moment before answering as truthfully as he could, "I haven't met any so far, Father, but then I haven't been at it all that long, so it's probably a bit early to say."

"Spoken like a true diplomat," Linhurst interjected. "Now we had better get you that drink."

Joe Delany and his wife, Linda, were on duty behind the bar. "How did you get on?" Joe inquired.

The priest forced a grin as he pointed an accusing finger at Linhurst. "He took a pound off me without even working up a sweat. Those lessons you're giving him are working miracles. Wouldn't surprise me if he won the tournament with the score he's just brought in. He'll lose a shot off his handicap, that's for sure. No harm either, the way he's playing."

Linda beckoned Loopy over to where she was serving at the other end of the bar. "I'm really in a bind. I have to get something for the dinner before the shops close. Could you ever take over here right away?"

Loopy was behind the bar when Pat O'Hara made his entrance, just moments after Father Spillane had rushed off to hear confessions in the nearby church. The schoolteacher joined Linhurst and Joe Delany, with Loopy on duty behind the bar counter. O'Hara had been discharged from hospital that morning after undergoing a series of tests, about which he declined to elaborate except to remark that all doctors were bastards. His slurred words suggested that this was not his first drink of the day.

The talk was desultory before focusing on Loopy's swing. O'Hara thought the "loop" should be eliminated from the lad's swing as soon as possible. He insisted that it was like a child stammering at school—

the sooner it was corrected the better. Joe Delany did not agree, thinking it too early yet to tinker with Loopy's natural swing as a hurler. He
might have had more to say had not O'Hara, who had up to now been
in no way aggressive, suddenly exploded in anger. In a voice loud
enough to carry into the farthest corners of the bar, he cursed the
game of hurling to the bottomless pit of hell, adding for good measure, "If you don't believe me about hurling being only a game fit for
savages, you need look no further than our barman!"

Furiously he pointed a trembling finger at Loopy, who was standing
openmouthed behind the counter. He had never seen O'Hara behave
quite like this before, and it wasn't over yet. Angrily brushing aside
Joe's restraining hand on his shoulder, O'Hara struggled unsteadily to
his feet, bellowing across the bar, "Take a good look at that young fella!
He nearly had his bloody leg cut off by some thug from Lisbeg. Now
he can't play hurling anymore."

After a brief lull as O'Hara swallowed a hiccup, he continued,
"Best bloody thing that ever happened to him, if you ask me! Means
he can give more time to his golf and I'll tell you another thing—"

What he might have added to the sum of human knowledge the
world would never know because of the sudden commotion in the far
corner of the bar. A large man, purple with rage, was clambering to his
feet and shaking a fist at O'Hara as he warned all and sundry, "If someone doesn't get that drunk out of here in double quick time, I won't be
responsible for my actions!"

In the blink of an eye Joe was behind the counter, whispering ur-
gently in Loopy's ear, "Here's the keys of his car. Now get him out before that big guy in the corner kills him. He's the father of the center
forward that did for your leg. He's not taking kindly to his son being
called a savage and a thug!"

By the time Loopy had come out from behind the bar, Linhurst
had persuaded O'Hara that the air in the parking lot would do him no
end of good. From there it was easier than expected to bundle the

teacher into his own car and head for home with Loopy at the wheel. Linhurst went back inside to await the results of the tournament.

The journey was less than five minutes to the neat, ivy-covered house where O'Hara had lived since being appointed to Trabane National School some thirty-six years previously. However, it was more than an hour before Loopy could escape from Pat O'Hara. He had manhandled the teacher into his house without anyone seeing them and was about to leave when O'Hara, in a surprisingly clear voice, instructed him to sit down. When Loopy protested that he had to get back to relieve Joe, the instruction was repeated in a manner that brooked no argument. With no reference whatsoever to the upset in the bar just minutes earlier, the schoolteacher embarked on a lecture. It had but one theme—the benefits of a good education. It took a long time, and the mantra *knowledge is power* was repeated over and over.

At every pause, Loopy made as if to leave, but was told to sit down again in no uncertain terms. When it did end, O'Hara's last words were "I know you are not taking in a fraction of what I say. I really don't know why I bother trying to get it through your thick skull that leaving school early is madness. It's something you'll regret for the rest of your life. I *know* you think you have to earn money for your mother, but it won't always be like that. If you don't go back to school now, you never will. And if that happens, believe you me, you'll live to regret it. I'm telling you for the last time, *knowledge is power*. Remember that. Now you'd better get back to the bar."

Loopy did not need to be told twice. As he walked into the crowded bar, it was announced that Edward Linhurst had won the tournament. Moments later the winner made himself heard above the general hubbub in a brief speech that thanked one and all. It was done effortlessly with the grace of someone to whom public speaking came easily. Yet, to Loopy, it sounded as if it came straight from the heart, especially the part where Linhurst thanked everyone for making him feel so at home in Trabane. Loopy decided there and then that it would be much easier for him to win the tournament than to make the winner's speech. Maybe O'Hara had been right about finishing school after all.

Moving from table to table, serving drinks and emptying ashtrays, Loopy could not help but overhear snatches of conversation. While some were about that day's competition, most of them dwelled on the recent job losses at the Maltings and the scarcity of tourists in Trabane. He couldn't be sure but he thought he heard someone mutter, "Leo's bloody bank could be the next to go, from what I hear."

Suddenly Linhurst was murmuring across the counter that the drinks for the rest of the evening were on him. By closing time, Loopy estimated that Linhurst had drunk eight or nine gin and tonics. As he was writing a check for the tab, he seemed to have some difficulty in signing his name. Tearing off the check along its perforation was proving so troublesome that Linhurst chuckled happily, "Do you know something, young man? I think I'm pissed as a coot!"

Loopy could not think of a suitable reply, but when he saw Linhurst, last to leave, weaving unsteadily toward his car, he summoned up the courage to run after him. Up to this he would never have had the nerve, but with the parking lot deserted, he somehow found the self-confidence to say, "Mr. Linhurst, is there any chance you'd let me drive you home?"

There! It was said and done. If the man took it the wrong way, then so be it. Loopy had been pouring gin and tonics into Linhurst all evening. Should anything happen to him, Loopy would feel responsible.

To his relief, Linhurst paused in midstride, straightened himself, and appeared to give the suggestion serious consideration before turning back toward Loopy. "What a damn good idea! You seem to be as much in demand as a chauffeur as you are a caddy and barman. Multitalented, I'd say."

With that, Linhurst climbed into the passenger seat, and the journey to The Old Rectory passed without incident. Loopy hadn't seen the house since Linhurst had moved in. The avenue was now a smooth ribbon of tarmac, flanked on either side by carefully tended rhodo-dendron bushes. The sweep up to the big hall door was even more im-pressive. An acre of green lawn, smoother than any pool table, surrounded the elegant stone building. But Loopy had barely enough time to be impressed. The door flew open to reveal a beautiful girl— and she was furious.

"Dinner's ruined—absolutely *ruined*! You are *hours* late, Dad. No wonder Mummy couldn't stand it any longer."

She broke off to address an awestruck Loopy, who was discreetly trying to steady her father, who was now swaying dangerously.

"As for you, whoever you are, you can hand over the keys of the car here and now. I'm not going to stand for every Tom, Dick, and Harry joyriding around this dump of a town in Daddy's car when he's obvi-ously pissed out of his mind!"

Wordlessly Loopy handed her the keys and, wordlessly, turned on his heel down the avenue. He walked the three miles to the farm-house, his mind seething with the events of the day. His last thoughts as he drew the covers over his head were that if Pat O'Hara's dictum *knowledge is power* were true, then maybe he should not have had to walk those long miles home in the dark.

Just after ten o'clock the next morning the phone in the bar rang.

"Trabane Golf Club."

"Is that Larry Lynch?" The voice was unmistakably Linhurst's, even if it was hoarser than usual.

"Yes, it is, Mr. Linhurst."

"Good, you're the man I want. First of all, thanks for last night. Very good of you to drive me home, then take all that abuse that Amy dished out like a man."

"No problem, Mr. Linhurst." Loopy nearly added a fatuous *Any-time*, but thought better of it.

"Silly of me to get that pissed. I can tell you I got hell from Amy. I'll tell her it wasn't your fault, nothing like it, just as soon as she cools down. She really does owe you a serious apology. The idea of blaming you for my condition is crazy, but there you are. I'm driving her to the airport later on this evening, so I'll probably stay overnight in Dublin. The trip there and back is a bit too long"—a dry chuckle—"especially when one is not feeling the best."

Loopy said nothing but wondered where all of this was leading. He did not have long to wait.

"Reason I called was that despite the excesses of last night, I *did* remember what you said about not being able to get rid of your hay so late in the year. I have a friend, more of a business acquaintance really, and he ships cattle all over the world. Just now he happens to be shipping beef on the hoof from Cork port to Egypt, of all places."

Another lengthy pause left Loopy still none the wiser.

Linhurst pressed on briskly, "Anyway, the point of all this is that I spoke to him this morning and he is very much in the market for hay. Apparently he loads it onto the cattle boats and feeds the animals with it for the week or so they are at sea. As he is paid by their weights at the other end, naturally he only feeds them the best. I told him you had the best hay for miles around, and he wondered if six pounds a bale collected from your farmyard would be okay. I told him I would have to check it out with you first. Better still, I'll give you his telephone number. If you're interested, I think you should call him back right away and be *sure* to mention my name. By the way, I can guarantee that his credit is good, so if he offers to pay by check, no need to worry."

He called out the number, asked Loopy to repeat it, then ended with "That's alright then."

He had hung up before Loopy could even begin to stammer out his thanks.

An hour later, Linda took over for him behind the counter.

"Where are you off to now? More golf, I suppose. Joe tells me you are making progress, and that's high praise coming from him, I promise you."

Loopy wisely ignored the hint of bitterness in her voice as he made his way out the door of the bar. "Not this morning. I think I'll take a walk along the beach."

"Big wind out there by the sound of it. Don't get blown away or anything."

"I'll do my best not to" was Loopy's parting shot as he disappeared from view.

The walk from the clubhouse to the beach brought him past the old stone school building, which looked even more bedraggled than usual. Empty soda cans and candy wrappers had been blown by the wind into untidy heaps against the low wall that kept O'Hara pupils off the road that ran through Trabane. From there it meandered along the coast to Lisbeg, a deadly rival both in commerce and sport for longer than anyone could remember. Loopy would follow it for a few hundred yards until it ceased to be Trabane's main street and resumed its role as the only road to Lisbeg and points west. As he looked over the schoolyard wall at the unaccustomed litter, never quite still in the sharp gusts blowing in off the sea, he wondered about Pat O'Hara. As recently as six months ago a scrap of litter anywhere near his school was a cause for one of his indignant outbursts. With the veins in his forehead standing out like power cables, he would inquire of his charges in a voice dripping with sarcasm, "Do you want to be known for the rest of your lives as ignorant litter louts who don't know any better than to scatter rubbish wherever you feel like it? Do you want where you live to be known as the dirtiest town in all of Ireland just because you can't be bothered to pick up rubbish whenever you see it? No wonder the tourists are staying away from here in droves. Who wants to visit a bloody pigsty?"

Then he would dismiss the class for as long as it took to clean up the school and its surroundings. But he didn't seem to be doing so anymore. Loopy wondered if the old schoolteacher had given up on it as a waste of time or was simply too old and tired to bother. Then as he recalled the angry sermon O'Hara had given him the night before about leaving school too early, he decided that there was still some life in the old dog yet. He quickened his pace as he passed Norbert's Super Store. A familiar smell was borne on the wind. Seamus Norbert was making his daily contribution to global warming by firing up his rusty incinerator with waste of every description.

Passing the graveyard, Loopy was joined by Norbert's watchdog, a German shepherd of uncertain age and temper. Loopy had earned its friendship by smuggling it a pork chop every now and then when Norbert wasn't looking. That was a year ago, but the animal seemed to remember and was staying with him now until he got another one.

Boy and dog turned off the main road just after the graveyard and walked down a short, rutted path to the beach. They were protected by stands of tall dune grass, now blown almost flat by the wind coming in off the Atlantic, so it wasn't until they reached the beach that they felt the full force of the gale. It had whipped the sea, gray under a leaden sky, into foam-flecked fury. The tide was almost fully out, leaving a vast expanse of wet sand soft underfoot. The only sign of life, apart from themselves, was a flock of gulls wheeling and diving just beyond the pounding surf. They filled the air with frustrated shrieks that suggested lunch was not easily come by in weather like this.

Suddenly they were no longer alone. In the distance a tiny figure appeared. Minutes later it was still half a mile away, but now it became apparent that it was accompanied by a dog. Remembering the uncertain temper of Norbert's watchdog, who was currently sniffing a large jellyfish stranded by the outgoing tide, Loopy noted uneasily that neither animal was on a leash. Tiring of the jellyfish, the bigger dog raised its head and saw the distant animal. In a flash it was sprinting toward the intruder, deaf to Loopy's despairing shouts.

There were no preliminaries. None of the sniffing and snarling that usually precede a dogfight. Without preamble they hurled themselves at each other in a snarling, whirling explosion of rage. By the time Loopy got near them, the contest was almost over. Though the smaller dog had given a good account of himself, the size of Norbert's animal proved telling. They were still struggling as Loopy grasped the bigger dog by the collar and, evading its best efforts to bite him, gave it a sharp kick on the backside. With a pained yelp, the hopes of another pork chop now well and truly dashed, Norbert's dog took to its heels and fled back from whence it came.

Loopy picked up the other combatant, a young spaniel. It was shivering with fright and bleeding from bite marks on its neck. It also seemed to have something wrong with its rear leg as it had toppled over in trying to get up and run back to its frantic owner. She was now quite close but too out of breath to say or do anything for the moment.

Loopy scarcely noticed her arrival, being fully occupied in trying to calm the distressed spaniel. Cradling it in his arms like a baby, he whispered soothing words in its ear.

"How is he? . . . Will he be alright? . . . Why don't you keep your fucking dog under some sort of control?"

The questions exploded around his head like grenades and spurred the spaniel on to further manic struggling in Loopy's arms. Something about the accent was familiar, even though the face was mostly hidden behind a long scarf. A bobble hat pulled well down over her ears left just her dark, furious eyes visible. They were the same eyes that had glared at him the night before as he'd deposited a drunken Edward Linhurst on his doorstep. This time Amy appeared, if anything, even angrier.

"Here, give me back my dog . . . There, there, po-o-o-or Jake. Did the bad man's dog hurt you, my poor baby?"

At the first lull in this rather one-sided conversation between Amy and her dog, Loopy sought to correct her on the ownership of the offending animal.

"Listen, that other dog has nothing to do with me. He just followed me along the beach. He wouldn't go home no matter how often I told him to. What's more—"

She cut in briskly, her voice now lower by several octaves, "Don't I know you from somewhere? Weren't you the guy that brought Daddy . . . ? Oh, Christ, it's *your* fault I'm out here in the first place!"

This left Loopy none the wiser, but before he could think of anything to say, she was off again.

"I'd better try to make myself a bit more clear. First thing this morning Daddy explained to me after you had dropped him off at the door and I had been so rude to you that it was all his fault. He said you had absolutely nothing to do with his getting pissed as a coot, that you were only acting as a Good Samaritan and driving him home as he was too pissed to do so himself. He also suggested that I had better get in touch with you and apologize before I fly back to London tonight. So here I am out here exercising Jake and trying to think how I'm going to pluck up enough courage to phone you at the Golf Club and say how sorry I am for being such a bitch—"

Loopy tried to interrupt but she held her hand up. This caused the scarf to slip away from the lower part of her face, revealing a pert nose and lips fuller and more perfectly shaped than any he had ever laid eyes on before.

"—then your dog comes along and you know the rest."

They looked at each other in silence for a long moment. She was out of breath and he was unable to think of anything sensible to say. Eventually, still holding her gaze, he could manage nothing better than to repeat, "Like I say, it wasn't my dog. The idiot just latched onto me and wouldn't go home for himself. Listen, we had better get Jake back to town to the vet. That's a nasty gash he has on his ear, probably needs stitching. There's something wrong with his hind leg, too. Here, let me carry him for you—it's a long walk back."

By the time they reached the vet's clinic, two doors down the street from Foley's pub, Jake seemed to have calmed down somewhat and the bleeding had almost stopped when they rang the bell. When there was no response after several rings, Amy yelped, "Says here he's closed Mondays. Oh, *shit*, I might have guessed. Today would have to be a bloody Monday, wouldn't it?"

Loopy got straight to the point. "Your dog needs to be fixed up right away. It won't wait till tomorrow."

"So what do we do? There must be another vet somewhere."

Out of respect for Loopy, who was still cradling her dog in his arms, she didn't add *in this godforsaken dump.*

"There is, but he's miles away in Lisbeg. We could phone him from Foley's, the bar over there, but he could take forever—always supposing that we could contact him in the first place. This time of day, he's probably out on a call."

Loopy bit his lip as he considered their situation. "Unless you have a better idea, I think we'd better bring him back to your place right away. It's only a mile or so from here."

They were now halfway to The Old Rectory and Jake was struggling ever harder.

"Do you want to let him walk for a bit? You must be wrecked from carrying him all this way." She had noticed him limping for the last few hundred yards. "Is there something wrong with your leg, too? Jake and you are quite a pair, both without a leg to stand on."

"Better not let him loose on the road. Might get knocked down by a car or something. They drive like lunatics round here."

"So I've noticed. Speaking of driving"—she patted his shoulder affectionately—"that was jolly decent of you to drive Dad home."

She stopped in her tracks and put her hand to her mouth in horror. "Oh my God, did you have to *walk* home all that way after I nearly ate the head off you last night?"

"Yeah, I did."

This time she stopped in front of him, her face only inches from his. Only Jake still cradled in Loopy's arms prevented her from hugging him.

"I'm *so* sorry. I completely misjudged you. I must have been an idiot to think you could ever be responsible for keeping my father out drinking. He told me this morning that you don't drink at *all*! Is that true? An Irishman who doesn't drink?"

She gave him a cheerful and wry grin. He thought how beautiful she looked when she smiled.

"'Fraid so. I haven't started yet anyway." He didn't add that he couldn't afford to, even if he had wanted to. "As for the limp, I got a belt of a hurley a while back and it comes against me every now and again. Nothing to worry about."

"So you play hurling. I've never seen a game, but is it really as rough and tough as I hear?"

"Sometimes. The better the teams the less likely you are to get hurt. In the All-Ireland for instance—that's much the same as the Super Bowl or Soccer Final in England, practically no one gets hurt."

"Why's that?"

They were halfway up the avenue leading to The Old Rectory. In the daylight, Loopy could see that the rhododendrons lining the avenue were a riot of color. Every few yards, at regular intervals, a large stone urn, dripping with a flower of piercing purple, was set in a half-moon of perfectly trimmed lawn. The effect was stunningly beautiful even before the house itself came into view.

"Skill levels. The guys who make it to the All-Ireland know what they're doing. They're tough as nails but fair. In those games there's very little fouling or hitting someone with a hurley when the ref isn't looking their way."

"So how did you get hurt then, if it's all so clean and sporting?"

Something in her voice told him that she wasn't just trying to be polite or anything like that, but that she was genuinely interested. How could he know that she was already quite taken by him and wanted to know everything she possibly could about him?

"I play—or I used to—on a much lower level. Every year Trabane plays Lisbeg, the town nearest to us. The two teams have been at each other's throat for as long as anyone can remember. It's in games like that, that you can get hurt, with the hurleys flying in every direction and the supporters on both sides yelling for blood."

"So that's what happened to you?"

"Yeah, I won't be hurling again for a while. Doesn't affect the golf though, so it's not so bad."

"Dad tells me that you're going to be a terrific golfer."

She was turning the handle in the massive front door, studded with nails like a medieval fortress. The sight and smell of familiar surroundings was causing Jake to struggle even more.

"I don't know about that. It's more fun than I thought it would be, though."

She closed the door behind them. "Why not let him down now. We'll see if he can walk now without falling over."

When Jake sprinted for what proved to be the kitchen, they followed him at a more sedate pace as Amy continued, "That's interesting. That you find golf fun, I mean. Dad's been playing it for as long as I can remember, and it sounds boring as hell to be honest with you. As for his golfing friends, they all wear these silly clothes, talk about nothing but golf, and drink like fishes."

During this, they had been trying to catch Jake, who was now looking much chirpier but still bleeding. In fact, a trail of blood led from the front door, along the polished parquet floor, and across the white kitchen tiles. Loopy found some old newspapers and put them on the kitchen table.

"We'd better have a look at his cut and see if his leg is alright. He seems to running round on it okay, but just in case, I think we should take a look at it."

"We . . . ?" Amy shuddered and turned pale as a ghost. "You, maybe, but not me. I can't stand the sight of blood."

"That's okay. Why don't you boil some water and see if you can find a bottle of disinfectant. Whiskey or gin will do at a pinch."

Amy returned with a bottle of gin and a glass. She poured a generous measure into the glass, saying, "This is for me, the bottle is for you and Jake. Also the boiling water. I won't even offer you a drink since you said you never touched the stuff."

They caught the dog, who somehow knew what lay in store for him and put up an impressive struggle before they could manhandle him onto the table. Loopy rummaged around in the fur on his neck to find the wound. There were two, one quite severe, the other much less serious. He washed the cuts first, then rubbed in the gin as Jake yelped in pain and tried hard to bite him on the hand.

"There, there, poor boy, you're going to be just fine," Loopy murmured to the struggling spaniel as the spirit worked its way into the cuts. Now Loopy needed Vaseline or something like it to rub over the wound. He had already waggled Jake's hind legs while keeping a firm grip on his throat. Though the dog yelped again, Loopy was fairly certain nothing was broken.

Amy was nowhere to be seen so he shouted, "Amy, do you have any Vaseline?"

She came back into the kitchen. The glass she had poured her gin into was now brimming with ice and tonic water. "Sure you won't have one of these? No? Right. Well, you probably think I am a complete idiot, but I really, really cannot stand the sight of blood. Makes me want to throw up on the spot. Now, what were you saying about Vaseline? Because I don't think we have any. Or if we do, I haven't a clue where to find it. Would face cream be any good? I've loads of that."

"Yeah, might be." Loopy was concentrating on working the hind legs up and down, much to Jake's annoyance. "Nothing broken anyway. His legs are fine, but they'll be a bit sore for a while yet."

Still working the dog's legs up and down with one hand and holding the mouth closed with the other, thereby stifling any further plans Jake might have had to sink his teeth into his benefactor, Loopy didn't notice Amy approaching from behind. She cupped his head in her hands and drew him toward her.

"You are a truly wonderful person! I was *so* wrong about you. How can I ever thank you for what you did."

With that, still holding his face in her hands, she kissed him long and hard on the lips. Then, breaking away after what seemed to Loopy to be quite the most delightful feeling he had ever experienced in his life, Amy grinned.

"I'd better get that face cream now while I can still remember it."

While she was gone, Loopy tickled Jake behind the ears and was rewarded with a wag of his tail. He confided to the still-struggling spaniel, "You're going to be fine, and do you know something, Jake? So am I."

CHAPTER FIVE

It was a perfect evening. The sun was dipping below the horizon, tracing a golden path along the shimmering, restless ocean. With just a few minutes left of twilight, the two golfers approaching the green quickened their steps. Silhouetted against the ocean, they were now in full view of Loopy. He had been gazing idly out the window as he polished the glasses. He would hold each one up to the light from the window for a final inspection before putting it back on the shelf.

The bar had a low ceiling into which lengths of timber had been embedded, then painted to look like rafters. From them hung a collection of glass, silver, and pewter beer mugs. The rustic effect was further enhanced by an assortment of earthenware jars, varying in size from one to five gallons. They all bore the modest legend, "Trabane 5 Star Special—The Finest, Purest, and Best Whiskey Obtainable."

The claim could not be proven since the brand had disappeared off the market sixty years earlier. The glazed jars, however, had proven more durable, and the first task Loopy had been given when he'd started work in the bar had been to polish them until they gleamed. He marveled at the thought of farmers, maybe his ancestors, carrying home their weekly supplies from town on a horse-drawn buggy weighed down with sacks of flour, salt, sugar, chewing tobacco, and a jar of Trabane 5 Star Special.

The walls of the bar were festooned with framed advertisements for long-defunct brands of tea, cigarettes, and mineral waters. Beer, too. One he particularly liked showed a smiling farmer effortlessly holding aloft, far above his head with one hand, a huge workhorse. The other hand clutched a pint glass of dark beer as he bellowed, "Murphy's stout gives you strength!"

A rival brand on the opposite wall was even more to the point: "Guinness is good for you!"

Loopy mused that unlike Trabane 5 Star, both beers were still brands his customers asked for regularly, even if the extravagant advertisements had been toned down over the years. The bar counter had a top of black marble that was the very devil to keep clean. Barstools upholstered in red leather stood like sentinels against a heavy brass footrail bolted to the wooden floor.

As he was putting the last glass back on the shelf, he saw in the big mirror behind the bar the reflection of two golfers playing the final hole. He turned around to watch their progress through the big window that looked out on the eighteenth fairway.

As they drew closer, he saw one of them veer off the fairway, looking for his ball. It was Leo Martin. Quite by chance, Loopy had seen Leo's ball bouncing off a tree and coming to rest behind it. Leo would have to chip the ball out sideways before playing his approach shot to the green. Loopy glanced across the fairway at the other player, now recognizable as Tim Porter. Tim was focused on lighting a cigarette in the stiffening breeze as he waited for Leo to play.

It was then that Loopy saw the banker give his ball a surreptitious kick with his shoe. The ball shot out from behind the tree and stopped on a level patch of grass from where Leo now had a clear shot to the green. Tim was still trying to light his cigarette and was too far away to have observed any skulduggery when Leo waved at him to indicate that he had found his ball. He then hit a high wedge to within ten feet of the flagstick. Had Loopy not seen what had happened *before* Leo's wedge shot, he would have remarked to himself—for the bar was empty—on the excellence of the shot.

Disconcerted by his opponent's recovery, Tim hit a weak approach shot that barely reached the putting surface. He took two putts to hole out, then watched intently as Leo crouched over his putt for what seemed like an eternity. The whoop from the banker as his ball disappeared into the hole left no doubt as to who had won the match.

When they came into the bar, Tim said, "There you go, Leo, ten hard-earned notes. That was one hell of a shot you played to the last green."

Leo shot Tim an anxious look but could find nothing in his expression to suggest that his fancy footwork had been detected.

"Thanks. Yes, it certainly was one of my better efforts. What can I get you?"

"A whiskey and soda, I think. Must make a phone call first though. Shan't be long." With that, he was gone.

With no one left to talk to, Leo addressed Loopy, "Two whiskey and sodas, like a good man. Make mine a large one while you're at it. Might as well celebrate, seeing as your friend Tim Porter is paying for it. To the victor, the spoils, eh? Just managed to pip him on the last hole with a big putt. Ran into the hole like a frightened rat, so it did."

Loopy stared hard at him. He longed to be the kind of person who could look Leo Martin in the eye and tell him straight out that he had seen him cheat. But this was nothing more than wishful thinking. Imagine Larry Lynch, son of the local bankrupt, shelf-stacker and general ignoramus, daring to challenge the bank manager who also just happened to be treasurer of the Golf Club! It was laughable, but nevertheless he felt a sudden surge of anger. This was not the way things should be, having to kowtow to cheats like Leo Martin.

Yet things like that were changing fast, not just in Trabane but all over the country. Look at the way, he reminded himself, he had felt too humble to drive Edward Linhurst home when he had taken one too many because Loopy regarded him as in some way his social superior. On that occasion Loopy had found the courage to stifle his inferiority complex. If he could find that same courage once more, it might just set things right for his friend. He hated to see Tim Porter cheated out of his money even if he had more than he needed. In a flash his mind was made up. He swallowed hard, then looked Leo straight in the eye.

"Yes, sir, it was a good putt. But the wedge onto the green was quite a shot, too, wasn't it? I had a great view of it from here altogether." Loopy nodded toward the window, and both pairs of eyes immediately zoomed in on the tree from behind which Leo had kicked his golf ball.

Again Loopy had to swallow hard before suggesting with a calmness he did not feel, "Weren't you dead lucky that tree didn't interfere with your shot."

There was another, longer pause during which neither of them spoke nor looked at each other. Loopy was still looking absently at the tree, and Leo had found something of interest to him in the ashtray on the bar counter.

By now Loopy was growing more confident by the second as he added, "Mind you, 'twas a great shot all the same, Mr. Martin, when you actually got 'round to playing it. I'd say Mr. Porter was really surprised, too—you were *more* than lucky, the way I saw it!"

With that, Loopy turned away to fill the drinks, leaving Leo staring uneasily at his back. When he turned round again with the drinks, Leo's manner had undergone a marked change. Tim had not yet returned, so the bar was still empty as the banker remarked in a casual, man-to-man drawl scarcely louder than a whisper, "I rarely talk shop here at the club, y'know, but I must say I'm very impressed with the way you're trying to pay off your father's overdraft despite your injury. A pity more 'round here couldn't do likewise. Anyway, be that as it may . . ." Then, as if the thought had just struck him: "Why not drop in to the bank tomorrow? I might have an interesting proposition for you."

Then, with what was meant to be a conspiratorial wink, Leo

leaned across the counter, adding, "Now let's forget all about the tree, shall we?"

At that moment, before Loopy could reply, Tim reappeared and joined Leo at a table by the window.

The Allied Banks of Ireland in Trabane was in a cut-stone building with round, marble pillars flanking a heavy oak door. Only the garish, backlit plastic sign indicated that it was a bank rather than the headquarters of some obscure religious sect. It stood on a corner of the main street and a lesser thoroughfare that lead to the church. This, unsurprisingly, was called Church Street. When Loopy called to the bank, it was almost empty. He wondered if the wild rumors were correct after all.

Moves were indeed afoot to close it down, though at this early stage only Leo Martin was privy to this. The suboffice in nearby Lisbeg had already shut up shop, and Trabane was scheduled to follow suit. To avoid the inevitable uproar when the closure was made public, the townspeople would first have to be persuaded that this was not necessarily the final nail in the coffin for Trabane. By now Leo had been carefully briefed as to how to proceed with this delicate exercise in public relations. The directors had already come up with a draft of something they called a Code of Practice for dealing with customers and local communities affected by such closures. From the little sense that Leo could make of it, it meant ingratiating himself as much as possible with the local people, though how this was to be achieved was left up to him.

The post office would remain open, but anyone needing proper banking services would have to travel to the next town, eleven miles away. Already some of the ground had been prepared in advance of the closure. Leo had easily been won over by the promise of a transfer and promotion to Dublin. Though sworn to secrecy, he was sure that Rosa, his wife, would welcome the move from this dismal backwater.

The intercom on his desk buzzed like an angry wasp: "Young Lynch to see you, Manager—says he has an appointment." The assistant manager made no effort to hide his surprise. He would have seen the stern letters addressed to Lynch's mother and wondered why her eldest was seeking audience with Leo.

"Send him in!

"Ah, Lynch, how nice to see you. Sit yourself down over there"— Leo gestured toward a chair on the far side of the paper-strewn desk as he peered at a computer screen—"while I bring myself up-to-date on your father's account."

Loopy did as he was told and said nothing.

After some tentative key-bashing, Leo let out a deep moan like a wounded buffalo. "Ah, yes. A matter of almost one thousand pounds. Overdrawn, I see, and without sanction."

"I beg your pardon, sir?"

Leo harrumphed and raised an eyebrow. This was intended to register his amazement that anyone in this day and age could not be familiar with this, the simplest of banking jargon. "*Without sanction?* Well, young man, it means that your father cashed checks all over the place without first okaying them with me. That's what *without sanction* means. And when you do that sort of thing, there are penalties."

"Penalties?"

"Yes, penalties." Leo was becoming testy from having to explain even the simplest of banking terms. Still, he reminded himself, it had to be done if his reputation was not to be ruined by this whippersnapper alerting all and sundry to his fancy footwork. "Penalties, in this instance, come in the form of surcharges."

He had thought to joke that these penalties were quite different from the sort Loopy was accustomed to taking for the Trabane Gaels, but decided against it. Too complex and not worth the effort. Instead he explained what surcharges were.

"Surcharges are in addition to the penalties, so that when you add both of them on the interest charged on an unsanctioned overdraft, it all adds up very quickly, I can tell you!" A pause to let this sink in. "However, in the light of our little chat yesterday, I have decided to review your father's account. The bank had originally viewed him as having defaulted on the loan, but that does not now appear to be the case."

Leo shot a glance at Loopy to make sure that he was taking all this in before pressing on. "I see there have been some repayments made, and small though they are, I am reclassifying the Lynch account from an unauthorized overdraft to the status of a regular long-term loan. All penalties charged to the original account will be canceled, and the interest rate will be substantially less."

Here Leo paused to adjust his glasses, which were threatening to fall off the end of his nose. "In plain English that means that with all these adjustments, the Lynch account now stands at something just short of *seven* hundred pounds, rather than the thousand or so that was owed to the bank when the account was in your father's name."

"Does that mean, Mr. Martin, that we owe three hundred pounds less than we did ten minutes ago?"

Martin harrumphed quite a bit before admitting, "Well, yes, you *could* put it like that, I suppose. Everything now depends on your mother signing these papers I have drawn up for her—oh, yes, and, of course, your discretion in that other matter, as well."

Now it was Loopy's turn. "You're trying to bribe me, aren't you?"

Leo turned purple, but before he could reply, Loopy continued, "We both know you cheated Tim yesterday, and now you think that you can buy my silence by taking a bit off the overdraft."

Leo had got his breath back by now. "How dare you, it's nothing of the sort. If you think—"

Loopy had found an inner strength from somewhere as he cut Leo short. "What I think, Mr. Martin doesn't matter. What does matter is that by the end of the month I'll have a check for three thousand pounds lodged against the account. When it is cleared, I want you to use it to cancel that overdraft and put what's left over on deposit in my mother's name. You can do what you like about the interest and penalties."

Without waiting for a reply, Loopy stood up and left. He visited the fort on his way home. As he sat cross-legged in the center of the standing stones, his mind emptied. Leo and his bank might have been a million miles away. After a while he saw his father's face in his mind's eye. A short man in his forties, red-faced and going thin on top. Loopy thought long and hard about his father. Would he have been proud of his son and the way he handled the banker? How would he have reacted to Leo's change of heart? It wasn't every day the bank reduced a debt by three hundred pounds. Would he have considered it nothing more than a lucky break—as if one of his rank outsiders had unexpectedly strolled home an easy winner? Or would he have clapped his son on the back, laughing: "Good man yourself, well done!"

Might he buy him a pint to celebrate? Not likely, Loopy decided.

And what of himself, Loopy wondered, what would he have done if his father were standing beside him in the fort just then? Would they have shared a laugh at Leo's expense? Or would he have let out an ecstatic *Whoopee!* and playfully punched his father's arm? Hardly, he thought. Father and son had never had anything to celebrate together, Loopy reflected sadly. As for the playful punch, it would, most likely, have been misunderstood and sparked off a real row instead. A row like the one on the night his father had slammed the door behind him and strode across the cobblestones and out of their lives, leaving a trail of debt behind him. His father had taken the easy way out without a care for his wife or family. Yet Sean Lynch for all his faults was Loopy's father, and nothing, absolutely nothing, he told himself, could ever change that.

Loopy wondered how he would react if his father did come back. Would he embrace him as a son should or would he act cold and distant to the man who had abandoned them? Why had his father not got in touch? Where was the money he had promised to send home as soon as he got a steady job? Probably in some bookie's satchel. Loopy realized with a start that he had come to hate his father. Then, as he remembered the times he had seen his mother sobbing quietly when she thought no one was looking, he hated him even more. This was a memory he had blocked until now. Whether it was the exhilaration at besting Leo Martin, the strange magic of the fort, or a combination of both that had freed his mind to enter dark places that had been off limits up to this he would never know.

Another thing he could not know was that his father was having a rough time of it in Birmingham. Anything other than the most menial of jobs was denied to him. He was forced to share a dingy room with an ever-changing cast of workers who drifted in and out like the fleas that infested the beds. The cockroaches seemed the only permanent residents as Sean tried—and failed—to pluck up courage to write home without enclosing the promised money order.

The tingling sensation had returned. It was as if the blood in Loopy's veins flowed faster. It was not an unpleasant feeling even if it did make him feel giddy and set the hairs on the nape of his neck standing on end. What made it so different this time was that long after he had left the fort, the tingling persisted.

When he told Brona of his visit to the bank, he did not mention the incident of Leo and the golf ball lest she might think that he had been indulging in a little subtle blackmail. The very thought made him smile, for who would have thought that the shy and self-effacing Larry Lynch would have faced down Leo Martin in his bank? Certainly not his mother. She would have ascribed their good fortune with the hay and the bank to the goodness of God and his Blessed Mother. Yet he knew her to be nobody's fool, and she might well have had an inkling that it had something to do with the Golf Club as well.

In the afternoon he dropped in again to the fort on his way back to work at the Golf Club. This time he remained standing, feeling a bit ridiculous even though only a few cows, lazily chewing the cud, were there to watch him. He felt his mind empty of everything. Norbert, the hay, Leo Martin, even Maire, vanished and he was left in a weird, almost frightening void. All he could feel was a strange sense of empowerment, as if no task were too great for him to accomplish. Again the feeling persisted long after he had made his way out through the narrow gap in what had once been the ramparts of the old fairy ring.

That afternoon as he was about to finish his stint behind the bar, Joe phoned from the driving range. "I've just had a cancellation. If you come up here right away, we can have almost an hour before my next lesson."

Loopy walked, almost ran, the half mile up the hill to where Joe stood, a solitary figure swishing a club one-handed with practiced ease. Joe handed him the driver. As Loopy set up to hit the first ball, he felt the hairs on the back of his neck start to tingle, exactly the same feeling as he had experienced in the fort. His mind emptied itself of everything. All he could see was the small white ball inviting him to smash it to smithereens. Instead of exploding into tiny fragments it took off like a missile.

Joe Delany murmured, "Hit another one."

He did so. Several times. Each time the ball flew like an arrow, straighter and farther than ever before.

"Okay, stop right there." Joe's voice sounded different. Hoarser, strained even. "We'll just have time to play the fourteenth. Then it's time for my next lesson."

Loopy had never played with Joe up to this. It had just been a matter of hitting balls on the range with Joe offering bits of advice every now and again. This was different. He would be using Joe's clubs, too, new and shining with grips so thick he could barely get his fingers to wrap round them. The fourteenth hole was a long par five, with the ocean on one side and mountainous sand dunes on the other. The fairway was bordered on either side by thick rough. It was pure linksland in the sense that the fairway was a narrow ribbon of green meandering through grass-covered sand dunes. Between these the pounding surf of the Atlantic could be seen—and heard.

The hole measured just short of five hundred yards with the entrance to the green jealously guarded by two sand dunes, standing solemnly and threateningly as sphinxes. Joe Delany estimated that in today's conditions playing into the wind, it would require three good shots to reach the green. Loopy had, however, unleashed a drive of enormous length. It was fully fifty yards beyond Joe's, but at the very last moment, it had trickled off the fairway into the first cut of rough.

Joe played a solid three wood for his second. It came to rest well short of the dunes protecting the green. He smiled to himself as Loopy took a four wood from his bag. The ball was lying much too low in the grass for that kind of shot. He thought of saying as much, but then decided that it would be better if Loopy found this out for himself. After a moment's thought, Loopy put the wood back in the bag and selected an iron instead. Joe couldn't quite see which one, but it looked like a five iron.

With more than two hundred yards to the flag, it seemed as if Loopy were following Joe's example and laying up short of the green. As he stood poised over the ball, Loopy again felt the tingle and the hairs prickling on the back of his neck stronger than ever. He focused every fiber of his being on the ball, or what he could see of it peeping out from the spiky dune grass that made the rough in Trabane so difficult. For a brief moment time stood still, and even the gulls swooping overhead seemed to pause in flight as the club descended, then sent tufts of grass and earth spewing in every direction. The ball exploded skyward. It cleared the big sand dune guarding the left side of the green with something to spare before disappearing from view.

Awestruck, neither spoke for what seemed an age. Loopy still had the club in his hand when Joe asked quietly, "What iron was that?"

"Five."

"Jesus, I don't believe it. Let me *see* it!"

Slamming it back in his bag, the pro strode off wordlessly. He played his third shot, a high wedge toward the hidden green. As they passed through the narrow entrance between the dunes, two balls were on the green. One lay almost thirty feet from the hole, the other less than four feet. Joe, examining the ball farthest from the hole, grunted, "Mine."

Loopy stood over his short putt, waiting for the tingle. None came. He missed the hole by a good two inches. Joe exhaled noisily but said nothing until they were back at the driving range. As Loopy was about to go back to the clubhouse and resume his stint behind the bar, Joe remarked casually, "I think it's about time you learned how to putt."

Some days later, his mother had two items of news for Loopy over breakfast. The Englishman had called about the hay, left a check for over three thousand pounds, and would send lorries to collect it as soon as the check had cleared. She had also had a visit from Joe Delany. He had tried as best he could to explain the unique golfing talent her son possessed. He had suggested it might be possible to make a living from golf if Loopy was prepared to work hard at the game. Joe had offered to coach Loopy free of charge in return for his helping out in the pro shop when he wasn't on duty in the Golf Club bar. It seemed odd that Joe should approach his mother before first checking with him, but maybe, Loopy thought, that was the way Joe did his business. Anyway it was great to hear, albeit secondhand, that Joe believed Loopy had a talent for the game. It certainly beat stacking shelves and getting nothing but abuse from both Norbert and Maire, though Joe still hadn't offered *him* the job personally.

When he reported for bar duty next day, Linda said that Joe wanted a word with him on the practice range and that she would look after things until he came back. Joe was giving a lesson and indicated that Loopy should wait until it was over. Workmen were pouring concrete into shuttering as if a house were being built at one end of the practice ground. With the lesson finished, Joe strolled over and jerked a thumb in the direction of the construction.

"The new driving range. They're the all-weather practice bays. Should be ready by the autumn. The club wants a proper driving range, automatic ball machine, the works. Trouble is, they want me to look after it, along with everything else in this bloody place. Did your mother tell you I called out to see her?"

Loopy nodded but said nothing.

"Yeah, well, I told her you might, just *might* make a golfer. That par five we played together made up my mind. Now listen carefully 'cause I'm only going to say this just once. If you work hard, do as I say, and don't mess around with drink or women, you might, just *might*, make a living from this game. Are you interested?"

Loopy thought the question demanded something more than a nod, so he blurted out, "Yes, I am. Very much."

"Right." The pro puffed his cheeks before expelling a long breath. "Here's the deal. Like I say, I'll say it just the once. Ready?"

Loopy nodded, trying hard to look calm even though his heart was thumping like a jackhammer.

"You help out in the shop and here on this driving range when it's up and running. That means you collect the balls—I'll show you later how it's done—make sure the ball machine is fully loaded and working properly. Every night you empty out the machine of coins and bring them to me. When you have the balls collected, you cut the grass if it needs it. In short, *you* are running this facility, though you are doing it for *me*. In return I will coach you every day and show you everything I know. You will have free run of this practice area and all the practice balls you want for free. We'll both review the situation at the end of every month. I'll decide if you are working hard enough—both for me and on your game. You can decide if you want to continue on with the arrangement or pack it in—as you wish. There may come a time when

I'll have taught you all I know and you may want to go somewhere else to complete your education as a golfer. On the other hand, you may get fed up of hitting golf balls day after day and want to call the whole thing off."

Joe paused for breath and looked at the boy. "Well, what do you think?"

Loopy looked at the ground first, deep in thought for a moment or two, then looked up with a grin. "When do I start?"

"No time like the present. Get the putter out of my bag and I'll show you how to putt."

Loopy could hardly wait to get home and tell Brona that the new job was in the bag. She seemed happy for him, observing that when Seamus had brought the groceries that morning, he had not been his usual cheery self. It wasn't so much anything he had said but more what he had *not* said. Up to now he had always asked about the injured leg and wondered when Larry would be fit enough to play for the Trabane Gaels again. This time his remarks were confined to the weather and the difficulty in getting rid of hay at this time of year. When Brona told him that some Englishman had taken the whole lot, he merely grunted and said nothing. All of which prompted Brona to ask her son, "Did you and Seamus have a falling-out by any chance?"

"It's like this, Mam. Mr. Norbert has really changed since he heard I can't play for the Gaels for a while. Nothing I do is right anymore, and everything's *my* fault. What's worse, Maire's nearly as bad as him. Since he put her in charge of the checkout, it's gone to her head."

"What do you mean 'gone to her head'? A little bird told me you were sweet on her, is that what's the matter?"

Loopy reddened but stood his ground. "Whatever little bird told you that got it wrong, Mam! No, it's just that she never stops bossing me round the place. It's 'Do this' and 'Do that,' and to tell the truth, Mam, I'm getting fed up with it."

He was so upset that she took his hand and squeezed it gently.

"If you don't like working at Norbert's anymore, why don't you hand in your notice? Don't think I'll be standing in your way. I never thought I'd hear myself saying this, but maybe you might be better off working at the Golf Club and getting lessons from that nice Mr. Delany."

B reaking the news to Seamus was worse than Loopy had expected. When offered a month's notice, Norbert preferred that he took his leave right away. "Don't want any halfhearted sailors on *my* ship!" was how he put it, leaving Loopy in no doubt that the supermarket was well rid of him.

Maire was no different. "I knew, I just *knew*, that you'd be joining those snobs up in the Golf Club the first chance you got."

This seemed unfair, especially when Maire herself was spending more and more evenings working part-time as a waitress at the club. Because both the kitchen and the dining area were some distance from the bar and the pro shop, he did not see that much of her.

As for his mother, Brona was a different woman now. Less timid than before, she dressed better, stopping to chat with old friends on the street rather than trying to avoid them, and went to a hairdresser once a week. There was still no word from her husband, but it had been months since Loopy had last seen her quietly sobbing to herself.

CHAPTER SIX

Loopy was spending every spare moment he had on the practice ground hitting golf balls until his hands blistered. Brona once asked him how his golf was getting on, and he spent half an hour showing her that by just changing the position of his thumb on the golf club, he had found he could hit the ball better than ever.

He had to admit that of late, he had been interested in nothing but golf. It was the only thing that got his attention day in and day out. He wondered anxiously if it was possible to be a really good golfer and still have a normal life. The sort of life where people socialized, went out on dates, fell in and out of love, and all that sort of thing. He felt something for Amy, much more than he had ever felt about Maire, but he wasn't sure if it was love or something else. He thought about it for quite a long time before going back to hitting more golf balls. He was using the driver that O'Hara had given him, the same one he'd used to drive the green the day it had all started for him. The reality was that his whole world had been taken over by golf.

His handicap was down to three, one shot more than Tim Porter. They had become good friends, despite the difference in age and up-bringing. Whenever Tim was around, they played together, and an intense but friendly rivalry had sprung up between them. It was as if

Loopy had a jinx on Tim. Nine times out of ten, he could beat him in a level match, despite the handicap rating. But it was not enough to beat Tim regularly—Loopy wanted more than anything else in the world to have the lowest handicap in Trabane Golf Club. It was not simply the prestige; Joe Delany had promised him a new driver if he managed it. Not just any driver, but one of the new high-tech ones that cost a small fortune.

Of course Tim Porter had one, just as he also had the latest BMW to travel round the country selling wine. His father was far too wise an old owl to let Tim loose on Porters, the core wine-importing business that dealt in classic French vintages for the better hotels, restaurants, and wealthy collectors. Tim was brand manager, a title he rather fancied, for the miniature wine bottles sold through bars and off-licenses. His father had entered this market with the greatest reluctance, for here it was price rather than quality that counted. However, it *was* a fast-growing market sector, and one that did not require any great knowledge of the wine industry. In truth, all it needed was frequent servicing, which meant that Tim had to meet his customers regularly, listen to their complaints, and either play golf with them or take them out to dinner as circumstances dictated. It was the perfect job for an only son whose greatest talent was his ability to get along with all and sundry.

In the wine trade, young Tim Porter was regarded as an artless if amiable upper-class twit. His education at one of the more expensive boarding schools sat lightly on his broad shoulders. He had been useful at rugby and tennis, played an adequate game of bridge, but golf was his first love. In golfing circles he was much more highly thought of than elsewhere. As well as sporting the lowest handicap at Trabane, for the past six years he had represented it in the prestigious Atlantic Trophy. Which was another way of saying that he was the best player by far—except that Loopy could now beat him nine times out of ten.

The Trophy differed from other amateur tournaments in that com-

petitors had to be *invited* to play. Sixty-four clubs were asked to send
one player each to compete in a knockout competition played over the
Easter weekend. In all the other "majors," players either qualified by
handicap, an open draw, or knockout competition. It was appropriate
that it be a bank-holiday weekend, for the Atlantic Trophy was sponsored by none other than Leo Martin's employers, the Allied Banks of
Ireland Group. The bank's corporate clients—mostly American, for it
was there the Allied Banks of Ireland had plans for expansion—were
the A-list invitees. After that came the teams from preferred golf
clubs.

It was no coincidence that golf clubs fortunate enough to be invited tended to bank with the sponsors, and the individuals competing
were invariably clients in good standing with ABI. The candidate selected by the invited clubs did not necessarily have to be the best
golfer available, merely the most acceptable to the sponsors. The golf
course in the popular seaside resort of Ballykissane, where The Atlantic, as it was generally known, had been staged since time immemo-
rial, was not unlike the links at Trabane.

Both courses were buffeted by gales blowing in from the ocean,
gusting and eddying between giant sand dunes, which made shotmak-
ing exceptionally difficult. There was the same wiry grass in the rough
with an added hazard at The Atlantic—clumps of thick heather that
flourished among the dunes. Hacking a golf ball out of these was an
uncertain science and required not just nerves, but also wrists, of
steel.

When Tim Porter announced that his business would bring him to
Ballykissane for an overnight trip and invited Loopy to accompany
him, Joe Delany insisted that the offer should be accepted without
hesitation.

On the long drive to Ballykissane, Tim Porter revealed that he had
never got past the second round of The Atlantic. He described this as
being "a bit of a pain in the arse" but hardly surprising since nearly all

of the Irish International golf team and many past Internationals made up the field every year. If that weren't enough, the sponsors invited their American clients, some of whom were—or had been— good enough to represent their country in the Walker Cup.

"It's really the last of the amateur events in the true meaning of the word. It's pure match play, not stroke—and it's a bloody tiring thirty-six holes *every* day. Your club pays the entry, but you have to cough up for your own hotel expenses, food, caddies, and lots of other things besides. The bank throws a big party on the last night, but that's about it!"

Loopy was more interested in the trophy. "When is the cup presented?"

"The Atlantic Trophy you mean? Immediately after the final round, outside the clubhouse. Win that, mate, and you're *made* for bloody life!"

Maybe so, thought Loopy, but only if you are in a position to properly benefit from it. Someone like Tim for instance. If he won it, he could dine out on it for the rest of his life. His customers would really be impressed and no mistake. He might even be invited to join the board of ABI at some future date. Quite what benefits winning The Atlantic would bestow on a country boy like Loopy were less obvious. They chatted easily about anything and everything as the big car ate up the miles.

The Royal Hotel at Ballykissane was a lavish affair. It had once been a railway hotel where trains deposited golfers from the cities to test their mettle against one of the best links courses on the planet. Now, with the railways long replaced by motorways, The Royal struggled to maintain at least some of its former glory.

Tim explained that they would be sharing a room. Tim's father handled the main account for the serious wine in the hotel's cellars, but the bar, in line with everywhere else, was selling more and more wine by the glass. The manager, at the urging of his bar staff, was anxious to upgrade the quality of wine that came out of the miniature, screw-top bottles that Tim supplied. Tim, believing that Loopy might be interested because of his work behind the bar of the golf club, explained at some length, "The stuff in most of those small bottles is absolute piss! There *are* a few, *damn* few actually, that could be classed as drinkable, but they are a damned sight more expensive. What The Royal want from me is the good stuff at the old price, and that simply can't be done. Still, we'll get a night at the hotel at half-rate, a decent dinner, and a free round of golf just for listening to their tales of woe and slipping the head barman a few quid under the counter. Absolutely *vital* to have him onside during The Atlantic—for the after-hours drinkies, y'know. Then, of course"—he was now talking to himself as much as to Loopy when he remarked wistfully and without any explanation whatsoever—"there's always good old Lily."

They had arrived at the hotel entrance by driving around, rather than through, the holiday resort of Ballykissane, still empty of visitors in early April. From the top of the flight of marble steps that led to the porch guarding the front door, Tim gestured toward a distant collection of mountainous sand hills in the distance, with the Atlantic ocean forming a glittering backdrop.

"That's the golf course over there. We'll check in first, then grab something to eat before we play. After that, dinner, and then, with any luck," he added enigmatically, "I might be leaving you to your own devices for a while."

At reception, they were handed two green-fee tickets and directed to their room. It was enormous and Loopy worried how he was going to pay for it, even at half-rate, when Tim, as if reading his mind, remarked casually, "By the way, in case you were wondering, this is all on the house. The House of Porter, that is, purveyors of fine wines for over a century. Actually," he added in a cheery tone, "I've always thought that Porter was an odd name for a wine merchant, but there you go. Beggars can't be choosers. They say you can pick your friends but not your relations—and that goes for your name, too, I expect.

Anyway, the long and the short of it is that this is a *business* trip and you are, for the purposes of the act, my guest. That includes green fees, which are, I'm glad to say, included in the overnight rate. So, Larry my boy, the only time you'll have to put your hand in your pocket is to pay for the odd drink and, of course, your caddy."

Loopy had been advised that it would be madness not to take a caddy for his first round on an unfamiliar course, especially one as testing as this. He had been expecting someone of his own age to caddy for him, so it came as quite a shock when the caddy master, after a whispered discussion with Tim, directed Loopy toward a disheveled bundle of rags sitting on a bench. The caddy struggled to his feet and tightened the belt of a heavy overcoat that had seen better days, even though the hot afternoon sun was splitting the stones. Loopy tried to hide his dismay at being put in the hands of a senior caddy, and such a dismal-looking one at that. The caddy master's introduction was brief and to the point: "This is Weeshy."

Weeshy gave a cough like a rasp on metal before he removed the remains of a cigarette from his lower lip and stamped on it with what had once, a long time ago, been a Nike trainer. Removing the last shreds of tobacco by flicking his tongue like a serpent, he spat them out delicately. They struck the ground inches from Loopy's feet. Weeshy eyed the golf bag with obvious distaste before hoisting it over his right shoulder and walking with a rolling gait toward the first tee.

Tim's caddy, a lad of about fifteen or so, muttered into Loopy's ear so as not to be heard by his senior colleague, "Mr. Porter tells me you hit a long ball, but I'd advise you to listen to old Weeshy. After he's seen you play a hole or two, he'll know what club you need better than yourself. He mightn't be much to look at, but he knows every blade of grass around here."

The first hole at Ballykissane stretched upward for what seemed an eternity. Though the ocean was not visible, its pounding surf could be clearly heard from behind the sand dunes, some of which were a hundred feet or more in height. Four hundred and forty-eight yards of ribbonlike fairway threaded its way around hummocks and hillocks to a small plateau high up among the dunes. The only indication that it was a green was the fluttering triangle of red in the distance. Loopy gave Tim the honor of teeing off first, and he striped one down the middle. Using O'Hara's old driver with the wooden head, Loopy hit a good drive, some twenty-five yards past Tim's and in the middle of the fairway. If Weeshy was impressed, he gave no indication.

Tim hit a four iron that made a gallant effort to reach the green before dropping just short of the target and trickling forty yards back down to the base of the hill. On reaching Loopy's ball, Weeshy handed him a seven iron without comment. Loopy was sure that it was not enough club to reach the flag that fluttered uneasily in the swirling sea breeze. Then he remembered what Tim's caddy had said, even though Weeshy had yet to see Loopy hit an iron.

He struck the seven iron sweetly, sending the ball high into a sky of the palest blue. It soared ever upward until, losing its forward momentum, it dropped back to earth, disappearing behind the ridge at the front of the green. He looked toward Weeshy for a nod of approval, but none was forthcoming. The caddy merely grunted, cleared his throat noisily, and shouldered the heavy bag before setting off on the steep climb to the green.

"How did you get on?" Tim had been too busy with his difficult third shot to take much notice of Loopy's second to the green.

"I dunno really . . ." Loopy stopped in midsentence to make sure he was out of Weeshy's earshot before confessing, "The caddy handed me a seven and I was afraid to give it back and ask him for a five. I hit it well, though, so maybe the old guy was right after all."

He was. When they reached the saucer-shaped green, both balls were within fifteen feet of the pin.

It was Loopy's putt first—for a birdie. Five yards down a slope, it would break at least six inches to the right, Loopy decided. He was so sure of the line that he didn't think it worthwhile to consult his caddy. He struck the putt exactly as he had intended. It missed by six inches.

The look in Weeshy's rheumy eyes said as clearly as if it had been em-blazoned in neon across his forehead, *I could have told you that if you had asked me!*

The second hole was a par three of two hundred yards. The second green lay just beyond a deep ravine, full of rocks and wild heather that surrounded a rancid pond. Out of this sprouted row upon row of tall, slender bulrushes, swaying gently in the wind. A pair of water hens cackled to each other across the water, oblivious to the four figures standing on the tee far above them.

Weeshy handed Loopy the same club again, a seven iron. This time the caddie actually spoke as he struggled to light another cigarette in the wind that tugged at their trouser legs on the exposed tee. As Loopy reluctantly accepted the seven iron and gave it an experimental swish before settling over the ball, Weeshy growled, "Ye needn't be afraid to *hit* it, anyways!"

Loopy hit the ball as hard as he dared. It landed past the flagstick, checked on the second bounce, then rolled back down the slope to within six feet of the pin. He had missed the birdie putt on the first but had still won the hole with a four to Tim's struggling five. As Weeshy retrieved the club and jammed it back in the bag, he grabbed Loopy by the shoulder. "Hole it this time, about a ball to the left."

With that, Weeshy was off down the narrow path that skirted the ravine, covering the ground faster than one would have thought possi-ble. As Loopy and Tim were already starting to perspire, how Weeshy, almost twice their combined ages, could wear a heavy overcoat *and* carry a heavy golf bag was a mystery. With the hem of his coat down to his ankles, he appeared to glide over the rugged terrain with that rolling gait of his. From behind the green Tim played a delicate chip shot to within a foot of the hole.

"That's good!"

It was match play, so short putts like this were conceded as a matter of course. Weeshy handed the putter to Loopy, confirming his reading from the distant tee: "A ball to the left, like I said."

Going down on one knee as if in prayer, Loopy lined up the putt from behind the ball. To him it looked dead straight. If anything, it looked as though it might break just a fraction to the *right*. Still uncertain, he got to his feet and repeated the exercise from the far side of the hole. From there the putt looked to be straight as an arrow. He stood over the putt for longer than usual, his mind a mass of seething contradictions.

Weeshy had called the putt from the tee, a good two hundred yards distant, as being a ball to the left. He had confirmed this as he'd handed Loopy the putter. Tim's caddy had told Loopy that Weeshy had been caddying here since Adam was a boy. Despite his missed putt on the first green, every fiber in Loopy's body told him that this putt was straight—and up to now he had always trusted his own judgment. He lined up the putt for the back of the hole and struck it straight and true. At the last moment it veered sharply to the right, missing the hole by two inches, the width of a golf ball.

No one said anything. His caddie slammed the putter back in the bag. From there on, Loopy got the message and followed Weeshy's advice to the letter, not just on the green but also on the blind shots where white stones set high in the dunes were the only indication of where a green might be. In so doing he had beaten Tim by the comfortable margin of four up with three holes to go. He had also won the "bye" over the last three holes despite giving Tim generous odds to save his money.

The last hole was long and narrow with bunkers deep enough to hide a grown man. Their sheer sides made it difficult to get the ball out, much less advance it in any meaningful way. Tim had played the last hole perfectly, leaving his ball some eighty yards from the green in two solid shots, one with the driver and the other a well-struck three wood. Loopy had hit an enormous drive that had caught the edge of the rough but found a tight lie that would prevent him from hitting a fairway wood. Obediently, he waited for Weeshy to hand him a club. It was the three wood.

"Give it a good cut with that!"

Loopy looked at the caddy and then at the three wood. Tim had shown him months back how to cut a six iron out of the rough, but the fairway wood was a different proposition altogether. Seeing the look of doubt, Weeshy snarled, "Cut it up, man, like I'm telling you, for Jaysus' sake! Aim well to the left of the green and *cut* it in. Go on." It was the first time Weeshy had appeared agitated all day. "I *knows* you can do it, anyways!"

Loopy placed the clubhead ever so deliberately behind the ball nestling deep in the wiry dune grass. Suddenly any doubts he might have had about pulling off the shot disappeared. They had been replaced by a familiar feeling, the tingling sensation in the hairs at the nape of his neck.

His mind emptied itself of everything. All he could focus on was that small white ball. He took the club back slowly. As he started the downswing, it was as if nature itself were holding its breath. The surf stopped pounding, the wind no longer whistled through the towering sand dunes, and even the seagulls stopped their squawking long enough for Loopy to execute the stroke.

He caught the ball square, despite its poor lie. It exploded skyward, hanging in the air for what seemed like an eternity before swooping down short of the green. Then, as if gaining energy from the tightly cut fairway, it bounded forward again. It scampered past an evil sand dune seeking to ensnare it in its grasp, then daintily sidestepped a deep bunker guarding the entrance to the green. Rapidly running out of steam, it came to rest on the front edge of the green, some 230 yards distant.

Tim was speechless. His caddy slapped Loopy on the back, shouting, "Bloody marvelous, best I've seen from there!"

Weeshy displayed no emotion other than to grab the three wood and stuff it back into the bag. Loopy searched his face in vain for the merest hint of approval. None was forthcoming. Tim pitched to within six feet of the hole. Loopy's putt was twice that distance and sharply downhill with what looked like at least three different breaks on its way to the hole. Weeshy handed him the putter, muttering, "Straight putt—*nurse* it down to the hole."

Loopy drew a bead on the front of the hole, imagined it to be about four feet nearer than it actually was, and stroked the putt ever so gently. The ball drifted to the left, steadied itself, then wandered off to the right for a few feet before swinging left again at the very last moment to tumble into the hole. This time Weeshy did not restrain himself. He winked at Loopy as if to say, *Look what happens when you do what I tell you,* then spat on the green, this time a respectable distance from Loopy's feet. Three at the par five eighteenth was that rarest of birds—an eagle.

As they walked toward the clubhouse, their round finished, Loopy was so elated that he scarcely noticed Tim babbling excitedly about how well Loopy had played. He had taken on one of the toughest courses and won, even though Weeshy still appeared put out by something. Could it have been that his advice had been ignored over the opening holes?

When Loopy tried to pay Weeshy the agreed ten pounds, the caddy waved it away disdainfully. "I'll get it—and more—from you the next time."

As there had been no mention of any *next time*, Loopy tried to insist that Weeshy take the money there and then, but the old man was adamant. "You look as if you need it more than myself, anyways. I tell you, I'll get it back from you the *next* time!"

With that he turned on his heel and shambled off, leaving Loopy and Tim wondering what he meant.

That night in the dining room of The Royal Hotel, Loopy's education took a further step. Faced with an array of spoons, knives, and forks, he found himself at a complete loss. No caddy this time, he reflected, to help him select the right implement. To make matters worse, the menu had so many foreign words in it that he didn't dare to catch the eye of the waiter hovering at his elbow. The waiter had already inquired a trifle too icily for Loopy's comfort as to what "sir" might like to start with when Tim came to the rescue. He suggested that they start with sherry and then discuss what they would eat.

"But you *know* I don't drink," Loopy protested once the waiter had glided out of earshot.

"Blast, I'd completely forgotten about that! Well, it looks as if I'll just have to drink for us both then, doesn't it?"

The laugh that followed was too hearty. Loopy sensed that for some reason Tim was not completely at ease. This struck Loopy as odd. He, if anyone, should have been the one to feel uncomfortable in these unfamiliar surroundings. The cause of Tim's discomfiture was not long in revealing itself.

"Larry, old chap, I have a problem."

Loopy looked startled. Was Tim going to confess to being gay and admit that was the real reason they were sharing a room?

"Oh, yes? What is it?"

"Well, it's like this. I have an . . . an . . . ." Tim struggled to find the right word. "An *understanding*, yes, that's the word I was looking for. Well, I have an understanding with a woman. Her name's Lily actually, who works in this hotel. You may have heard me inquiring about her when we checked in. Yes? Well, I *did*. And the upshot of it all is that she's, ah . . . ah . . . visiting me in my—I mean *our* room around nine o'clock. Do you get what I'm driving at?"

"Sure, I get you, Tim. You want me out of the way for a few hours while you're with Lily. That's no problem. I'll take a walk along the strand or maybe even hit a few balls on the practice range if there's still light. Just give me an idea of when I can come back. Now, maybe you can help me out."

"Yes, of course. Anything you need."

"For a start you can tell me which knife and fork I use first."

They laughed, and the awkward moment had passed. It proved too dark for the practice ground so Loopy strolled down to the pier as the sun was setting. Fishing boats rocked gently on the oily water, shot with the last rays of the sun. Seagulls swooped and dived, screeching as if trying to keep the darkness at bay.

He had to pick his steps carefully along the pier. Lobster pots with stinking bait inside, massive marker buoys tethered to coils of rope, and untidy heaps of filament nets were scattered everywhere. As he picked his way round the debris, he saw a lonely figure sitting with his legs dangling over the end of the pier. It was staring intently out to sea as the last glimmer of sunset sank below the horizon. Overhead a few hungry gulls dived into the darkening waters in search of a fish supper.

He was about to turn when he banged his foot against a lobster pot. The sudden noise startled the figure gazing out to sea, causing it to turn round. It was Weeshy. Too late Loopy realized the man was drunk, very drunk.

"Ah, if it isn't yourself!" The voice was slurred and the eyes bloodshot. "What brings a young man like yourself to the arsehole of nowhere at this time of night, anyways?"

"Just taking a bit of a walk, that's all. Nice evening, isn't it?"

Weeshy hiccuped, then cleared his throat with a hacking cough. Loopy was about to leave when Weeshy demanded aggressively, "Where's the other fellow? Tim, Tim Stout or whatever his name is."

"Porter."

"Whaa . . . What are you saying?"

"His name is Porter. Tim Porter. He's back at the hotel."

"The Royal?"

Loopy nodded, anxious to bring the conversation to an end. He wasn't much good at talking to drunks, and his time spent serving behind the bar had taught him that it was usually foolish to even try. He told himself to keep his answers, indeed the entire conversation, as brief as possible.

"Yes, that's it."

"I suppose your man is paying?" Without waiting for an answer,

Weeshy, his monosyllabic tongue loosened by drink, pressed on, "I seen that fella around here for the past few years. Plays in The Atlantic, so he does. Never gets anywhere and I'm not surprised."

"Why's that?" Loopy asked before he could stop himself.

"His shaggin' swing, that's his problem."

"It looks okay to me." Loopy was not going to let down his friend. Tim's swing looked just fine; in fact, Loopy often envied its studied slowness.

This must have stung because Weeshy now showed that he was a good mimic. *"It looks okay to me!* What the fuck do you know about the golf swing, anyways?"

Before Loopy could answer, Weeshy was off again, a trail of angry spittle punctuating his every word. "His bloody swing is like every golf book that was ever written. His backswing is Ben Hogan's—just watch his wrists. But then he lets go at the top and changes into Jack Nicklaus until he's halfway down. By then he thinks he's a mixture of Bobby Jones and Fred Couples. Trouble is"—there was a pause while Weeshy belched loudly—"by the time he gets the clubhead to the ball, he doesn't know who the fuck he is."

"Maybe so. I've never read any of those books so I wouldn't know much about—"

Weeshy cut in viciously, "You're a damn sight better off. Be yourself, anyways. That loop of yours is better than Jimmy Bruen's, God rest him. Let no one change it on you, d'you hear me?"

By now Weeshy was shouting angrily and waving his arms around as if to emphasize what he was saying. Loopy nodded and made as if to go.

"And another thing"—another loud belch—"when you come back here again as you surely will, remember, I'm your caddy."

With that Weeshy abruptly turned his back on Loopy and resumed his examination of the horizon, by now a deep shade of purple streaked with darkening gold. As Loopy made his way back down the pier, the stars were already piercing the clear night sky and the gulls had gone silent. Hurrying up the road from the pier to the main street of Ballykissane, he turned to give a last backward look at his caddy. He was just visible, a lonely, huddled figure at the end of the pier.

Back in the room, Tim was already in bed. "Very sporting of you, Larry old chap. Lily and I have had this thing going for the past few years. We met quite by accident during the first Atlantic I played in. I'd been knocked out in the first round and was thoroughly fed up with myself. Went out and got pissed. So pissed in fact that I fell out of bed without knowing it. When the chambermaids came to do my room, they saw yours truly lying on the floor and thought I was dead. That's when they called Lily. She's the housekeeper, y'see. Well, I need hardly tell you, we hit it off a treat right from the start. She's married to some frightful fellow and sees me as a kind of knight in shining armor." Tim paused to gauge how all of this was going down with his roommate. "Must say, though, she knows her stuff. Know what I mean?"

Loopy did not bother to answer. He pulled the bedclothes over his head and pretended to sleep. When he did drop off, it was not Tim Porter's couplings but the huddled figure at the end of the pier that haunted his dreams. It had toppled in and was flailing about in the water, desperately trying to stay afloat. Loopy, alone and unable to swim, could only look on helplessly as the drowning Weeshy shrieked, "Let no one change it on you, d'you hear me? Remember, I'm your caddy!"

CHAPTER SEVEN

News of Tim Porter's illness spread like wildfire. Linda, Joe Delany's wife, heard for a fact that he was in the intensive care unit of the capital's most fashionable clinic, while others insisted that it was something to do with his pancreas and had him lodged in St. Luke's cancer hospital, undergoing tests. It was a considerable relief, therefore, to everyone, especially the committee of the golf club, to learn that in truth he was confined to bed in his father's elegant retreat some twenty-five miles from Trabane. And there, it was confirmed, he would remain until the kidney infection cleared up. In the interim he was to be allowed few visitors and only those of his own choosing. Which was how Loopy came to be driving up the long, winding avenue to Castle Porter, having first identified himself and Pat O'Hara to the speaker attached to the remote-controlled entrance gates.

The driveway must have been the best part of a mile long, Loopy estimated, with post-and-rail fencing on either side—the hallmark of a successful stud farm. In some of the paddocks, foals played around their mothers. In others, sleek racing machines frisked and played games of tag with each other, aloof as supermodels on a catwalk. Here and there mighty stallions, always alone and fenced off from temptation, stalked dejectedly to and fro, whinnying at a distant herd of black-and-white cows that grazed contentedly, oblivious to everything but the fresh grass under their noses. The peace and tranquility of the scene reduced both driver and passenger to a stunned silence. Even more impressive was the stately pile that loomed up before them. Castle Porter was enormous, a square manor house built centuries ago out of limestone blocks sturdy enough to withstand the most determined assault. The entrance door was set in a porch at the top of a steep flight of steps, down which a long, lean figure of a man was hurrying. He introduced himself as Tim's father and ushered them through a hall door studded with evil-looking spiked nails. The hallway was paneled in dark wood and its walls were festooned with the heads of long-dead animals. Sam Porter, a lanky, angular man dressed in heavy tweeds, examined the visitors through hooded eyes of piercing blue. These contrasted sharply with his aquiline nose, which was of the deepest purple.

"Welcome to you both!" Grasping Loopy by the shoulder, Mr. Porter addressed him first. "You must be Larry Lynch. Tim speaks most highly of you, especially your golf. Tells me you beat him recently. And you"—turning to O'Hara—"must be Pat O'Hara. Can you really be retired and you looking so young?"

O'Hara, who had been roundly cursing the landed gentry all the way up the long, rhododendron-lined avenue, seemed mollified by such outrageous flattery and conceded that it was indeed he.

"Good, then come inside. The patient is in an upstairs room and likely to be there for some time if old Doc Hegarty has his way. Follow me."

With that Mr. Porter bounded up the wide stairs at the end of the hall, taking the steps two at a time. At a landing at the top, more dead animal heads lined the walls, interspersed by the occasional African spear. They were ushered into a large bedroom, brightly lit by enormous windows looking out over the rolling pastures of the Castle Porter estate.

Tim's bulky frame was almost lost in an enormous four-poster bed. Propped up on pillows, he was looking sorry for himself as his father announced the two visitors before slipping silently out of the room. Loopy and O'Hara drew up chairs to the bedside.

"Bloody ridiculous to catch this stupid infection. Probably from drinking too much of my own wine, eh, Loopy?"

After some small talk, all of a sudden Tim became more businesslike. Turning to O'Hara, he declared without preamble, "It looks like I won't be fit for the Atlantic Trophy next month, so I just wanted to tell you in person, Pat, that I believe young Loopy here is the right man for the job."

O'Hara stared at Tim in disbelief as if he could not believe his ears. He had never heard anything so ridiculous inside or outside the classroom. How could anyone, even someone as dim-witted as Tim Porter, even consider the possibility? A lad with such humble origins had about as much chance of being asked to play in the Atlantic Trophy as being elected pope. He did not try to hide his feelings as he growled, "Is that why you dragged us all this way down here? Just so that you could let us in on the news that you wanted our friend here to take your place in the Atlantic Trophy? Jaysus, you've got some neck, Tim Porter, so you have!"

Exasperated, Tim struggled with the pillows to prop himself up higher before replying with more spirit than might have been good for him, considering his condition, "Listen to me for once, will you." Turning to Loopy, Tim explained as if O'Hara were not there, "Y'know, that's the trouble with all these bloody schoolteachers—they never bloody *listen*. I suppose they get into the habit of yakkety-yakking on and on in the classroom, and God help anyone who dares to butt in."

Tim continued in a calmer voice, "Now, if Pat will shut up for a second, the reason I asked you *both* here at such short notice is that I knew I couldn't convince either of you over the phone. And as I'm not much good with the pen, writing it all down would have been no good either. I had to see you both and convince you—"

O'Hara cut in impatiently, "Oh, have a bit of sense, Tim. Supposing, just supposing, that you could convince me *and* Larry here. What about the bloody committee, especially Mr. Leo bloody Martin? You know as well as I do that it's *his* bank is sponsoring The Atlantic, and that Leo has always had a big say in who represents Trabane. Up to now, there's been no problem because *you've* always been the obvious choice. Not just because of your golf either, but also because of all this . . ." O'Hara flapped a hand around at the luxurious surroundings in which Tim was convalescing.

As Tim tried to interrupt, he was waved into silence as O'Hara stubbornly held the floor. "Now *hold* on a minute, Tim, let me finish. You know as well as I do that anyone playing in The Atlantic has to be"—O'Hara paused, seeking a way to phrase what he wanted to say without causing offense—"shall we say, *well-off*. And it's no harm to be a client in good standing with Allied bloody Banks of Ireland. An expensive education is no harm either. Surely it must have occurred to you, lying there in your bed with all the time in the world to think about it, that Loopy has none of these attributes. So how do you propose getting round that obstacle, for starters? Then there's the question as to whether the lad is actually good enough to play in a big tournament so soon."

Having said his piece, O'Hara sank back in his chair, feigning exhaustion at his efforts to talk sense.

Tim, however, was not to be put off. "I daresay much of what you say is true, old cock. The Atlantic *is* full of snobbish nonsense, more so than anything else I've ever played in. Not just our own lot but lots of Brits and Americans, all top golfers mind you, but with big jobs in banking, insurance, and God alone knows what else. But so what? Loopy's manners are as good as theirs, and he's the obvious choice to replace me. Even if I were in the whole of my health, he would still be the best pick. As you know, he beat me easily over the Ballykissane course."

O'Hara looked startled. "That's news to me. I never heard a word about it. Nor did anyone else at the club, as far as I know."

They both eyed Loopy, who remained silent as Tim explained, "Oh, yes, indeed he did. We played the Ballykissane course not so long ago, off the back markers just as they do for The Atlantic. He beat me four and three and won the bye as well. I wouldn't mind, but it was his first time ever setting foot on the course. He played so well even the caddies were clapping him at the finish."

O'Hara looked accusingly at Loopy. "Why didn't you tell me?"

Loopy blushed, then tried to shrug it off with a diffident "You never asked, that's why."

O'Hara was spluttering in disgust at anyone being so stupid as to behave like that. "Jaysus but you're the odd fish, and no mistake! Sure, this changes *everything*. Now I can face up to Mr. Leo bloody Martin and tell him that our friend here not only knows the course, but he has beaten you. By how much did you say?"

"Four and three *and* he played some bloody marvelous golf into the bargain. Best I ever witnessed, in fact."

The schoolmaster was practically beside himself with excitement. "That's *it* then! All we need now is a letter from you to the committee, saying that you won't be available for this year's Atlantic Trophy and that you strongly recommend that Larry be your replacement in view of the fact that he has already beaten you over the Ballykissane course."

"Write down exactly what you want me to say, will you, like a good chap. As I said earlier, letter writing is not my thing, not by a long shot. There should be a notepad on the table over there, under the magazines."

O'Hara did as he was asked and, when he was finished, handed the draft to Tim. "We'll be on our way if you don't mind. Send that letter to the committee, and I'll see to the rest. Don't worry about a thing."

As O'Hara spoke, Tim's father appeared framed in the doorway. "Came to see how you were getting along. The doc said he wasn't to tire himself, but I see you are already leaving. Can I offer you a drink or anything?"

Before O'Hara could accept, Loopy responded quickly, "No thanks, Mr. Porter. I must be back in Trabane by six o'clock."

The older man nodded sympathetically, murmuring, "Yes. Well, maybe some other time." Before leading them downstairs, he stopped in the hall to address Loopy.

"Tim was telling me that you work in the bar of the Golf Club and are thinking of taking up golf as a career, is that right?"

Loopy was taken aback. "I . . . I . . . haven't made up my mind yet, Mr. Porter. It all depends . . ." His voice trailed off and the older man did not press him further. Instead Tim's father changed the subject abruptly.

"Either of you interested in horses at all?"

This time O'Hara was quicker off the mark. "Yes, *I* am."

"Right, well, let me show you what's in the stables before you go." Turning to Loopy, Mr. Porter whispered half-apologetically, "Won't take more than ten minutes, I promise."

He led the way out onto a large cobblestone courtyard surrounded by stables. Horses poked their heads through the upper section of some of the stable doors, examining the threesome with interest as their owner expounded on their breeding and prospects. O'Hara, whose only real interest in horses lay in how fast they could run and at what odds, struggled to look interested, while Loopy hung back as he tried to hide his impatience at the delay. As much to make conversation as anything else, O'Hara, struggling to show a polite interest in the tour of the stables, wondered aloud if stableboys were more difficult to come by nowadays.

"Oh, absolutely, this blasted Celtic Tiger has everyone in the horse industry driven absolutely round the bloody bend. Impossible to get new recruits, and when you do find any, they up and leave for a better-paid job just when they are getting useful. The other thing, of course, is hay."

This got Loopy's attention. "Hay?"

"Yes, hay. In the old days we had more than we knew what to do with. Every Tom, Dick, and Harry wanted to sell us hay because the horse breeders and trainers paid more for good hay than anyone else. Now no one is making the stuff, and if they are, it's poisoned with bloody fertilizers and God alone knows what else."

Loopy heard himself say confidently, as if he were doing old Sam Porter a favor rather than asking for one, "We're in the hay business. Mind you, all of this year's crop is sold, but you might be interested in next year's crop. We do about fifty acres a year and it's all for sale."

"Very interesting. I would be even more interested in leasing the hay meadows from you. That way I get *exactly* what I need. Horses are very choosy about what they eat, y'know. Some weeds actually poison them, while your cattle will chew them all day without any apparent harm."

Loopy nodded sagely, indicating that he was already aware of this. Thinking it impolite to pursue the matter further at this stage, he suggested that they might discuss it again some other time, but Tim's father would have none of it.

"I'd like to get my man to walk your farm and report back to me. If he says everything is okay—and I can see no reason why it should not be—then we can get down to business right away even though we'll be talking about next year. That alright with you?"

By now they had reached O'Hara's car. "That will be just fine, Mr. Porter. You can contact me at the Golf Club most days or leave a message there and I'll get back to you. Thanks for everything, and I hope Tim gets better real soon."

With that they were off down the avenue. This time the gates were activated as they approached, causing O'Hara to remark, "Must be great to have money!"

When Loopy did not reply, O'Hara continued in pensive mood, " 'Twas a good day's work for you, anyway. If you play your cards right, that man will take all your mother's hay for the foreseeable future. Your mother will be beside herself when she hears about it."

Again Loopy said nothing, staring fixedly at the road ahead.

"You're very quiet in yourself. What's wrong?"

"I dunno really! The shock, I suppose. How am I ever going to play in The Atlantic? I can't afford the hotel. I know because I saw the rates written up on a card on the back of the bedroom door. Even if I could find a cheap bed-and-breakfast place, what about the caddy? I paid him a tenner for just one round. At least I would have if he hadn't refused to take it from me."

O'Hara seemed shocked by this. "A caddy refusing to take money? Jaysus, that's one for the book and no mistake. How did that happen?"

"I dunno. He just said I needed it more than he did, and that he'd catch me the next time. I didn't know what he meant by 'next time,' but I was afraid to ask him. I think he was half-mad, to be honest."

"Oh, yeah"—O'Hara remained skeptical—"he certainly sounds mad. I never before heard of a caddy refusing money—though I often heard of them looking for more than was offered to them. What did he mean by 'next time'? I wonder."

"I dunno. Looks like he was right though, doesn't it?"

They both laughed at this, then O'Hara wondered aloud, "Does this prophet have a name?"

"Weeshy something. I never found out what his real name was. He was real scary. Wore a big heavy coat even though it was a really hot day. He'd hand me a club and I'd be afraid to argue with him even though I was *sure* 'twas the wrong one."

"And was it?"

"What?" Loopy had been distracted in his efforts to pass a slow-moving truck along the narrow, winding road.

"I asked, was it the wrong club?"

"No, that was the amazing thing, he was always right. I played out of my skin and it was as much due to him as it was to myself. Especially with the putts."

"You mean he gave you the right line?"

"You bet he did. The first few times I ignored him and followed my own line." Loopy laughed out loud at the memory. "I missed a few short ones early on in the round and he got sour as hell. After that, I did everything he said. Went around in two over par, actually."

"Pretty good, but not good enough to win The Atlantic in good weather."

"No? What usually wins it?"

"Depending on the wind, it's usually around level par in decent weather."

"Do you really think the club will pick me for it?"

"Hard to say. All I can promise is that it won't be for want of trying."

After that they sank into a comfortable silence until the road sign announced proudly that were entering the town of Trabane.

The committee room had a small service hatch connected to the bar, which was closed while the meeting was in progress. The captain of the club was ex officio chairman of the general committee. That a captain's tenure lasted just a year was a consolation to the eight committee members seated round the table as they endured with varying degrees of impatience his long-windedness. Those who had voted him to this high office had expected a lawyer, usually well paid for his words, to use them sparingly when no financial reward was on offer. This was not so.

Rising to his feet on the stroke of eight o'clock, the captain prefaced his remarks by advising his audience to stock up on their refreshments before the hatch was shut. Twenty minutes later he was still stressing the extreme gravity of what they were about to discuss without actually spelling out exactly what it was.

O'Hara, who had already left the room once for a refill, was about to repeat the exercise. By now the only one paying the slightest attention to the proceedings was Leo Martin. In his capacity as honorary treasurer and vice president elect he was not going to give anyone cause to think he might not be the automatic choice for the presidency at the next Annual General Meeting. This had occurred just once in the history of the club, when the vice president had run off with someone's wife to make a fresh start in Western Australia. Leo had no intention of joining him on the roll of infamy. He was only too well aware that the directors of Allied Banks of Ireland approved of their staff playing an active role in their local community.

In the coming year it would be vital that Leo be in a position to influence local opinion when the bank announced the closure of its Trabane branch. This had been confirmed that very morning. A registered letter, the contents being far too explosive to entrust to any other form of communication, had landed on Leo's desk. His bank was indeed short-listed for closure. The letter stressed that the information was strictly confidential and for Leo's eyes only. When the news of the closure had been released and the initial outcry had died down, it would be Leo who would make soothing noises to the objectors, and where better to do so than from the presidency of Trabane Golf Club? A quiet word here, a veiled threat there, and the closure of the bank branch would prove nothing more than a nine-days wonder. A few important clients, such as Edward Linhurst and Seamus Norbert, would be "looked after" in the nearest branch eleven miles away. Then, and only then, could Leo pack his bags and move to Dublin, where, he was sure, a broader stage awaited his undoubted talents. It would also, he hoped, cheer up Rosa, who had been moaning about what a dump Trabane was ever since she had set foot in the place. Though, he now reminded himself, she had not been banging on quite so much about it since taking up golf.

Such were the thoughts going through Leo's mind as he watched the captain droning on and on, pausing just long enough to take a sip from a pint of Guinness. Wiping the creamy froth from his wispy mustache, the captain cleared his throat more noisily than usual, a hopeful sign that he might at long last be coming to the point.

"So it now behooves me to address the vexed question of who we are to select to represent us in next month's Atlantic Trophy."

The captain stopped to further refresh himself from the pint as O'Hara's stage whisper of "And about shagging time, too" echoed off the walls of the small committee room. The captain chose to treat this insult from an already half-drunk schoolmaster with the disdain it deserved.

"It is my duty first of all to read you a letter I have received from Tim Porter, who—as you will no doubt be well aware—has so ably represented us for the past several years—"

"Never got past the second round, if that's what you mean by *ably represented*!"

This time there was no ignoring O'Hara, halfway down on his third large whiskey and showing all the signs of it. "Mr. O'Hara, you will have ample time to give us the benefit of your thoughts on the matter later. In the meantime I would be more than grateful if you allowed me to get on with it."

This occasioned a deep sigh that seemed to come from near the soles of O'Hara's shoes, and a fainter, though still audible, encouragement to "Get on with it so, for Jaysus' sake!"

If O'Hara were not supposed to be taking the minutes of the meeting—no one else being prepared to do so—the captain might have taken him up on that last comment. Instead he again ignored it.

"Now where was I? . . . Oh, yes, Tim Porter's letter."

With one hand he rummaged among the papers at his elbow, using the other to raise what remained of the pint to his lips. He drained it, leaving a succession of creamy rings inside the empty glass.

"Here we are. I'd better read it out to you:

Dear Captain,

Sorry to have to tell you that I'm laid low with a kidney infection and my doctor assures me that I will be confined to bed for at least a month. That being so, I have no chance whatsoever of playing in the Atlantic Trophy—in the event of the committee being kind enough to select me yet again.

However, I would very much like to recommend someone who is well qualified to take my place and who, I have every confidence, will properly represent our club in such a prestigious event. He is Larry Lynch and you all know him well. A while back I played him in a level match over the Ballykissane course and he beat me easily—four and three. He showed a great liking for the golf course and I confidently expect him to do well there again. I can further assure you that he will represent our club most ably as his behavior both on and off the course is beyond reproach.

I leave the matter in your able hands, secure in the knowledge that you will act—as always—in the best interests of the club.

> *Yours sincerely,*
> *Tim Porter*

The captain waited for a moment for the import of Tim's letter to sink in, then looked straight at Leo Martin as he spoke.

"Well, gentlemen, there's no doubt who young Porter thinks should represent us. Even though, as Pat O'Hara reminded us, Tim never advanced further than the second round, there can be no doubt that he represented Trabane in a proper fashion. He dresses well, speaks well, and enhances the image of Trabane Golf Club wherever he goes—"

"Mr. Captain!" The interruption came, as might have been anticipated, from O'Hara. "Mr. Captain, I trust that you are not in any way implying that young Lynch might not, as you so elegantly put it, enhance our image by representing us at Ballykissane! You and the rest of the committee must surely know that he is the best golfer in this club, even though he has only been playing a relatively short time. I myself—"

It was the schoolmaster's turn to be interrupted as Leo cut in, "Mr. Captain, if I may interject—"

O'Hara was not to be put off so easily and countered, "Mr. Captain, I believe *I* have the floor. May I suggest friend Leo wait his turn!"

The captain remained calm. "Gentlemen, please! . . . As a matter of fact I still have the floor. I had not finished when first Mr. O'Hara and then Mr. Martin wished to speak. I assure them both that they will have ample time to express their views—but only *after* I have said what I want to say."

O'Hara's apology was not as contrite as the captain might have wished when he confessed, "I beg your pardon, Captain. After half an hour or so, I mistakenly believed that you had concluded your remarks. I can only crave your forgiveness." With that he went to the serving hatch and returned shortly thereafter with a full glass.

Leo, ever mindful of his position as president-in-waiting, muttered a more intimate. "Sorry, skipper."

"That's all right, gentlemen. I'll throw the discussion open to everyone in a moment, but I just want to emphasize, and I can't emphasize it too much, that whoever we choose, his behavior off the course is just as important as his accomplishments on the course. What we don't want is someone who might let the side down. Other than that, and all things being equal, I suppose we have to pick the best player, and, let's face it, we will not find a stronger player than Tim's candidate, young Lynch. Now, Leo, you have something to say."

O'Hara again interjected, this time more heatedly, "Mr. Captain, *I* had the floor long before Leo."

"All in good time, Pat. Let Leo have his say first, then you can come in immediately after him, and then, of course, anyone else who feels they might have something to contribute to the discussion."

Leo rose to his feet, delighted to have jumped the gun on O'Hara, whom he heartily detested.

"I will be as brief as possible. As you know, my bank has the honor of sponsoring the Atlantic Trophy. I'm sure you will agree that it is a special event in certain respects. As you well know, the other major amateur tournaments are by qualification. Those wishing to play in them must either have a sufficiently low handicap or else have qualified to play in them through a series of eliminating rounds. Either way, the organizers have no say in who plays in their tournaments just so long as the entrant has qualified in the specified manner. I would remind you, however, that entry into The Atlantic is by invitation only. You can have the best amateur in the world in your club, but if he doesn't measure up to the required standards, then he will not be invited."

With that, Leo sat down, and the captain indicated to Pat O'Hara that he might now have his say.

"Captain, we should all be grateful to friend Leo for reminding us of the rather unusual entry requirements for The Atlantic. No doubt he has a special insight into the minds of the sponsors, being one of their valued employees. That said, there can be no argument as to whether young Lynch is the *best* golfer in our club. Tim Porter's letter leaves no doubt on that score. Anyone who doubts his word can check with Joe Delany, who says quite simply that Larry Lynch is the best amateur he has ever seen, full stop. So, gentlemen"—he paused for a moment to look around the table at the other members of the committee in an effort to gauge their mood before he came to the nub of his argument—"what we are really talking about here, even though no one so far has dared to admit it, is whether young Lynch's manners and background are up to scratch. I see my friend Leo shaking his head at this, but nevertheless I am sure that most of you will agree with me on this. Now I'll grant you that there never was any problem in that regard with Tim Porter. He has a boarding school education, knows what knife or fork to use and holds them in the approved manner. He knows a good wine from a bad one and, even more important, can pronounce their names properly. That's all well and good and no doubt pleases the sponsors of The Atlantic no end. He is also, more than likely, a client in good standing of the bank, though we can hardly expect friend Leo to take us into his confidence in that regard. As far as young Lynch is concerned, I am led to believe that he, too, has an account with Allied Banks of Ireland, so that should not be a problem."

O'Hara shot a smug glance at Leo, who was staring fixedly at the ceiling with an expression on his face that said louder than words, *When is this buffoon going to sit down and shut up?*

"As for his table manners, well, we can always give them a quick brushing up, should that prove necessary. Personally I have always thought it more important how he handled a golf club rather than a knife or fork, but there you are—doctors differ and patients die. Now I can see that our captain—and others—are becoming restive, so I'll just make one last point before I finish. Times are bad enough 'round here already—talk of businesses losing jobs, if not closing down altogether, and when was the last time anyone saw a tourist in Trabane. Well, we don't want to go and make things even worse by telling the world and his wife that this place is so full of bloody snobs that the ordinary person can't even get a look-in. Now we all know that, for the most part, this is pure balderdash. However, if it should go out from this meeting that young Lynch wasn't picked to represent us at The Atlantic because we weren't sure if he could hold his fork properly or knew how to pronounce *Beaujolais Villages*, then our critics would have a field day at our expense. As you know, young Lynch was a talented hurler before taking up golf, and Seamus Norbert is trying to get him back playing again for the Trabane Gaels. He has a path worn out to Lynch's farm trying to persuade the lad's mother to get him back hurling again. He might offer him a job at more money than he gets here. That's not to be sneezed at the way jobs are disappearing at the moment. Yet I know for a fact that young Lynch wants to stay on here. He likes the club and is dead keen to improve his game. Now you tell me, what sort of a message will we be sending to him, not to mind every Tom, Dick, and Harry with a grievance—real or imaginary— against our club if we select anyone else? That's all I have to say to you for now."

His speech was received in silence. The captain sounded solemn as he summed up, "I'm sure we are all immensely grateful to both speakers for their contributions to the discussion. Now, is there anyone else who wants to say something?"

He waited for a while, one eyebrow cocked expectantly, then when it was obvious that no one else wished to add anything, he tapped a pencil on the table and said, "Right, gentlemen, we must vote on it then. Would someone please propose a motion that we can vote on."

O'Hara struggled to his feet and said, not as distinctly as he might have wished, but nevertheless clearly enough for all to understand, "I propose that young Loop—I mean Larry Lynch represent Trabane Golf Club at the forthcoming Atlantic Trophy."

When the hands were counted, Leo's was the last to be raised, making the decision unanimous.

CHAPTER EIGHT

The days between his selection for The Atlantic and the start of the competition flew quicker than Loopy could have thought possible. O'Hara promised to drive him to Ballykissane, where a widowed sister-in-law had a house outside the seaside resort and about five miles from the golf course. There they would stay for as long as necessary. O'Hara explained that the invitation had been long-standing, but that he had been reluctant to take it up since his brother had died some years back. The Atlantic Trophy presented an opportunity to fulfill his obligations in that regard and to avail themselves of free accommodation in an area that had been booked out months in advance of the golf tournament.

The one blot on this otherwise perfect scenario was that, as O'Hara confided to Loopy, the widow was a "lighting bitch." Margaret O'Hara regarded alcohol as the devil's brew and not to be tolerated within the four walls of her house. Her late husband had had to take a lifelong pledge against alcohol before she would even entertain the idea of marrying him. Pat O'Hara hoped that by using The Atlantic as an excuse, he could fulfill the "duty" visit to his sister-in-law without spending much time in either her house or her company. The way he saw it, looking after Loopy would allow him to spend as long as he liked on the golf course or in the bar without incurring Margaret's wrath.

Moments after he was picked for The Atlantic, Loopy had telephoned the caddy master at Ballykissane to inquire if Weeshy would be available to caddy for him. The caddy master was dubious, suggesting that Weeshy would probably be carrying his regular bag, that of a wealthy businessman from Northern Ireland who had once played at international level. It was a long-standing arrangement and the caddy master thought it unlikely that the caddy could be lured away from such a profitable assignment. Nevertheless he agreed to pass on Loopy's request.

That evening, Weeshy phoned back. From the outset, it was obvious that he was uncomfortable speaking on the telephone. One moment he was shouting into the mouthpiece, the next he had obviously moved it some distance away and Loopy could barely catch what he was saying. He did, however, catch enough of Weeshy's words to realize that the caddy was prepared to give up his usual client, thereby dropping a substantial paycheck, to work Loopy's bag. Weeshy did not state, and Loopy did not dare ask, the reason for this strange but welcome decision.

Joe Delany would be unable to make the trip to the Atlantic Trophy but presented Loopy with two complete outfits, from the peaked visor down to the spiked shoes. As Joe said without a hint of sarcasm, the outfits were interchangeable so that Loopy could wear a different combination each day right up to the final. The shirts, sweaters, and visors bore the crest of Trabane Golf Club, and Loopy's heart swelled as he tried them on in the pro shop with Joe and O'Hara clucking their approval like a pair of old hens. When he tried to stammer out his thanks, Joe would have none of it.

"Just wear them with pride and remember you're as good as the best of them and better than most!"

Oddly, Seamus Norbert, supermarket supremo and trainer of the

Trabane Gaels, used precisely these same words before sending his charges out to do battle on the hurling pitch. There had been only one setback to Loopy's progress as a golfer. He had spent an hour on the practice ground hitting every shot imaginable when he say Amy walking toward him. He hadn't seen her since the incident with Jake the spaniel, but they had spoken quite a lot over the phone. She was carrying a parcel.

"I just got in from London, and Dad said I might find you here. I brought you this."

Loopy eyed it speculatively. "What is it?"

"A present—well, not really a present. More of a replacement really."

"A *replacement*? A replacement for what?"

"Why not open it and see!"

It was a cashmere sweater with *Loopy* woven into it as a crest. He had never seen anything like it before.

"It's . . .," he stammered helplessly, "it's fantastic. But why? What did I do to deserve this, Amy?"

"Well, for one thing, you ruined the one you were wearing carrying Jake back home. He's fine again, by the way, all thanks to you. So I saw this place in London that did personalized sweaters and I thought you might like it."

"Might *like* it, I absolutely love it! How can I ever thank you?" As he pulled on the sweater, Amy quipped, "You know something, I must be the only one round here who has never seen you hit a golf ball."

"Well, that's easily fixed. I'll show you my very best shot." With that he threw a ball on the ground and plucked Porter's old driver from his bag. "Joe Delany, he's the professional who plays with your father and coaches me, well, he tells me that no one else can hit a driver off the ground like me. I don't know if it's true, but it sure as hell makes me feel good about myself anyway, so here goes."

With that he swung at the ball as hard as he dared. Whether it was because of his elation at Amy's gift, or that Porter's trusty driver had finally decided to call it a day, was something that Loopy would never know. All he could be sure of was that as the ball soared away into the evening sky, the head of the club shattered into tiny fragments. Loopy tried to reassure her that it was no big deal, though deep inside he would have been happier if it had not happened. Joe had been trying to persuade him to change to a newer model for ages. Now he would have no choice.

In the days that followed his selection, Loopy had time to think of little else except golf. He would have liked to get in as much practice with the new driver that Joe Delany had presented to him as he could, but as luck would have it, the lorries to collect the hay were arriving at regular intervals. He had to be at the farm to count and then sign for the number of bales in each load. When the barn was emptied, there was a final balancing payment of 322 pounds in addition to the advance of 3,000 pounds. Brona was beside herself with excitement.

From the day that she'd married, there had never been a time when the family was not in debt to the bank. There was a locked drawer full of letters and bank statements, all bearing the same grim news. Colorful phrases such as *The Lynch account has gone way over the limit agreed between Mrs. Brona Lynch and the Manager of Allied Banks of Ireland* in the portly person of Leo Martin. *As a result of this alarming rise in borrowings, the directors of the aforesaid bank have no choice but to instruct Mr. Martin to take whatever steps he deems necessary to recover the amount outstanding at the earliest possible opportunity.*

This conjured up a picture of the directors, dressed in swallow-tailed coats and striped pants, wringing their hands in a massive outpouring of collective grief. Their grief was occasioned by the fact that Brona Lynch, deserted wife and mother of a young family, was indebted to the largest lending institution in the state for the exorbitant sum of 623 pounds and some odd pence.

Now, all of a sudden, she had money on deposit, earning interest with the same Leo Martin who had, only weeks previously, been threatening to evict her from the farm her family had worked for generations. Better still, her son was representing Trabane in some big golf tournament sponsored by the very same bank. Sometimes Brona had to pinch herself to make sure it was not all just a wild dream.

One afternoon when the bar was empty, Edward Linhurst dropped in for a quick gin and tonic.

"Thanks for fixing up poor Jake. Amy tells me you did a great job on him. Most impressed she was—and take my word for it, she's not that easily impressed. Did the hay work out alright?"

"Indeed it did!"

"Good. You may have wondered why I was so interested. Well, not a lot of people know this, but I started out cutting hay by hand."

"By *hand*?" Loopy thought that Linhurst must be joking.

"Yes, by bloody hand! We had two acres of scrubland out the back of where I was born. Used to borrow a scythe from a neighbor and cut the hay myself with it. Then I'd sell it to him later on in the year."

"Sounds like hard work." Loopy sounded impressed.

"You'd better believe it! But it put bread on the table when we most needed it."

Neither one said anything for a while after that, each silent with his own thoughts, then Loopy remarked, more to himself than Linhurst, "Would never have guessed it."

"Guessed what?"

"That you of all people started out like that."

"Damn sure I did. Where I lived in Wales, coal mines were closing down right, left, and center. Not a job to be had anywhere."

"Trabane's getting like that now, y'know," Loopy confided. "That's why my father went to England."

He didn't mention the trail of debt he had left in his wake.

"My old man bailed out one day," Linhurst observed in a matter-of-fact tone as if it were the most ordinary thing in the world for a father to do. "Never saw or heard from him again from that day to this."

"We have that much in common, anyway," Loopy commented drily but without rancor.

Linhurst laughed out loud. "So we have! Cut from the same cloth, you might say." Then, brightening visibly, he added, "The reason I dropped in here in the first place was that I wanted to tell you that I'm not quite sure if I can make it to The Atlantic to see you play."

This was the first inkling Loopy had that anyone else apart from O'Hara would be there to watch him play.

"Had I been there, I would have taken you and Pat out to dinner. In fact I had already made the reservations. They're in my name for eight o'clock at The Royal, all four nights. That okay with you?"

Loopy didn't know what to say. When he tried to thank him, Edward Linhurst would have none of it.

"The very least I could do. Now please don't be offended, but since I can't be there myself, here's something to cover your expenses, caddies, drinks for Pat, and suchlike."

"I-I-I can't. Mr. Linhurst, I really can't. You've already done more than enough for me with the hay and—"

"If you don't accept it, I will be deeply offended. Now take it like a good fellow and not a word about this to anyone. Okay?"

Loopy took the envelope with some reluctance. "Thanks, Mr. Linhurst, I won't forget this—ever."

People came into the bar and the moment passed.

In fact, Loopy's father, unlike Edward Linhurst's, had every intention of returning home. Nightly Sean Lynch had agonized in his flea-ridden bed over what he would say when he walked in, unannounced, through the door of his own house. Would he time his arrival for midday when the children were away and only Brona would be there to hear his excuses? That was the problem, of course, *what* excuses? How could he properly explain to her his crippling shame of getting so deep into debt and not being able to do anything about it?

At first the only way out, as he saw it, was either to kill himself or make a new start in England. He had given serious thought to suicide. After much consideration, he decided that it would only bring further pain to his long-suffering household. The trouble was, that having taken the boat for England, how could he now explain to them that it had been as easy to back losers in Birmingham as it had been in Trabane?

The *Irish Post* was a paper for Irish emigrants that sometimes carried news of Trabane, as it did of most small towns back home. Whenever he could lay hands on a copy, he would eagerly devour every scrap of news.

The trip to Ballykissane in the elderly Ford took far longer than in Tim Porter's coupe. This was not solely due to the difference in performance between the two motors. There had been many stops along the way—the first of them at Loopy's request. Without explaining why, he'd asked O'Hara to stop at the fort.

It was a sunny morning and the ocean breeze rustled the leaves of the mighty oak trees standing guard around the fort. Shafts of sunlight penetrated their canopies, bouncing off the rough, gray stones that had stood in a circle since time began. It made them feel more welcoming than before as they seemed to give out vibrations stronger than ever. Loopy felt a greater sense of relaxation than ever, not unlike the anesthetic he'd received at the hospital. He found a place in the grass that was free of nettles and lay down, facing upward. Around him, the slabs of gray stones stood sentinel, stark against the huge tree trunks. He felt drowsy as he stretched out lazily, like a cat in the long grass. Closing his eyes, his mind seemed to empty itself completely.

The tension that had been building up day by day as The Atlantic drew ever closer seemed to seep out through the pores of his skin, leaving in its wake a familiar inner glow. That glow turned into something akin to a mild electrical charge, and it seemed to be coming from the gray limestone slabs that encircled him. Though their origins had been lost in the mists of prehistory, legend had it that the tribes who'd put them there were sun worshipers with magical powers. Later these ring forts were thought to be the home of the little people, as fairies were called in Trabane.

Even today, some people in the locality claimed to have heard strange music and sound of singing coming from the fort on May Eve, a night special to the little people. Pagan superstition mingled easily with Christianity in Ireland, and the forts with their mythical inhabitants had long been treated with a mixture of fear and respect. This despite the best efforts of the clergy down through the centuries to wean their flocks from such pagan beliefs.

It would be going too far to say that Loopy actually *believed* in fairies, but like his father, he sensed the power of this stone circle to give him inner strength. His mother pooh-poohed the whole idea, insisting that superstitions like that were not only ridiculous but offensive to Our Holy Mother, the Church. Nonetheless she sprinkled her hens and cows with holy water every May Eve—when the little people were supposed to leave their fairy forts and roam through the countryside.

Memories like these ebbed and flowed as he lay in the grass, but for the most part he thought of absolutely nothing. His mind had become a vast, empty cavern, disturbed only by the buzzing of insects and the insistent warbling of a skylark high overhead. It was a trance-like state deeper than ever before. When he did manage anything like it on the golf course, his game improved beyond all recognition. Instead of worrying about keeping his head still, completing the backswing, and the myriad other tips that Joe Delany had passed on to him, he would just stand up and hit the ball out of sight. It was then that he realized with a startling clarity that if he could get into the same state of mind at Ballykissane, he might yet acquit himself creditably in The Atlantic.

He got to his feet after what seemed an age, but a glance at his watch told him that he had been in the fort less than five minutes. As he left, he brought with him a sense of some indefinable power, a self-confidence such as he had never felt before.

Back in the car, O'Hara remarked, "I see you still believe in the old ways. Well, do you know something? All my life I used to laugh at that kind of thing. Wrote it off as ignorance and superstition—nothing more than a stupid legacy from pagan times. That is, until I saw the way you played golf after you had been in there." Cocking a thumb back toward the fort, which was fast disappearing in the rearview mirror, O'Hara chuckled, "Now I'm not so sure. In fact, strictly between you and me, I might even try it myself one of these days."

Loopy shrugged but said nothing. As they drove along the twisting roads, conversation was sporadic. O'Hara seemed listless most of the time. He would perk up briefly after stopping for a drink at one of the pubs that dotted the road between Trabane and Ballykissane. These were mostly small, whitewashed buildings with a thatched roof and a sign over the door that proclaimed them "licensed to sell beer and spirits." At that time of the day, they were often the only people there, but that did not deter O'Hara in the least. Quite the opposite in fact.

"Best bloody time of the day for a drink," he insisted. "No one around to talk nonsense at you!"

Loopy wondered if there was ever a bad time of the day—or night—for a drink where his traveling companion was concerned. Yet the stimulating effects of the drinks did not last long. In no time at all, O'Hara would lapse back into another long silence. All the while Loopy's thoughts kept returning to The Atlantic. Up to now he had been playing just for himself. Win or lose he had only himself to blame. Success or failure had been his alone. Now, for the first time, he alone was representing Trabane. It wasn't like the hurling team, where other players shared the credit or the blame. This time he was on his very own. He might have reflected that being accepted to play in The Atlantic was a notable victory in itself were he not still thinking about the new driver nestling in his bag.

· · ·

Sure, he reminded himself, he might have been better off with the old one, but that was now broken beyond repair and that was that. A worry perhaps but no grounds for real concern. Anyway, he was hitting the ball better with the new one every day, he told himself, and all he needed was a bit more confidence in it. This would come, he thought, in the practice round the day before the tournament proper got under way, when past winners, sponsors' guests, and competitors would play together for The Plate. It was as much a social as a competitive occasion, and those competing in The Atlantic could invite a friend to play with them. This was how Pat O'Hara would fulfill the ambition of a lifetime by playing on the sacred turf of Ballykissane.

CHAPTER NINE

Better check in at the golf club first before we try to find this sister-in-law of mine. She told me over the phone how to find her place, but there was so much old talk out of her about everything under the sun that I never got 'round to writing it down."

There was little difficulty in finding the clubhouse, however. To judge by the signposts, it seemed as though, sooner or later, all roads led to the famous links. Like Trabane, Ballykissane, too, was a seaside resort—but there the similarity ended. Driving down the main thoroughfare, even the usually impassive O'Hara was impressed by the elegance of the houses and the obvious wealth of their inhabitants. Striped green lawns, lovingly manicured and dotted with flowering shrubs, separated the homes from the tree-lined street. As they drove along the seafront, it seemed as though every house had a sea view, for Ballykissane stretched like a ribbon along the cliff top with only the road between it and the Atlantic.

Far below them, at the base of the tall, black cliffs, lay an unbroken stretch of golden sand. The sea was calm with a gently heaving surf sending tiny wavelets to lap the shoreline. Close to the cliff face but still on the beach stood a line of elderly bathing huts mounted on rusty wheels. Here modest bathers, fearful of offering even the smallest glimpse of bare flesh, could change into their bathing costumes safe from the ogling eyes of the day-trippers who descended on the peaceful resort at the weekend. The wheels allowed the huts to be trundled up the shingle to safety before the onset of the winter storms. Overhead, seagulls rode the thermals with wings outspread, their graceful ballet cut short by sudden dives into a sparkling sea. Mostly they would reemerge from the water with an empty beak, screeching furiously at their failure, with droplets sparkling like diamonds in the sunshine on their snow-white plumage.

When Tim Porter had brought Loopy here, they had skirted the town, still barely stirring itself into wakefulness after the long winter hibernation. The Royal Hotel, where they had stayed overnight, was beside the golf links, so Loopy had not seen Ballykissane until now. On this occasion, however, he had little choice but to examine it minutely, for O'Hara was set on exploring its every nook and cranny. Alternating between admiration and anger, he gave vent to his feelings with sporadic outbursts at what he called vulgar ostentation. Not for the first time Loopy wished his old teacher would use words he could understand properly.

"Jaysus, will you look at that place. Must have cost a bloody mint. That's what wrong with this bloody country, y'know . . ."

Unsure whether these remarks were directed at him, Loopy did not reply. He wished they could abandon the sightseeing and get to the clubhouse. There he would have to register for the tournament, find his locker, and most important, confirm that Weeshy had not suffered a last-minute change of heart and was still prepared to caddy for him.

Tim Porter had warned Loopy about Weeshy: "Bloody great caddy, that old fella, but mad as a hatter. Disappears for days on end and no one can find him. Drinks like a fish, of course."

This was really something, Loopy fretted, coming as it did from Tim—who himself was no stranger to strong drink. At times like these, Loopy worried inwardly that his destiny seemed to be almost entirely in the hands of would-be alcoholics.

Alcohol, largely whiskey and stout, seemed to fuel every social occasion that Loopy had ever attended. Birthdays, funerals, christenings, weddings, or postmatch celebrations were all lubricated by vast quantities of booze. All too often they ended in tearful brawls with the next day spent nursing hangovers. The Lynch family was an exception to this. Loopy's father was a moderate drinker, gambling being his failing, and Brona had never taken alcohol in her life. As for Loopy, he simply did not like the taste of the stuff.

O'Hara was still ranting away as Loopy dragged himself back from his woolgathering to the here and now. ". . . too much power—and money—concentrated in too few hands. It's bloody religion, too, of course."

Loopy was curious about this. "How so?"

"Obvious, when you really think about it. The native Irish, Catholics like you and me, have been under the heel of the Brits for over seven hundred bloody years. Easily known you never listened to a bloody word of history while you were in school. That," O'Hara added glumly, "makes you no different from the rest of them, mind you. Anyway, when we stopped fighting the Brits, that didn't mean they gave us back all the big factories and the good jobs. No, sir, not by a long shot! Them that stayed on after the War of Independence still held on to the reins of power. They mightn't have made it quite as obvious as before that they were running the show, but they still held on to enough power to keep themselves in houses like these. And, it goes without saying, with more than enough money to play all the bloody golf they want."

"Like Tim Porter?"

"Yeah, *exactly* like Tim. Not that he's the worst of 'em. Not by a long shot. More like his father, actually."

"He seemed nice enough that time we went to see Tim when he was sick, remember?"

"Of course I remember," O'Hara protested crossly, but Loopy was not to be put off so easily.

"Well, do you remember that it was Tim who had to convince *you* that I'd be okay to play in The Atlantic? Not the other way round?"

"H-m-m-m, you might have a point there. I've nothing against Tim, that's the truth. Except of course that he's got more money than sense."

"That's not his fault. The money, I mean. He inherited it, didn't he?"

"That's true but—"

"I mean, you hardly expect him to give it back, do you?" Loopy persisted defiantly, determined to press home his advantage. It wasn't often he came out ahead of O'Hara in an argument.

"Do you know what's wrong with you, young fella?"

Loopy thought it best not to answer.

"You're getting so bloody smart you'll soon be passing yourself out!" Then O'Hara ruffled Loopy's hair to show that there were no hard feelings.

This was as close as O'Hara came to praise and Loopy knew it. He only wished his mentor would take better care of his health, because everyone at the Golf Club said he was drinking himself into an early grave. The thought of this terrified Loopy—now more than ever. In the long silences during the drive from Trabane, he realized for the first time how dependent he was on this frail figure of a man. Despite his gruff exterior and a tendency to become irascible when drunk, he had always been a rock of good sense where Loopy's future was concerned.

When O'Hara had finally come to accept that his pupil was never going to finish school because of circumstances outside his control, instead of bemoaning the fact the schoolteacher had set about preparing him for what was to come. Of late there had been less talk of *knowledge is power, my lad*. Instead O'Hara dinned into Loopy at every opportunity that the strength he imagined he got from his visits to the old fort came, in reality, from within. While Loopy was yet to be fully convinced of this, he had the good sense to realize that O'Hara was trying to instill in him a self-confidence that had, until recently, been conspicuous by its absence. When Joe Delany had told him that he was as good as the best of the competitors and better than most, that, too, had provided the extra fillip he needed to approach The Atlantic with a positive mind. Just then, a wooden sign announced BALLYKISSANE GOLF CLUB—1 MILE.

The road hugged the cliff, and when they looked back over their shoulders, they had a stunning view of a fairy-tale village perched high on a cliff, overlooking a golden beach fringed by a placid sea. They crossed a humpbacked bridge over a stream that meandered through giant sand dunes. It flowed across the beach, splitting into a hundred tiny rivulets, before vanishing forever into the sea. From the top of the bridge, the golf course was suddenly there before them, laid out in all its glory. Now, instead of the stream, ribbonlike green fairways threaded their way through the enormous sand dunes. Occasionally red or yellow pennants peeped out from behind a sand dune to indicate a putting green. Overhead, against a backdrop of pale blue sky recently laundered by a passing rain shower, shrieking gulls mocked the best efforts of little knots of golfers who were making their way around the hostile moonscape that was the famed Ballykissane golf links.

The clubhouse nestled snugly among the sandhills. Loopy had never seen anything remotely like it. It was a huge, rambling structure, built largely of timber. Three stories high and topped by twin weather vanes that shifted uneasily in the breeze, it was nonetheless dwarfed by the towering dunes that surrounded it. White-painted balconies of ornately carved wood sprouted from its upper windows. From these, tiny figures lounged in wicker chairs, sipping drinks as they gazed nonchalantly down on the golfers below doing battle with the elements.

O'Hara parked the car in the visitors' carpark and they walked the short distance to the front door in silence. A polished brass plate informed them that gentlemen must wear jacket, collar, and tie within the clubhouse. Luckily Tim Porter had forewarned them of this, otherwise they would have been turned away by the gruff man at the door.

"Yes, gentlemen, how can I help you?" The question was barked out like a drill sergeant's on a parade ground.

O'Hara, determined not to be put down, responded with an equal lack of warmth, "We're here for The Atlantic. Show us where we sign in." He didn't actually say *and be quick about it*, but it was implicit in his tone of voice.

The drill sergeant eyed both of them speculatively, as if checking them for concealed weapons, then with a jerk of his head muttered, "Follow me."

He set a brisk pace across the parquet floor of the front hall, through swing doors that led into the reception area. Pausing only to wordlessly direct them toward the reception desk, he executed a smart, military about-turn before disappearing back through the swing doors.

O'Hara muttered to Loopy, "A sour bollix, isn't he? Hope the rest of 'em are better than him."

Loopy nodded and went over to the girl behind the desk. "Laurence Lynch, miss. Trabane Golf Club."

In contrast to the doorman, the girl was politeness itself. "Welcome to Ballykissane, Mr. Lynch. Is this your first time competing in The Atlantic?"

"Yes, it is, miss."

"Well, the very best of luck. I only asked because, as it *is* your first time here, I'll explain where the locker rooms are. You're in locker number forty-three, by the way. Just through that door there, the one marked LOCKER ROOMS. I have the time sheet for tomorrow's Plate here. Now, let me see. . . . Here it is—Laurence Lynch and Patrick O'Hara, is that right? . . . Good, well, you are both off the first tee tomorrow morning at nine fifteen a.m. Breakfast is served in the dining room from seven thirty should you wish to avail of it. That seems to be everything, Mr. Lynch. Enjoy your time at Ballykissane. . . . Oh, yes, I nearly forgot. There's a message for you."

She handed him the envelope. Loopy tore it open there and then. When he read its contents, he could barely suppress a whoop of delight. It was from the caddy master. It confirmed that Weeshy had been assigned to him for the Atlantic Trophy. It added that his caddy would be waiting for him outside the caddy master's hut the following morning at 9 a.m. Loopy thrust the envelope into his pocket and sprinted after O'Hara.

As he caught up with him, they went through the door and followed the arrows carved from mahogany with LOCKER ROOMS in brass letters screwed onto them down a long corridor. This was thickly carpeted and had other doors leading off it with even more brass plates to indicate what lay behind them. There were, it seemed, private rooms for everyone. The captain, president, secretary and catering manager. Outside the Members Bar a large notice reminded them that it was strictly reserved for MEN ONLY.

Every wall from hall door to the locker rooms was paneled with the same dark wood, giving it a somber air as if entering a courthouse or a place of worship. Above the shoulder-high paneling hung a series of framed photographs, many yellowed with age, of stern-looking men. The caption beneath each indicated that they were all in some way associated with the running of this bastion of privilege over the past 150 years or so. Many of the faces had long sideburns and the ruddy features of the well-off of another age. The one similarity they all shared was to stare sternly at some unseen object in the middle distance. There was not a woman among them.

"Bloody merchant princes to a man, that lot. It's a miracle they let us in through the bloody door! Reminds me of the local bank when I was a kid. My mother used to send me there for change for the sweetshop she ran at the time. I nearly peed in my pants every time I went there, I was that nervous. It was all that shagging dark paneling and the portraits of elderly farts looking down on you from the walls. All designed of course to scare the bejaysus out of you. Gave me the creeps, I can tell you. Still does, actually."

O'Hara was determined not to be overawed by any of it. The

haughty stare of the long-dead worthies seemed to treat his comment with the contempt they would have thought it deserved. At the end of the corridor, two large swing doors faced them. One bore a brass plate with the faded inscription LOCKER. The other, ROOMS. These pair of signs had become faded, unlike the others, by countless members brushing against them as they pushed open the swing doors.

Back in Trabane the changing room had recently been enlarged and renovated and was the pride and joy of the club. The accumulation of odd shoes, abandoned socks, and old golf clubs had been thrown into a skip. In their place were installed shiny metal lockers with slits for ventilation, two modest showers, and a vanity unit where the golfers could smarten themselves up a bit before joining their colleagues in the bar. Until now, it had been the smartest changing room Loopy had ever seen. When he had turned out for the Trabane Gaels, the changing facilities were round the back of a shed that housed the groundsman's equipment. As for the after-match ablutions, these were conducted in a nearby water trough. On some of the grounds he had played on, this trough also served to water the sheep and cattle who kept the pitch grazed bare in the off-season.

Pushing the swing doors open, they were inside what looked like a small cathedral. Instead of pews, row upon row of lockers stretched for almost as far as the eye could see. Each locker had a small brass cardholder with the member's name on it.

O'Hara examined some of these with interest. "Presumably, if you don't have a business card of some sort, you don't get a locker. That would automatically eliminate most of our members back home," he cackled gleefully before adding, "mightn't be such a bad thing at that."

Loopy barely heard him. A large notice board close to the entrance was festooned with lists of members' handicap adjustments, forthcoming social events, and forthcoming members' competitions. The sole indication that Ballykissane Golf Club was about to host yet again one of the country's major amateur tournaments was a sheet of paper, rel-

egated to an obscure corner, headed ATLANTIC TROPHY COMPETI-
TORS. It informed its readers that the lockers assigned to those playing
in the Atlantic Trophy were at the far end of the room and had their
names attached thereto. In heavy Gothic script it again reminded
competitors, lest they had failed to notice the large brass plate at the
front door, that jacket, collar, and tie must, at all times, be worn within
the clubhouse.

After some difficulty they located the locker assigned to LAURENCE
LYNCH, TRABANE GC. They went out through a side door marked
CARPARK and retrieved his golf clubs and sports bag from the car. Taking a careful look around to get his bearings in this vast cavern of lockers, Loopy noticed that directly over his locker hung a portrait in oils
of Jimmy Bruen, one of the greatest amateur golfers that Ireland had
ever produced.

O'Hara never tired of relating Bruen's exploits to anyone prepared
to listen. Described at the time as the best golfer, amateur or professional, in the world, Bruen led the British and Irish Walker Cup team
as a teenager before going on to win the British Amateur in 1946. Of
late though, O'Hara tended to lay emphasis on an even more unique
aspect of Bruen. This was his golf swing. It had an exaggerated loop at
the top, as a result of playing the game of hurling as a boy. Bruen retained the loop until his untimely death, by which time he had lost interest in the game, emerging from the shadows—like the late Bobby
Jones—only to feature in the occasional exhibition match.

When some of the club members in Trabane urged Loopy to
change his grip on the golf club to a more orthodox method and
thereby remove the loop that was part and parcel of his backswing,
O'Hara would explode. Done with swearing, he would then glare at
the individual bold enough to suggest the change to orthodoxy and remind him in no uncertain terms that Ireland's greatest golfer had precisely the same loop at the top of *his* backswing. O'Hara would end the
discussion by snarling that what was good enough for Jimmy Bruen
was good enough for him—and Larry Lynch.

It seemed, however, that O'Hara had not seen the portrait of his idol, for he was already on his way to the bar.

As Loopy elbowed his way through the swing doors, he caught a glimpse of O'Hara's back disappearing round the corner at the far end of the corridor. He hurried after him, but was momentarily distracted by a scorecard dated August 1947, which was in a small gilt frame and spotlit by a powerful lamp. It was the course record for Ballykissane before alterations to the layout had consigned it to history. The score was 65, and the player was none other than Jimmy Bruen. Another omen? Hardly, he decided. It was ridiculous to imagine that the ghost of a long-dead golfer could help him now—even if they shared a "loop" in their swings. Nonetheless he felt strangely elated as he strode confidently into the public bar.

Public, of course, meant that it served those who were not members but had passed the scrutiny of the doorman. The bar was even more like a cathedral than the locker rooms. Again there were acres of wooden paneling on every wall, with enormous French windows looking out onto the putting green and, in the distance, the first tee. Some of the windows were open, allowing the ocean breeze to dissipate the pall of tobacco smoke coming from tall, winged armchairs of deep red leather dotted randomly over the huge polished floor of the bar. Most of the parties were hidden, sunk deep in the plush leather, behind newspapers, though others were grouped around low tables and talking animatedly among themselves. Loopy made his way to the bar, where he took a stool next to O'Hara, who was already halfway down a tumbler of whiskey.

"This place gives me the creeps," Loopy confided. "It reminds me of the courthouse I had to go to the day my father . . ." His voice trailed off. The memory of that day of ignominy he preferred not to recall.

"The day they were suing him for the money, you mean?"

"Yeah." The edge to Loopy's voice did not escape O'Hara.

"Don't know why that bothers you so much. Half of Trabane have been up in that court at one time or another. I was up myself—"

"I know. I know. For drunken driving or something. That's nowhere near as bad as not being able to pay your debts."

O'Hara gave a hollow laugh that seemed to come all the way from the soles of his feet. "H-m-m-ph! Glad you think so. There are plenty who think different, my lad. Don't worry about it, for God's sake. He didn't go to jail or anything like that."

"Only for my mother standing up in court and pleading with the judge to go easy on him, he would have done. Or so Mr. O'Sullivan, the solicitor, told us afterwards. Not that I gave a damn what sentence they gave him. They could have locked him up and thrown away the key as far as I'm concerned. I never want to see him again as long as I live. 'Twas my mother I was worried about."

O'Hara waited for a moment or two before dropping the subject with a gentle "I know, lad, I know."

In the silence that followed, both of them took stock of their surroundings.

The walls of the bar were easily twenty feet high. One was adorned with plaques listing the names in gold leaf of former captains and presidents and the years in which they had held office. Elsewhere there were framed photographs of previous winners of The Atlantic. Some of the earlier ones were sepia prints of knickerbockered worthies with long mustaches and even longer double-barreled names and a sprinkling of *Right Hons.* thrown in for good measure. Loopy found it almost a relief to see that last year's winner was a blond youth in his twenties with a severe crew cut and a Harvard sweater, whose name, according to the caption beneath the photograph, was Albert Neumann. A scorecard more modestly framed than Bruen's proclaimed that Neumann was the holder of the course record for the present layout.

Loopy went over to the scorecard to examine it more closely. This was a much more recent scorecard than Bruen's. A closer look revealed that it was, in fact, from The Plate of the previous year, the competition that he had been told no one took really seriously since it was merely a warm-up round for The Atlantic! Well, it seemed that the crew-cut Albert Neumann, had taken it seriously indeed because he had gone around Ballykissane in three under par. Impressed by this feat, Loopy rejoined O'Hara, who was already well down on his second whiskey. As they sipped in silence, out of curiosity Loopy picked up a typewritten sheet, one of several strewn around the bar counter, and glanced idly at it. It was the draw for the first round of The Atlantic. The peace and tranquillity of the bar were shattered by a startled yelp. Loopy had found his name right at the bottom of the draw.

"I'm up against last year's winner in the very first round. There's his picture over there on the wall. What's more, he holds the course record!"

If Loopy was expecting any consolation from O'Hara, he was to be disappointed. "Just as well you stopped off at that famous fort of yours then, isn't it? You'd better pray that its effects last for at least another forty-eight hours!"

With that, the schoolmaster put the glass to his lips and drained it in two quick gulps. Looking at Loopy's half-full glass of Coca-Cola, he added reproachfully, "Better finish that up quick. We don't want to be late for Maggie. My sister-in-law never tires of saying over and over again that punctuality is the courtesy of kings. How she came by that bit of misinformation is anybody's guess."

CHAPTER TEN

The next day dawned bright but windy. The sun ducked in and out from behind clouds that looked like giant wads of cotton wool. Such hide-and-seek constantly changed the ocean from duck-egg blue to a menacing gray, speckled with white horses driven by offshore gusts—then back again. This volatile weather cocktail was clearly visible from the bathroom of Margaret's house, which overlooked the sea. Loopy was shaving with great care for he wanted to look his best when he strode to the first tee, wearing his new golfing outfit emblazoned with the crest of Trabane Golf Club. He could hear O'Hara shuffling around his room, preparing to confront another day. At least he wouldn't have a hangover, Loopy reflected. Margaret ran a dry ship and a religious one as well. The night before they had barely finished a meal of boiled mutton, cabbage, and potatoes when she'd announced that they would say the rosary.

Moving into the sitting room, they'd knelt on the carpet, facing the armchairs they had been sitting on earlier. Loopy lowered his head and droned the responses in a singsong voice he hadn't used since his earliest days at the National School. Margaret led the prayers, in a high-pitched, nasal voice that made Loopy want to giggle. His and O'Hara's role was a to chime in with the responses. As with the golf swing, in this, timing was everything. To begin the response before Margaret had finished would make her feel that she was being unduly hurried. To come in late was just as bad, implying that the attention of both men was wandering and not on what clearly was, for Margaret, the crowning moment of the day.

It came as something of surprise to discover that when the last Gloria of the fifth and final decade of the rosary was completed, the performance was, in fact, only getting into stride. Margaret went on to solicit numerous favors and blessings from a collection of saints, many of whom Loopy had never heard of before. Though her approach seemed scattershot at first, it soon became obvious that she believed there was safety in numbers when seeking saintly intercession on her behalf. Loopy noticed with regret that Andrew, the patron saint of golf, was not on Margaret's shopping list. As he waited for the rosary to end, Loopy wondered idly if he might yet have cause to invoke Andrew's saintly help before his stay in Ballykissane was over.

At breakfast, they discussed their plans for the day. Margaret was going to mass in the local church. There, she promised, she would pray for them both that they would emerge unscathed from the pagan stronghold of the golf club. To her, it was a bastion of privilege, inside whose walls she would not venture in the unlikely event of her ever being invited to do so. Worse still, it was a nest of Protestant and Presbyterian vipers waiting to lure the likes of an impressionable Loopy away from the one true faith. To protect them both from such blandishments, she sprinkled holy water from a bottle on their shoulders before hurrying off to mass.

With relief, Loopy watched her go. When O'Hara had described her as a "lighting bitch," he had not lied. The house was, like herself, a monument to rectitude. No sooner had he or O'Hara risen from a chair but Margaret was over, like a flash, to pat the cushion back into shape. If as much as a crumb fell from the kitchen table, she would rise from her seat wordlessly and retrieve it with brush and scoop.

Then with a self-pitying sigh, she would deposit the errant crumb into the pedal-bin. The bin had a crocheted cover that matched the tea cozy. Breakfast consisted of cereal, tea, a boiled egg, and one slice of toast. As O'Hara remarked while she was out of earshot, it was hardly the breakfast of champions, vowing that from then on they would breakfast at the golf club.

When they reached the golf course, the flagsticks were bending in the gale blowing in off the ocean. As good as his word, Weeshy awaited them, huddled in his familiar long coat as he sheltered behind the caddy master's hut. Loopy grasped his hand and introduced him to O'Hara. Weeshy responded by way of a grunt and what might have been the merest hint of a nod. As O'Hara unloaded his golf bag from the car and went to see about hiring a trolley to carry it, Loopy and his caddy went to the locker room to retrieve Loopy's clubs.

On the first tee, Weeshy seemed to be the only one present who was suitably dressed for the weather. Though he was wearing the same old heavy overcoat as before, now his neck was swathed in several scarves. Instead of trainers he wore rubber Wellingtons, though no rain had yet fallen.

The starter called, "Laurence Lynch of Trabane Golf Club and partner!"

They were off. O'Hara struck a safe three wood down the middle of the fairway. Loopy took out the new driver Joe had given him and, after a few tentative practice swings, hit a long but far from straight ball off the tee. It finished deep in the dune grass and tucked neatly in behind a clump of heather. Loopy's first attempt to extricate himself from the rough failed miserably. Though he dislodged a sizable chunk of Ballykissane, leaving a divot big enough to bury a fair-sized cat and wreaking mayhem on the heather, the golf ball scarcely moved at all. O'Hara was too far away to witness this disaster. As for Weeshy, he merely grunted, this time more forcefully, but said nothing.

Loopy's next attempt was more successful in that the ball, again followed by a thick wedge of turf, just made it to the edge of the fairway. This left him with a long iron for his fourth shot to the first green. To his credit, he caught the three iron flush on the ball. It cut through the wind like a hot knife through butter, finding the front portion of the green but still a longish way from the pin. Weeshy maintained a stony silence, not even offering to point out the line of the long first putt. More by luck than skill, Loopy stroked the putt with just the right pace, but misread the line by five feet. He was relieved to see his next putt stagger into the hole. He had carded a horrendous six, two over par. O'Hara, who had charted a steadier course down the middle, knocked his ball along the fairway to reach the green in three, taking two putts to card a highly respectable—for him—five.

"One up," he announced to no one in particular, and strode purposefully to the second tee. This was a difficult, downhill par three, which was halved in fours. O'Hara still had the honor at the next tee and struck off first. Again he scuttled the ball a short distance along the fairway. Loopy duplicated his drive off the first tee by hitting the ball a tremendous distance into the wind. For most of its flight his ball maintained a low trajectory, keeping it above the narrow fairway yet below the main force of the wind. However, toward the end of its flight, it suddenly gained height and was caught by a crosswind that unceremoniously dumped it in the second cut of rough. This time there was no heather to contend with, but the dune grass prevented clean contact between the club and the ball. Still, Loopy told himself, he was within a hundred yards of the pin.

Since they had started out, Weeshy had not uttered a single intelligible word. He confined himself to a selection of grunts, but these were growing increasingly animated. They became even more so when Loopy plucked a pitching wedge from the bag. Weeshy retreated backward from the ball, clucking angrily to himself and glaring at Loopy and his choice of club, leaving no doubt as to his feelings.

Determined not to be intimidated by this, Loopy stayed with his choice of club. It was, he reminded himself, supposed to be a practice round, a warm-up for the tournament proper. To hell with Albert Neumann and his course record. These college boys, he told himself, had the time and the money to get in twenty practice rounds before The Plate, never mind the tournament proper. What's more, they could afford to stay in The Royal Hotel, where, he knew from experience, the breakfast alone was sufficient to keep a man going for the rest of the day, unlike Margaret's spartan offering.

As he squared up to the ball, he tried to banish from his mind that, on the opening hole, pretty much the same shot had ended in disaster. He tried to think positive, reminding himself that this time there was no heather to contend with and the green was much nearer.

He exhaled slowly in an effort to calm his jangling nerves. Taking a deliberately slow practice swing before addressing the barely visible ball, he was only too aware of Weeshy's eyes drilling twin bullet holes in his back. He flicked the club downward in a steep curve, just as Joe Delany had taught him to do when digging the ball out of really thick rough. He prayed that the sharp leading edge of the pitching wedge would slice through the wiry dune grass, causing the ball to pop up out of the dense undergrowth and float in a lazy arc to the green. He even opened the clubface a touch more than usual to encourage the scything action that would prevent the blade of the pitching wedge from getting entangled in the grass before making contact with the ball.

However, the dune grass at Ballykissane made a nonsense of his best effort. The ball broke free but only just. It flew only a few feet—flopping down again like an exhausted bird into lighter rough, not much nearer to the green. Exasperated, Loopy cried out in a strangled voice, "Will someone *please* tell me what I am doing wrong?"

Though the question was yelled at the sky, Weeshy saw his chance. "I'll tell you what's wrong, young fella. You're not hitting the fairway, that's what's wrong. Unless you're on the fairways round here, you can throw your hat at The Atlantic, anyways."

Looped stared at the ground for a while, then looked up at Weeshy.

"This new driver, I hit it great on the practice range back home. I was sure it would work out here."

Weeshy gave him a scowl, grunting, "These newfangled drivers are more temperamental than Old Moll herself. You can't just come here with any old driver, y'know. What you need is one that was built for this course—one that keeps the ball low and straight, anyways. That contraption of yours is ballooning the ball up all over the place and getting it caught in the wind. Just go back to your old one and we'll be right as rain."

Loopy again stared at the ground, more crestfallen than ever. "I can't. I shattered the head while I was practicing back home. My boss gave me this one instead. Said it was the best on the market."

"The dearest, mebbe. Sure as hell it's not the best for 'round here, anyways. You're rightly banjaxed without your old one, that's for certain. You're hitting that yoke"—here Weeshy pointed disgustedly at the offending club—"all over the bloody place. Leave in your bag for the rest of the round. Use the spoon."

"The spoon?"

Loopy was completely mystified. By now Weeshy was almost beside himself with fury.

O'Hara, who had played his shot from the fairway, came over to see what was wrong. "Weeshy means the three wood. It used to be called a spoon when I started playing the game."

For the rest of the round, Loopy struggled round the course, using the unfamiliar three wood off the tee. What he lost in distance, he more than gained in accuracy. Now that he was playing his approach shots from the fairway rather than the rough, his game improved as the round progressed, but to nowhere near the level at which he would offer anything more than a token resistance to the experienced Neumann. Nevertheless, Weeshy seemed in much better humor by the time they played out the last hole. Loopy had blasted out of a deep bunker and sunk a tricky downhill putt to halve the match with O'Hara, a feat that earned an appreciative grunt from the caddy.

They shook hands with each other as they left the eighteenth green. It was just after one o'clock and O'Hara was talking in terms of lunch. Even had they so wished, Weeshy could not have joined them because caddies were not allowed to set foot inside the clubhouse. It did not matter, for Weeshy had other plans for his man. He beckoned Loopy over to him with the crook of a finger and, out of earshot of O'Hara, muttered vehemently, "If ye want to have any chance at all against the Yank, ye'd better listen to me here and now. I didn't want to be telling you what you're doing wrong out on the course—anyways that's not my job."

"Tell me now, so. It's the driver, isn't it?"

Weeshy nodded. "Yes, yes, that driver's no bloody good to you. Not here, anyways. Not for this kind of course with narrow fairways and thick rough. You saw yourself that once you got the ball on the fairway off the tee, you were fine. Trouble is, using the spoon means you're leaving yourself too far from the green."

"So what'll I do?" Loopy tried hard not to make the question sound like a wail, even though that was exactly what he felt like doing—wailing.

"I'll tell what you'll do." Weeshy's voice took on a new intensity as he explained what he had in mind. "And if, mind you it's a big *if*, you'll do what I tell you, we might still be in with a chance."

Loopy gave a hollow laugh. "You mean I've a chance to *beat* Neumann?"

"I'll put it another way, young fella. If you don't believe with all your heart and soul that you're going to beat him anyways—and beat him well—then you haven't a snowball's chance in hell."

"I'm not quite sure I understand."

"Of course you don't. How could you? Sure, what are you, only a grown-up child, anyways? Anyone in his right senses would have seen

that taking a wedge for that first shot out of the rough was pure madness. The grass will catch you every time. They sent you out here to do
a man's job, though, and make no mistake."

There followed a long pause. Loopy wasn't sure that Weeshy had
finished, so he, too, remained silent. After what seemed like a lifetime,
Weeshy spoke again, this time in a quieter, less impassioned tone.

"Y'see, I'm thinkin' I have this oul' club back at the house that just
might do the trick. As a driver, I mean. Don't ask me where I got it because you won't be told. You can be sure 'tis a damn sight better article
than that excuse for a golf club you have in your bag, anyways."

Loopy didn't even try to argue. He knew that Weeshy had given up
a lucrative bag in exchange for his. The least he could do was to humor
the old man and see what use he could make of this mysterious driver.

Weeshy was speaking again: "You go off with your man and have a
bite to eat, anyways. I'll go home for that club, and I should be back
here inside an hour with any luck. Meet me on the practice ground
and then we'll see what we can make of you."

Lunch for Loopy was a hurried sandwich and a cup of coffee.
O'Hara was in a celebratory mood, having performed way above his
norm and on a links he had never dreamed he would ever get a chance
to play. To him, God was in his heaven and all was right with the world.
His feeling of well-being to all and sundry was being enhanced by a
succession of whiskeys. The shepherd's pie he had ordered from the
bar menu remained untouched. As the drink took hold, he grew ever
more expansive.

"Your caddy was right, you know. That new driver is no good to
you. On this track—"

*Oh, God, he's talking as if he owned the course after playing one
half-decent round,* Loopy groaned inwardly.

"—if you're not on the fairway, you're dead as a bloody doornail.
Your man Weeshy—or whatever his name is—said as much. My advice to you is to do whatever he says. He's a sour old bastard to be sure,

but I'd say he's forgotten more about golf than the rest of us would know after ten lifetimes. You've no choice anyway but to put yourself in his hands. If you play like you did today against the Yank, we'll be on our way home by lunchtime tomorrow with our tails between our legs. Now, why don't you take yourself off out to the practice ground. It's bound to be quiet during lunchtime, and you can get in a bit of practice while you wait for your man to come back with this famous club of his."

Then, almost as an afterthought, O'Hara added nonchalantly, "I'll stay here for a while. I might even chance my luck and join the high and the mighty for a quick nap in the members' lounge. I preferred the look of them leather armchairs to Margaret's ones in the parlor. Then I'll join you on the practice ground later and see how you and Weeshy are getting on with each other. Does that sound okay to you?"

Loopy nodded and made his way out through one of the French windows and past the practice putting green, which was now full of people stroking putts as if their very lives depended on it. On his way to the practice ground, he paused to let a threesome hit off the first tee. One of them stood out from the others. His hefty frame and blond crew cut would have marked him out in any group. His face and forearms were bronzed from the sun. The last shred of doubt as to his identity was dispelled when he ambled over to a golf bag with HAR-VARD emblazoned on it. The bag was so big that his caddy had to bend almost double to heave it on his back. Swishing the driver as if it were no heavier than a toothpick, he took a few long, leisurely practice swings. Then he squared up to the ball and, with a lazy stroke, smooth as silk, propelled it straight and true down the middle of the first fairway, to the admiration of his two playing partners.

"Great shot, Al, you really caught that one."

Loopy hurried to the practice ground. He had no wish to see any more of the man he was to face tomorrow. Neumann's majestic progress toward the first green was in too stark a contrast to his feeble efforts at the same hole only a few hours earlier. Further proof, if such were required, that he had much work to do on his game between now and when he faced the blond giant the next day.

Loopy sensed Weeshy's presence rather than hearing him approach. Loopy had been practicing high long irons, the kind of second shot necessary to hold the iron-hard greens of Ballykissane. Unlike those of most modern courses, the greens here were not watered. No watering system would ever be allowed to sully this proud links, and consequently, after a spell of dry, windy weather such as Ballykissane had recently been experiencing, the greens were slick and hard. Which, of course, made them unreceptive to approach shots that were not high and loaded with backspin. Luckily it was a shot that Loopy, with his unorthodox grip and looping backswing, was able to hit with relative ease. He had just struck six in a row of such blows with his four iron and was pleased to see that the half dozen balls had finished within a few yards of each other when Weeshy's voice stopped him in his tracks.

"That's good, that's exactly the kind of shot you'll need tomorrow. It's going to blow for the rest of the week anyways if I'm any judge of the weather. The gulls are high and so are the clouds, so ye'll get no rain to soften out them greens. All to good, I'm thinkin'. Yanks don't like hard greens, anyways. They're used to carpets soaked in water, so they are. That's why that Yank destroyed the course last year and no mistake. It rained for a month before he arrived. Then he spent a week practicing. New balls, if you don't mind. Brand-new Titleists, for Jaysus' sake! Never thought I'd live to see the day. And they call him an amateur."

Weeshy paused to signal his disgust by hawking noisily, gathering up enough ammunition to spit expertly at a dandelion two yards away from him.

"Well, I can tell you this much and it isn't one word of a lie, anyways. He's going to find Ballykissane a very different kettle of fish in this weather, and no mistake. With the greens hard as a jockey's bollocks, he's going to be in for a few surprises when he plays any of his three wedges onto them, and that's not a word of a lie either."

This had been Weeshy's longest monologue by far, and Loopy found it strangely exhilarating. He longed to get a proper look at the club Weeshy was clutching beneath his coat but decided to bide his time.

Weeshy's next move caught him unawares. "Do you know how to play the bump and run, anyways?"

Not wanting to show his ignorance, Loopy played for time with "You mean the low chip shot?"

"All dependin' what you mean by *chip*, young fella. Here, give me your six iron and I'll *show* you what I mean."

Weeshy handed the club he had been concealing under his coat to Loopy and hit a few low, running shots with the iron. True to their name, they were airborne for less than half the length of the shot, bumping and running along the hard ground for the remainder of the journey. The balls stopped some forty yards distant, but so close to each other that Weeshy's cap would have covered all three. The display of the short approach was worthy of a professional, but Loopy barely noticed.

Instead his gaze was riveted on the antique driver, a piece of ancient golfing memorabilia, that he held in his hand. The grip was of shiny leather. It was glued onto a shaft of steel, speckled with rust spots and scarred by innumerable scrapes and scratches. The shaft fitted over the hosel of the clubhead and was secured to it by a length of tightly wound waxed cord. One end of the cord had worked loose, leaving three inches or so flapping in the breeze. Most alarming of all, however, was that the clubhead itself, like the delicately carved hosel, was made of *wood*.

He had seen photographs of such clubs, but this was the first time he had ever actually laid eyes on such a relic from bygone days. He held the clubhead up close in a vain attempt to find a maker's name on the soleplate. All that was visible was a worn number 1 and beside it something that might have read Nicoll O'Leven. Then he noticed that the hosel had several hairline fractures that ran right through it, and the scuffed wooden head had been repaired more than once as several glue-filled cracks revealed. The face of the club had a large red inset made of some hard plastic substance, which, like the soleplate, was affixed to the wooden head by four countersunk screws. It occurred to him that Weeshy's antique deserved a place of honor in a museum rather than to be substituting for the most modern driver that money could buy.

"Och, it's old, sure enough. But give it a few swings and see how it goes, anyways."

Loopy teed up a ball and, because he was afraid the clubhead would shatter into a hundred wooden fragments, swung the club more gently than usual. Much to his relief, the clubhead remained all in one piece. The sound it made as it impacted the golf ball was weird. Instead of the sharp metallic click that he was accustomed to, the wooden head and plastic inset gave off a dull, unfamiliar thud. It was more the sound of an ax felling a tree than a golf ball being driven straight and true.

For that is what it did. It took off on a low trajectory straight as an arrow, never more than twenty feet off the ground. On landing, it scurried forward farther than he would have thought possible, until Loopy thought it might disappear into the gorse that marked the farthermost boundary of the practice ground. The shot was greeted by an awed silence from both player and caddy. Wordlessly Loopy hit another ball with much the same result. Then, with a growing realization that this relic from the past could well be his salvation on the narrow fairways of Ballykissane, he hit another dozen in quick succession. As he paused to get his breath back, Weeshy took the club back.

"That's enough for today, if you please. We don't want to tire her out too much on her first day back. I'll look after her until tomorrow, anyways. Clubs have been known to go missing y'know, and I wouldn't like to lose her now. She's been around too long for that to happen. You can have a loan of her for the tournament, anyways, seeing as how she seems to like you. Just remember she's a woman—and God knows, they can be fickle enough at times. Treat her right by swinging her easy and slow and she'll do anything you ask her. Try to bully her, though, and she'll land you back in the heather where you were this morning."

Weeshy put the club back into its canvas sack and laid it carefully on the grass beside the golf bag. From it he picked out the six iron he had been using earlier and handed it to Loopy.

"Now let's see if you can play that bump and run, because if you can't, now's the time to learn. Not when you're up against that Yank tomorrow."

CHAPTER ELEVEN

A muffled hiccup signaled O'Hara's arrival. He watched intently as Loopy stroked a succession of balls toward his golf bag some fifty yards distant. He noted with satisfaction that his erstwhile pupil both in school and on the golf course seemed to have mastered the subtleties of bump and run under Weeshy's watchful eye. The delicately struck approaches flew straight and low, landing about halfway and then bouncing forward and scampering along the turf, before trickling to a halt inches from the bag.

O'Hara could wait no longer. Turning to the caddy, he asked nervously, "How did the driver work out in the end?"

"Fine!" Weeshy, who had become increasingly chatty with Loopy, did not waste words on strangers such as O'Hara. Then he relented, adding almost affably, "We're working on the bump and run, as ye can see."

O'Hara watched a few shots and remarked, "He seems to be getting the hang of it alright, doesn't he?"

Weeshy was noncommittal. "Let him hit the last few balls anyways and then we'll call it a day."

With the last ball struck, Weeshy picked up his driver, still shrouded in the canvas sack, and tucked it inside his overcoat.

"Don't be fooled by today, young fella. It's goin' to blow like hell to-morrow or I'm a Dutchman. Remember, if we beat the Yank anyways, there's still another match that evening. You'll be wanting to hit a few balls to warm yourself up before we start at ten o'clock, for it's going to be cold and windy for the rest of the week, you can bet on that any-ways. Make sure the lad has enough clothes on him. Nothin' worse than a cold golfer."

With that, Weeshy was gone.

O'Hara, stifling yet another hiccup, asked, "How did you *really* get on?"

"Not bad! Weeshy arrives with this driver of his. It's about a hun-dred years old I'd say, and he won't talk about it. I mean, *her.*"

"Her?"

"Yeah, he calls it her. Said she's a woman and if I treat her right, she'll look after me."

"Maybe he's right at that."

O'Hara chuckled as Loopy continued excitedly, "I hope so. She re-ally worked for me, y'know. At the start I thought the wooden head was going to fall apart the moment I hit the ball. If it had, he would have murdered me for sure. But, no, it held together okay. It's much heavier than the other one, so I have to swing it easier."

"Distance, how about distance?"

"Not all that much difference. The ball flies very low and it lands much earlier. But then it takes off like a bat out of hell and runs and runs."

Another stifled burp preceded O'Hara's observation. "Sounds like just the kind of thing you want to be able to do if the wind comes up, like Weeshy says it will."

"Yeah, absolutely. Same with the bump and runs. Weeshy has me hitting them really low with a six iron. The ball runs along the ground nearly as much as it flies. Even when it *does* fly, it keeps low, real low."

"Just look at how I poked the ball along in front of me and I damn near beat you. You hit the ball okay, but every time it took off, it was blown away to hell."

"Into the rough. Weeshy told me if I took the wedge out of my bag tomorrow, he'd take it off me and split my skull with it."

O'Hara thought this hilarious. "Let me tell you something. I'd say he meant every word of it. I'd stay with the chip and run, if I were you. Now get changed. You'll need to put on a collar and tie as I'm sure you remember that your friend and benefactor, Edward Linhurst, is treating us to dinner tonight and for the next three nights as well at The Royal Hotel, no less. So put on a clean shirt and tie and let us be off without delay to join the great and the good. No more boiled mutton and soapy spuds for us, my lad. Attired in our very best bib and tucker we shall see what culinary delights await us."

Loopy could not help but notice that the more O'Hara had to drink, the more flowery his language became. Loopy hoped that for once this mellow mood would last throughout the evening and not degenerate into surly ill-humor. He really liked his old schoolteacher and thought of him as the father he would have wished to have had. He was kind and wise and had helped Loopy more than anyone else he knew, but at times late at night in the bar of Trabane Golf Club, Loopy felt that he had more than repaid that debt. Those were the bad times when O'Hara, transformed by drink into a loudmouthed, argumentative bore, would find himself shunned and abandoned by all but Loopy. The task of driving O'Hara home had been Loopy's for some time, and his duties did not end there. There followed the job of persuading the schoolmaster not to have a last nightcap, then helping him upstairs, undressing him, and putting him to bed. All in all, Loopy decided, the balance sheet, as of now, read about even.

The Royal Hotel was reassuringly familiar. This time Loopy marched confidently past reception and was heading for the dining room when he heard an agonized cry.

"Jaysus, we're surely going to have a drink before we eat. You go ahead and make sure we have a table, if you want, but for God's sake come back to the bar. Didn't you know no one worth their salt sits down to eat their dinner before nine o'clock!"

Loopy had a word with the headwaiter, who agreed to call them when a table became vacant. It was just after eight o'clock. Back in the bar, O'Hara had found a table by the window. It looked out on the ocean where a fading sun was starting to slip below the horizon. The wavelets that had earlier gently lapped the shore were now being whipped into sizable waves that crashed relentlessly onto the beach. Weeshy was right. The wind was already getting up.

O'Hara seemed oblivious to all of this. He was engrossed in a newspaper, clucking like an old hen as he read, and taking a sip every now and then from a whiskey that the barman had set before him. Clearing his throat, he read aloud without any preamble, "'The holder of the Atlantic Trophy, Albert Neumann of Harvard University, has returned to defend his title. It will be remembered that not only did he win last year but also set a new course record in The Plate, a contest that precedes the tournament proper.'"

Loopy interjected, "That was in fine weather. He didn't break eighty today, or so Weeshy told me on the practice ground."

"Good news, good news. Now, do you want to hear the rest of this?"

"I suppose so." Loopy got the impression that he was going to hear it anyway, regardless of what he wanted. Like most schoolteachers, O'Hara liked the sound of his own voice—and did not welcome interruptions.

"'. . . the tournament proper. This is contested between sixty-four invited amateurs, some of the best in the world. Despite the presence of several international players both past and present, it is expected that the American·will reach the finals without too much difficulty. There he is seeded to meet Sir Andrew Villiers-Stewart, a member of Royal County Down who holidays annually at Ballykissane and is therefore familiar with the difficult world-famous links course. It will be remembered that he just failed to beat Neumann in last year's final and hopes to reverse the result this time round.'"

Loopy was surprised but tried gamely to hide it. "That all? Not much, was it?"

"No, that's all, I'm afraid. No mention of anyone else, not even of the brilliant young golfer from Trabane with the peculiar loop at the top of his swing. That's the press for you. Wait till you knock out the Yank in the first round, though. Then the shaggers will be beating a path to your door, looking for interviews and the divil only knows what."

"I know you're joking, but now that my driving seems to be okay again, what do you think?"

"About what?"

"Can I really beat Neumann? Honestly, now, answer me *honestly*."

O'Hara emptied what was left in his glass before replying. "As true as God I have this feeling in my old bones that you *are* going to beat him tomorrow. Not because you're playing particularly well. The truth is I've often seen you play better. It's more"—he paused, trying to put his thoughts into words as Loopy waited, too experienced to risk O'Hara's wrath by interrupting—"more of a *feel* thing. I *sense* that there are things happening to you just now, a coming together of important strands in your life all at the same time."

"Like what, f'r instance?"

"Oh, I don't know, really. I suppose the first thing was when you stopped by the fort. I always thought all that kind of stuff was pure nonsense. Your father used to tell me he went there to cheer himself up and make him feel better, but this time I thought I felt something *off* you when you got back into the car. A kind of aura, I suppose. Then there was the business of the driver. I still haven't seen it, by the way, because Weeshy kept it inside that dirty old sack of his, but I feel that it is, in some weird and wonderful way, connected up with everything else."

O'Hara raised his hand as if to stifle any objections before pressing on, "Don't ask me *how* because I couldn't tell even if I wanted to. It's just a gut feeling. I think your session on the practice ground where Weeshy got you hitting the ball low and straight could be the thing that swings it all in your favor. All you need now is for that wind to blow like bloody hell for the next few days and you might surprise even yourself. So, after all that, to try to answer your original question, not only do I honestly, yes, *honestly*, believe that you will beat that Yank tomorrow, but I wouldn't be one bit surprised if you made it all the way. Just imagine playing thirty-six holes match play against someone with a name like"—he paused again while rummaging through the paper to find the name of the second seed—"like Andrew Villiers-Stewart. There's a mouthful of a name for you, and he's old enough to be your father."

Any further discussion was interrupted by the arrival of the head-waiter. "Gentlemen—your table is ready when you are."

They followed the portly figure, impeccable in full evening dress, as he glided past tables in the thronged dining room and waved them to their seats. Their table was next to a large group. Loopy noticed that among them was Al Neumann. The table for two behind them was the only empty one in the room.

The headwaiter plucked two leather-bound menus from under his arm and flicked them open with a deft movement of the wrist. "There you are, gentlemen. This is the table Mr. Linhurst specifically requested for you. As you may be aware, he has taken care of everything, and we are also expecting you for the next three nights, is that correct?"

They both nodded.

"Please take your time perusing the menu, gentlemen. If I may be of any assistance, please do not hesitate to ask. A drink perhaps, while you are making up your minds?"

Before Loopy could refuse, having decided that his dinner companion had already had more than enough, at least until he had got some solid food inside him, he found himself upstaged.

"A mineral water for the young man and a Black Bush for me. Might as well make it a large one while you're at it." O'Hara smiled winningly at the headwaiter and was rewarded with a beaming grin.

"Actually, sir, if I may recommend the hotel special. It is a sixteen-year-old Bushmills, single malt. I can personally recommend it."

"Sixteen years old . . ." O'Hara whistled appreciatively. "Now that's something you don't see every day. Yes, I would like to try it very much indeed."

The menu appeared to be unchanged from Loopy's last visit in that it was largely in French. The only part of it readily decipherable was the price of each individual dish, and that was impressive. They read through it in silence, O'Hara audibly clicking his teeth every now and again in evident disapproval.

"I thought I had a good smattering of French, but I can't make head nor tail of this. We'll get your man to translate when he comes back with the drink."

Which is what they did. Loopy opted for soup and a fillet steak, while O'Hara proved more adventurous. He settled on pâté followed by lobster thermidor. The wine waiter was consulted and O'Hara settled on a midrange Semillon, which Loopy was determined to sample, if only to leave that much less for O'Hara to drink—or get drunk on.

As the wine waiter was waiting for O'Hara to sample the wine, the headwaiter glided past their table murmuring, "This way, Sir Andrew, if you please. Will her ladyship be joining you?"

"Not tonight, Dominick. She's still in London. Arrives tomorrow, actually."

"In good time for the final, no doubt, your lordship."

"Hopefully, Dominick, hopefully. I see young Neumann over there. Who are those people with him?"

"His parents, your lordship, and the rest are friends."

"Staying here, are they?"

"Only the boy and his parents, your lordship."

"Some boy, Dominick. You'll remember how he beat me on the last hole."

"Indeed I do. A sad day for Irish golf, if I may say so, your lordship."

"Oh, I'm not so sure about that. The lad played well. However, I *am* rather looking forward to meeting him again, if fate decrees. Show him that there's life in us old dogs yet, eh, Dominick? Been getting in a spot of practice for a change. With any luck I should give a better account of myself this year."

"That's good to hear, your lordship. Now what can I get you?"

"Oh, the same as usual. Never changes. Unlike the bloody weather. It was blowing a gale just now as I was coming in."

Both Loopy and O'Hara shamelessly eavesdropped on this, and apart from a shared conspiratorial wink and a knowing grimace or two, neither of them gave any indication that they, too, were involved in The Atlantic. It was good to have Weeshy's weather forecast confirmed. Nor was it any harm to be reminded that Villiers-Stewart was a peer of the realm.

As if by an unspoken agreement, they discussed everything under the sun except golf but were well aware that the siting of their table might yield further insights into the number one and two seeds in The Atlantic. As O'Hara remarked, somewhat uncharitably, between forkfuls of lobster, this beat the bejaysus out of boiled mutton and spuds with the full rosary plus trimmings to follow.

Sir Andrew ate frugally—and swiftly. Standing up from the table, he was dabbing at the corners of his mouth with a napkin when a loud greeting assailed him from the crowded table nearby.

"Hi there, Andy, good to see ya!"

His lordship brushed past Loopy and O'Hara as he went over to pay his respects to the Americans. "Are we to meet again this year?"

Al Neumann's relaxed greeting contrasted sharply with Dominick's bowing and scraping. "All depends, I suppose."

His lordship replied in a noncommittal tone, "Who are you up against tomorrow?"

Neumann called across to a heavyset man who might have been an older brother, "Some wild card or other. Can't remember his name. No one's ever heard of him anyhow."

His father shrugged but made no answer. Nor did he make any effort to address his lordship, who was now edging his way toward the door.

"Well, good night, gentlemen. We older folk must get a good night's sleep. Thirty-six holes takes it out of one, y'know." With that his lordship slipped off into the night.

When he was out of earshot, the younger Neumann observed, "Decent old fart, I reckon. Wonder how he got the handle."

Another voice from farther down the table offered, "Didn't he buy it? Seem to recall his family owns a brewery or something like that."

The elder Neumann set him right on that one. "A distillery, I think. Somewhere up in the highlands of Scotland. He told me after last year's final."

"Didn't offer us a case or anything though, did he?"

"Sure as hell he didn't. Those English lords are close guys with a buck."

A new voice chimed in from the far end of the table, "Was that why he fired his caddy halfway through the final?"

Al set him right on this. "Don't think it was about money at all. Someone told me it was the caddy walked out on him—not the other way 'round. Who knows? Who cares?"

When the merriment that greeted this subsided, Al struck a more serious note. "D'you *really* reckon his legs are giving out? I mean, it would be useful to know for the last round on Sunday. He damn near had me last year, to be honest. Until that business of his caddy, I guess. After that he kinda went to pieces."

Neumann senior advised caution. "Son, forget about that guy's legs—and his caddy. I don't blame Andy for firing the old guy, he smelt like one of his distilleries. You'd better take each round as it comes and get it into your head that you've got five guys to beat before you even reach Andy. Apart from the wild card that no one seems to have heard of, the rest of the guys you're up against will probably have played for their country—if not Walker Cup."

"Doesn't worry me. Not one little bit. I thought we agreed before we came over that this is just a warm-up for the British Amateur. Not"—Al hastily corrected himself lest he give the wrong impression—"that I won't be trying my damndest on every shot. Still, I reckon this is the last night we can party before getting down to serious business. Anybody ever retained the trophy? I wonder. I mean, has anyone won it two years in a row?"

Under the table, Loopy stamped hard on O'Hara's foot to prevent him from answering the question. Which was just as well because O'Hara had indeed been about to rise to his feet and inform the young American that the late James Bruen had done just that—twice. Nor would it have cost him a thought to add that Bruen habitually ate Americans for breakfast and would have beaten the likes of Albert Neumann with one arm tied behind his back.

Having forestalled one incident, Loopy did not intend to push his luck any further. O'Hara was showing all the signs of his customary truculence when drunk, and it was a cast-iron certainty that one of the Americans, intent on partying the night away, would provoke him into some kind of ill-mannered outburst. On leaving the table, Loopy allowed Al Neumann and his father to get a good close-up view of him. Good enough, he hoped, for them to recognize him on the first tee tomorrow.

CHAPTER TWELVE

The house was in total darkness, which made inserting the key in the front door a difficult exercise even for a sober Loopy. For O'Hara it would have been an impossibility. By now it was blowing a gale, so severe that the car had swayed from side to side alarmingly on the way back from The Royal Hotel.

O'Hara observed to no one in particular, "She must be in one of her moods again. That's why the oul' bitch didn't leave a light on for us."

This was followed by an attack of giggles so infectious that Loopy could not help but join in. One would put his finger to his lips and say, "*Sh-h-h-h-h-h-h!*" The other would shake with suppressed laughter, trying desperately to ensure that the sounds of their merriment did not awaken the sleeping harridan. Somehow Loopy located the light switch in the narrow hall as O'Hara propped himself up against the banister, still giggling uncontrollably between bouts of hiccups. A note was on the hall stand: *Gone to bed. Phone messages on kitchen table.*

The first message read, *Best of luck. I love you, Amy. P.S. I got the job!*

Loopy smiled to himself and looked at the other one. From Joe Delany and his wife, Linda, it wished Loopy *all the luck in the world*.

"You'll probably need it" was O'Hara's parting shot as they climbed the stairs, trying to make as little noise as possible. From overhead came a menacing rumble that might have been rolling thunder. It was strong enough to be heard above the gale that howled around the house, making the windows rattle like staccato bursts of machine-gun fire. On their reaching the landing, the thunder proved to be Margaret snoring.

The job Amy referred to was an important viability study for a big British distillery. By a strange coincidence it was the parent company of the Maltings, though the Trabane operation was but the tiniest cog in what was a large machine. Amy had asked him about the Maltings, and he had told her its history and how important it was to the town that it remain open. He hoped that she might put in a good word for the Maltings when she came to write the viability report but would not have asked her do so in a million years. Yet that phone message from Amy gave him the boost to his confidence he would need so much in the coming days.

As they drove to the golf course in the early-morning light, the seagulls were no longer riding the thermals with a lazy flick of a wing. The few gulls brave enough to take wing were being tossed about like scraps of paper in the upper air. Their less daring colleagues contented themselves with squabbling noisily for morsels in the rubbish bins of Ballykissane.

After breakfast in the clubhouse, O'Hara and Loopy made for the practice ground, ten minutes before the time agreed with Weeshy. If what they'd overheard in the dining room last night was true, Weeshy had walked out on better golfers in midround for a lesser offense than showing up late.

The practice ground faced in the same direction as the first hole, so Loopy practiced what he imagined might be his second shot to the green. He experimented with several irons in an attempt to reduce the effect of the gale-force crosswind that blew hard from his left. He went back two clubs, to a five iron, as he drew a bead well to the left of the 150-yard marker. Gripping the club down the shaft, he seemed to get more control over the flight of the ball. By aiming so far to the left, he found he could, after some trial and error, hit a low shot that made use of the crosswind to finish close to its target. When he tried to hit what would have been his normal approach over this distance, a full eight iron, it was a disaster. The wind gathered up the golf ball like a seagull's feather, dumping it well short of the target and away to the right.

He was discovering for himself that a lower iron, hit with less than full power, was the only way to control the ball in these conditions. The more orthodox high, dropping shot, loaded with backspin, was golfing suicide in this wind. He could only have learned this from actually playing such a shot, for it was contrary to all his natural instincts. He would never have believed just how far he had to lay off to counteract the wind unless he had proved it to himself by trial and error. Part of his mind registered that among those other golfers warming up for their matches, there was no sign of Al Neumann. Perhaps, Loopy thought, the American did not consider it necessary to warm up before doing battle with a mere wild card. That made Loopy all the more determined to master the wind by making it his friend. He was so absorbed in hitting low approach shots with a variety of irons that Weeshy had been looking on for some time before Loopy noticed him.

The caddy merely grunted what might have been approval and, removing the driver from its canvas bag, passed it to Loopy with the warning "Do the very same with this and you'll be right as rain."

After a few early miscalculations, Loopy soon got the feel of how much he had to allow for the wind with Weeshy's driver. Just as he was getting the hang of it, Weeshy marched him off to the far end of the practice ground and made him go through the same routine all over again from the opposite direction. The few minutes remaining before their starting time were spent on the practice green. Here the wind actually caused the ball to wobble as Loopy lined up the putts. Weeshy had a word of warning about that, too.

"Out there a ball can be blown across the green by the wind. Make sure you're not lining up a putt when that happens or it'll cost you a stroke. That means you'll lose the hole."

"So how do I know when that's going to happen?"

"You don't. But I do. Don't put the putter anywhere near the ball, anyways, till I tell you. And widen your stance for all the shots from driver to putter. With your legs further apart you'll find you won't be blown around as much."

It was time to head for the first tee. A sizable crowd was already gathered there to watch the defending champion's opening drive in his bid to retain the Atlantic Trophy. The tee was festooned with large banners advertising Allied Banks of Ireland. These flapped noisily in the wind and looked as if they might be ripped from their moorings at any moment by the howling gale blowing in from the sea. From what Loopy could see, most of the Americans who had been at Neumann's table had turned up to support their man. Not that any of them felt he would need much support, drawn as he was against some golfing nonentity from the back of beyond.

Indeed, the selection by Trabane of this untested youngster with a dubious background had met with criticism from within the confines of the Private Members Room. The consensus was that if Tim Porter could not represent Trabane, then it might have been better to do the decent thing and give The Atlantic a miss altogether until such time as he was fully recovered from whatever ailed him. It was a bit ridiculous, they sniffed, to feed someone Loopy's age to the tigers that prowled the fairways during this most prestigious of tournaments.

As they chatted among themselves in a relaxed, confident manner, the Americans looked as if they had partied long into the night. Many of them were bleary-eyed and complaining of sore heads. Even Al Neumann's mighty frame seemed to sag a little, and his face looked a trifle less bronzed than yesterday as he strode purposefully onto the first tee. He wore a weatherproof suit of bright red with the word HARVARD emblazoned on the back in big white lettering. This made him look even bigger and more formidable.

An elderly man in a matching tweed cap, overcoat, and scarf stepped forward, inquiring, "Mr. Lynch?"

When Loopy nodded, the man explained that he was the match referee. "Have you met your opponent? No? Well, come along and I'll introduce you to him. That's how we like to do things at Ballykissane, y'know. Keeps everything nice and friendly, we find, which is how we like it."

They approached Al, who was making practice swings with his driver just off the tee.

"This is Laurence Lynch, your opponent. Laurence, meet Albert Neumann."

During the perfunctory handshake Al eyed Loopy closely. Looking somewhat perplexed, Al asked, "Larry Lynch? Say, Larry, I know your face. Haven't we met somewhere before?"

"Yeah"—Loopy grinned back at him—"last night in the dining room. I'm the wild card no one has heard of, remember?"

The American stiffened noticeably but said nothing. Instead he muttered to the referee, "Let's get on with it, ref."

"As you wish. Eighteen holes match play, gentlemen. Strict rules of golf. Referee's decision is final. Is that clear, gentlemen?"

When both men nodded wordlessly, he added, "Mr. Neumann, as holder of the Atlantic Trophy, has the honor off the tee and goes first. Best of luck to you both, gentlemen, and may the best man win."

The wind had changed from yesterday. Not only was it much stronger, but it was coming from a different direction. Now it was blowing hard from left to right across the narrow fairway. The opening hole ran uphill for all of its 448 yards. Its fairway was a thin ribbon running between immense sand dunes, which served to funnel the on-shore wind, making it more intense on some parts of the fairway than others. Standing on the tee, in the lee of one such monstrous sandhill, the players felt nothing more than a strong breeze. Yet when Neumann struck a towering drive, his ball was quickly snatched by the gale and deposited into thick rough on the right-hand side of the fairway.

As Loopy prepared to drive, an excited buzz and not a few loud chuckles came from spectators at the sight of his driver. He overheard someone remark, "Christ, look at his driver. It must have come out of the Ark."

Another could not keep the incredulity out of his voice: "Look at his *grip*! He's holding the club like a ruddy *hockey* stick!"

Setting himself up to hit the ball, Loopy blotted out the voices from his mind and concentrated his entire being on swinging Weeshy's driver as slowly and smoothly as possible. As he did so, he could just catch the unmistakable growl of O'Hara from somewhere in the crowd: "That's the grip of a hurler, you fool. And a bloody good one at that! Now keep quiet and don't put him off his stroke."

He caught the driver short, halfway down its shiny leather grip. As Weeshy had told him, he swung much more slowly than usual while aiming far to the left. The ball was heading straight for an evil-looking patch of rough that lay between two sand dunes. As it did so, it struck a violent jet stream cascading out between the two hills, which radically altered its flight pattern. The ball veered sharply to the right and came to a halt on the fairway, to a smattering of polite applause, some 180 yards from the pin.

The green was perched on plateau, high up in the hills. Only a fluttering red triangle indicated its presence in an otherwise forbidding moonscape of dune grass and heather. Putting yesterday's disaster at this hole out of his mind, Loopy cast his mind back instead to his game with Tim Porter months before when Weeshy had handed him a seven iron. At the time he had thought it was not nearly enough club, but the caddy was right.

This time Weeshy handed him a six iron. "Y'see the path to the left? Aim for the stone to the left of it."

"The white one?"

"Aye, that's the one. A nice low shot is all you need."

Loopy did as he was bid, and the wind again obliged and blew his approach far to the right and toward the flag. With the green out of sight, he could not be sure if his ball was on the putting surface, but more applause from the onlookers suggested that it was not far off it.

In the meantime, Al and his caddy had been looking for his ball. Only then did Loopy notice that Neumann senior was caddying for his son. When they eventually found it, the ball must have been buried deep in the wiry dune grass, for Neumann's most powerful slashing blow was barely enough to send it scuttling along the fairway, still some hundred yards short of the hole. From there he struck an elegant pitching wedge, allowing not quite enough for the wind, if Weeshy's grunt of satisfaction was any indication.

When they reached the summit, both balls were just feet apart, on the fringe. Neumann putted first to within six inches, and Loopy gave him the putt for a one-over-par five. With two putts for a win, Loopy was taking no chances. After consulting his caddie, he stroked the first putt to within a foot, then tapped the next one in without waiting for his opponent to concede it to him.

"Mr. Lynch goes one up after one hole," the referee announced in a calm voice that could not quell the buzz of excitement among the spectators, who had by now grown more numerous.

The second hole was the two-hundred-yard par three off an elevated tee. The hole played in the opposite direction so that the gale was now from right to left, bringing the out-of-bounds area to the left of the green very much into play. Having won the first hole, Loopy had the honor off the tee.

Weeshy handed him the same six iron. "Same shot as the last one. Aim for the biggest bunker on the right."

Had Loopy not decided to put himself completely into Weeshy's hands and follow his advice to the letter, he would have laid off another twenty yards at least to the right of the evil-looking bunker. Instead he did as he was told, fully expecting the gale to blow him out of bounds and give his opponent a chance to draw level after two holes. However the laws of nature appeared to be suspended for the duration of his six-iron shot. The ball hung in the air over the cavernous bunker for what seemed like an eternity, barely missing it as it dropped to earth onto the outer rim of the closely mown apron that surrounded the saucer-shaped second green. It bounded past the flagstick, skidded to a halt against the steep slope of the saucer, then rolled back down again to stop some ten feet below the hole.

So great was his surprise—and relief—that he barely noticed the excited clapping and cries of "Bloody fine shot!" and "Well done, young fella!" that assailed his ears. As for Weeshy, he merely grunted and watched intently as the Neumanns debated on what club to play and where to aim it.

"Seven iron—twenty to the right!"

"You reckon? I'd figure it to be an eight. And mebbe not that much to the right, either. That ball didn't move all that much, did it?"

Al was referring to Loopy's ball, now staring back at them mockingly across two hundred yards of nothing but grief and unplayable lies. Eventually Al played the eight iron. Perhaps mindful of his father's suggestion that it mightn't be enough club, he overhit it. The ball climbed steeply and was headed safely to the right, into the crosswind. Then, unlike Loopy's lower-trajectory six iron, it was grabbed by the wind and slammed to the left. It was lucky not to end up out of bounds. It struck the wire-mesh fence that separated the hole from the public road and took a lucky rebound off a fence post, leaving about six inches of clearance between it and the wire mesh.

Weeshy was moved to speech as he shouldered the bag and made for the green far below them: "That's Old Moll for you."

He did not explain this cryptic comment, so Loopy decided that his caddy had taken to talking to himself. It would be revealed to him later that Old Moll was the name of the sand dune that guarded the second green from the sea. Out of sight from the tee, she shielded a low shot like Loopy's from the wind. The American's forced eight iron, however, had soared high above her, and his ball was lucky to catch the fence rather than be swept clean over it.

When he saw his lie and realized that he had no room for a proper backswing, Al appealed to the referee. Quite what grounds there were for his appeal, Loopy did not know. He had just spotted Edward Linhurst and Amy among the spectators and suddenly felt a surge of confidence as he watched the anxious discussion between the referee and the Americans. The sensation he was now beginning to feel was the same as he had got from the standing stones that surrounded the old fort. He felt drowsy, yet relaxed with his mind empty of every distraction except the task that lay before him, the sinking of an uphill putt not more than ten feet. The excitement and bustle of those around him seemed to be part of another world that had nothing to do with him. He was lost in an oasis of calm like the eye of the hurricane. He knew with an absolute certainty that if he could maintain this mental state, no task was too difficult, no golf shot too demanding, for him to achieve. As Al Neumann might have put it, Loopy was now well and truly "in the zone."

"The bastard is looking for a free drop. Will he get it?" O'Hara's panic-stricken question, though directed at Weeshy, momentarily dragged Loopy out of the trance and back to reality.

The caddy seemed unconcerned and merely shrugged his shoulders as he muttered out of the side of his mouth, "Dinna matter whether or which. Our man's got the measure of him anyways."

The American *did* get a free drop. It was in a designated dropping area circled with a white line painted on the turf. Between it and the green lay a big mound. Neumann could either pitch his ball over the mound or putt it along the ground with enough force to climb over it and trickle down onto the green. In the end after another lengthy discussion with his caddy, he elected to fly it. A demanding shot, it had to clear the mound, yet land softly if it was to finish anywhere near the hole. To make matters worse, the green sloped away from him. The ball would have to drop like a butterfly on a downhill slope that had been dried out to a granite hardness by today's wind and yesterday's sun. If he caught it heavy, the ball would catch the mound and trickle back down to his feet. Were he to overhit the shot, it would scamper off the green and almost certainly end in one of the surrounding deep pot bunkers.

Neumann produced a creditable effort, a delicate, floating chip that earned a sprinkling of applause even though it scurried fifteen feet past the hole. With no way of applying backspin to such a short shot, he could hope for no better. Being farthest from the hole, he was first to putt. He looked as startled as everyone else when it rattled into the cup for a par three.

Again Weeshy merely grunted at this cruel setback. However, he did spend noticeably longer than usual lining up Loopy's putt. Cocking his head this way and that, he sank to one knee to get a better view of the terrain that lay between the ball and the cup. Eventually he rose to his feet and whispered, "No break. Hit it hard to the back of the cup."

With a ten-foot putt to win the hole and go two up on the defending champion, Loopy might have been forgiven for feeling nervous. But he wasn't. Not in the least. The trancelike feeling remained with him, as it was to do for the rest of the match. It had arrived as he'd watched his opponent bring off the two minor miracles in one hole that had rewarded him with the luckiest of pars. Miracle number one was that Neumann's ball had stayed in bounds after his errant tee shot, and then, when it was obviously unplayable, the American was awarded a free drop. Miracle number two was the sizzling putt that might so easily have skidded off the green had it not struck the back of the cup and dropped into the hole.

None of this troubled Loopy. It did not even enter his consciousness. All he could see was the ball and the hole ten feet away. Hovering over the putt, he could think of nothing else but the inside of the white-painted cup. Even before he struck the putt, in his mind's eye he could see the ball roll smoothly up the slope, check for the briefest of moments, then disappear into the hole. In reality, he struck the ball harder than he had intended. It hit the back of the cup quite hard and jumped up a few heart-stopping inches into the air before dropping back, exhausted, into the hole for a birdie two.

Two up after two. Life did not get any better than this. Complete strangers were walking up to him and slapping him on the back as he made his way to the third tee. Edward Linhurst sidled over with Amy on his arm. She gave Loopy a hug and just smiled at him as her father murmured, "Keep up the good work," before drifting off into the gaggle of spectators that was growing with every minute that passed. News was spreading across the course that the defending champion was in trouble against an unknown wild card. Other matches were being deserted by spectators eager to witness what just might be a sensational upset.

The third hole was a par five that almost, but not quite, paralleled the first. The public road that Neumann was so lucky not to have ended up on, even though he still lost the hole, ran the entire length of the par five. At 590 yards it was the longest hole by far of the eighteen. Sportswriters had christened it Neumann's Favorite after last year's championship. In the unseasonable heat wave with not even a breath of wind, the American had played it impeccably. He had birdied it every time he played it, but had saved his best for the final round of The Atlantic.

On the green in two mighty blows, he was one down to Villiers-Stewart, who was well short in two. Even though the American just failed with his attempt at an eagle, leaving a tap-in for his birdie four, the older man could manage no better than a par five. The match was now even, and although his lordship would rally several times to level the score, he never again led the beefy young American. It was generally agreed in the postmortems conducted in the Members Bar late into the night that those two monstrous blows to the third green had demoralized the older man even though he was ahead up till then.

Today, however, conditions could not have been more different at "Eternity"—so christened by the members because it seemed to go on forever. The wind continued to barrel through gaps in the dunes, creating pools of turbulence and calm within a few yards of each other along the winding fairway. As if these variations were not enough for the players to cope with, heavy rough bordered each side of the narrow fairway. To the right lay the road and out of bounds. To the left, an assortment of deep pot bunkers waited to trap a wayward shot. With the wind coming from the left but now also slightly into the players' faces, it made the hole a true test of nerve and skill.

One thing was certain. No one was going to make the third green in two today. Those watching from behind the tee could feel the full force of the quartering wind and agreed among themselves that reaching the green in three full-blooded shots would be the best that either player could hope for. This both players signally failed to do. Having had a close encounter with the out of bounds on the previous hole, Neumann naturally aimed well to the left, hoping that his huge drive would be blown back onto the fairway. He was unlucky, for it nearly did. Instead, however, it bounded into one of the deep fairway bunkers.

Loopy's drive was also caught by a sudden gust that even Weeshy had not allowed for and ended in the deep rough on the right of the fairway, but safely within bounds. He hacked out with the eight iron handed to him wordlessly by Weeshy. Left to himself he would probably have opted for the pitching wedge despite his bad experience with it in similar circumstances the previous day. He was pleasantly surprised at the distance the ball skipped along the hard fairway after nothing more than an average recovery. Weeshy's demeanor was as impassive as ever as he slammed the eight iron back in the bag and marched off on his own, his long, black overcoat trailing along the fairway.

It was now Neumann's turn to get out of jail, and he did so with a mighty explosion shot from the deep bunker that threatened to empty it of sand. Both balls were on the fairway about equidistant from the elevated green with the best part of three hundred yards still to go. Loopy was surprised to be handed a three iron. He had in mind a three wood, or spoon, as Weeshy would have called it, which would have chased up to the base of the green with any luck.

"Hit it well to the left and don't worry about the rough."

With some misgivings Loopy did exactly as he was told and finished up off the fairway and about seventy yards from the green. The spectators, most of whom were members of Ballykissane, nudged each other and winked knowingly. Neumann, sensing a chance at last of reducing the deficit, took his driver to a near-perfect lie on the smooth turf. Like Loopy, he had aimed to the left, and this time the perfectly struck ball flew as low as the three iron. It hit the fairway ten yards in front of the green, a monster of a shot that drew thunderous applause from one and all. To hit a driver off the deck into a quartering wind in a dead straight line is the kind of shot most golfers only dream about.

Neumann's dream was short-lived. His ball, instead of skipping up the slope like a frolicsome puppy and finishing on the putting surface, took an unlucky bounce and ended up in a bunker even deeper than the one from which he had but recently escaped.

Loopy used his pitching wedge for the first and last time that round and floated a nice safe shot onto the green from a perfect lie in the rough, just as Weeshy had predicted when he'd muttered *don't worry about the rough*. From that distance Loopy had been able to load the ball with backspin, making it skid to a halt some twelve feet from the pin.

The face of the bunker Neumann had found was at least six feet high, and its sides were lined with turf sods, built like bricks into its vertical face. To get out of the bunker and leave the ball anywhere near the pin, Neumann would have to blast his ball upward with a delicate splash shot out of powdery sand. To threaten Loopy's lead, he would have to get the ball to rise in an almost vertical trajectory, barely clear the top of the bunker, then trickle down toward the pin. To do so would require the delicate touch of a surgeon and the nerves of a steeplejack.

To his credit he nearly pulled it off. The ball sailed upward, caught the top of the bunker, and wobbled there for a tense moment before dropping backward into the white sand, almost at Al Neumann's feet. Understandably, he now lost what remained of his composure. Wordlessly but with a noticeable reddening of his cheeks and neck, he struck the next shot with rather more violence than required. This time it ricocheted violently off the vertical wall, barely missing him as it again finished in the sand. Picking up the ball, he climbed out of the bunker and then conceded the hole with as much grace as he could muster in the circumstances.

Three down after three holes is not a comfortable position for anyone, but with fifteen holes still to go, it is still far from being a lost cause. The Neumann camp, however, felt differently. Maybe it was the difficult conditions—for the wind was now turning cold as well as gaining in strength. Or perhaps the feeling was growing among them that this was just not going to be their day. Whatever the reason, the heart seemed to go out of Al Neumann the moment he conceded the third hole. Though he played bravely for the rest of the contest, the result was never in doubt.

The match finished on the thirteenth green, before a crowd now swollen to enormous proportions, as the referee announced, still in the most neutral of voices, "Match goes to Laurence Lynch. He wins six up with five holes to go."

Then, and only then, did Loopy emerge from the trance.

CHAPTER THIRTEEN

The first to pound his back as he left the green was Edward Linhurst. "Great win! Best of luck this afternoon! See you for dinner tonight."

His daughter, Amy, went further this time, giving Loopy first a hug, then a big kiss full on his lips. Followed by a whispered "Fantastic. Well *done*, Larry!"

He noticed that she still refused to call him Loopy. As for Pat O'Hara, he was nowhere to be seen. The Neumann camp looked desolate, but Al had shaken Loopy's hand after the last putt had dropped. The burly American's only comment on the thrashing he had just experienced was to say with evident sincerity, "Do me a favor and win this thing out. That way I won't look so bad."

The unexpected win had repercussions further afield than a Ballykissane that was already humming with excitement. Already there were heated arguments about whether Loopy had merely gotten lucky and would be wiped out in the afternoon round. By whom was still unclear as the other matches were still being contested all around the course.

Brona received an urgent phone call from Joe Delany. She had been feeding the chickens and had rushed in with her hands still caked with meal as she picked up the receiver. Daytime phone calls to the Lynch household were few and far between, the night rate being far cheaper. A telephone ringing around midday was a cause for alarm, and this was evident in her voice as she asked nervously, "Joe *who*? Delany? I don't know any Joe Delany . . . Oh my God, I'm *terribly* sorry, and you being so good and all to Larry . . . He's *what*? . . . Oh dear Holy God, sure isn't that grand for him. . . . Oh, you mean it isn't finished yet, just that he's beaten this American fella, is that it? . . . I see, well, sure all I can do is say a special prayer that he'll keep up the good work . . . Ah, no, I couldn't do that. Who would look after this place while I'd be gone? Anyway I've never set foot inside a golf club in my life, I'd only embarrass him, put him off his stroke or something . . . Sure I never even went to the hurling matches for fear of seeing him get hurt . . . Ah, no, Mr. Delany, but thanks all the same . . . Be sure to give him my love though when you see him . . . and tell him I'm praying hard for him . . . Good-bye now and thanks again for the call."

Telephones were also busier than usual at the Trabane branch of Allied Banks of Ireland. Leo was listening openmouthed to the PR officer for the ABI group screaming at him to get over to Ballykissane Golf Club as fast as he possibly could. "Didn't you hear? Some youngster from your own golf club has just beaten one of the top Americans six and bloody five. Wiped the floor with him, so he did."

Leo was astounded as the voice babbled on, "He's from *your* golf club, for heaven's sake, man, that's why I'm calling you. You're *what* in it, by the way? I mean, what position does our man in Trabane hold in his local golf club, Leo? *That's* what I bloody mean."

Here Leo was on firmer ground. "Treasurer and president-elect."

He thought it sounded better that way. Vice president sounded as if he were playing second fiddle to someone.

The voice was unimpressed. "Um-m-m, I see. You know yourself, Leo, how keen Personnel are for our people to play a leading role in their local communities. Makes the bank look like a caring mother hen, y'know."

Leo grasped at the opportunity to ask, "Speaking of mother hens, anything further on the closure, is there?"

The voice was reassuring. "A matter of weeks, months at the very most. Right then, Leo, I know I can count on you to look after things until we show up at Ballykissane then?"

Leo assured him that indeed he could, then sought confirmation that he was on the guest list.

"Yes, of course! Will your wife . . . Yes, of course, *Rosa*. Gawd, I'll be forgetting my own name next . . . She will? Good. The Royal tends to be rather crowded for The Atlantic weekend. The fact that it's a bank holiday is no help either. That's about it then, Leo. Show the flag for us till we get there tomorrow night."

"How do you mean?" Leo was mystified. This was the first he had heard about a flag.

The voice proved less than helpful on this score. "Oh, I'll leave that to yourself. At the very least get a picture of yourself and that young fella, what's his name, the child prodigy, standing in front of one of our signs. There's a whole raft of top-notch golfers in the lineup, so he may not be around for much longer, which means you had better get on to it right away. I suppose our esteemed director, Sir Andrew Villiers-Stewart, is the hot favorite, now that the Yank has got his walking papers?"

Leo admitted that he did not know.

"You don't *know*, Leo? Well, it's about bloody time you *found out*, isn't it?"

Content that he had inserted a king-size flea in Leo's ear, the voice slammed down the receiver. Leo glared at the silent telephone for a moment, then hurried to his car. He would drive to Ballykissane immediately, do as he was told by that idiot PR man, then return home. The next day he and Rosa would pack their finery and return for the weekend revels at The Royal Hotel. Best of all, it would not cost him a penny. He just hoped young Lynch could keep his afternoon match alive until he got there. It never occurred to him as he started the car and edged out onto the road that he was the one who had opposed Loopy's membership in Trabane in the first place.

Father Michael Spillane's conversation was briefer:

"Hallo, is that Corkery's? . . . Good, Michael Spillane here. . . . That's right, the curate. I want a bus to hold about thirty or forty people. . . . No, not for bingo. I want it to go to Ballykissane. . . . I want it *today*, for God's sake. About two o'clock or so. . . . I *know* it's very short notice but something quite unexpected has just come up. Can I count on you for that? . . . Right so, outside the church, two o'clock. How much? . . . Two hundred pounds? Are you gone mad or what? One hundred and fifty—not a penny more. . . . Right? God bless you. See you at two o'clock sharp." His phone was busy for another hour.

Pat O'Hara had not been idle either. From a high stool in the golf-club bar he was regaling a group of reporters with tales, some of them almost true, of Loopy's brief but meteoric golfing career to date.

"Y'see, the whole thing about young Loopy is that he started out as a hurler. . . . Yeah, that's right, just the same as that fella hanging up on the wall over there. Jimmy Bruen was the greatest golfer ever to come out of Ireland, no matter what anyone tells you to the contrary. Henry Cotton described him as the best golfer—amateur or professional—in the world, and old Henry knew a thing or two about the game of golf, I can tell you. . . . No, I'm *not* trying to tell you that he's as good as Bruen was. Not *yet*, anyway. . . . Yes, I *know* he hasn't won anything yet. For Jaysus' sake, this is the *first* big tournament he has ever been in. . . . How do *I* know if he'll win it out? What do you think I am—a shagging *prophet* or what? . . . Yes, the loop at the top of his swing *is* the reason we call him Loopy back home in Trabane. You wouldn't need to be a rocket scientist to figure that one out, now would you? . . . Yes, he used to play for the local hurling team till he got a belt of a hurley and can't play anymore. That's why he took up golf as a matter of fact. . . . No, I'm *not* his father. . . . No, he's *not* here, he's in England. I was his teacher, that's all. . . . Well, I showed him how to swing a golf club before anyone else, if that's what you mean. . . . No, not anymore, I don't. Joe Delany is the teaching pro at Trabane and *he's* coaching him now. . . . Why didn't he change his grip? That's a question you'd be better off asking Loopy—or Joe. Speak of the devil, here he comes now!"

Joe, his wife, Linda, and some thirty other supporters that the priest had managed to round up at short notice had got on the bus outside the church and made the journey as speedily as they dared to Ballykissane. Joe and Linda had been seeking out Pat O'Hara for details of the morning's stunning victory, and naturally the first place they looked for him was in the bar. Joe was unprepared for the barrage of questions from the media, but coped as best he could. He knew nothing of the old driver with the binding cord flapping in the wind like a fishing line. Nor could he enlighten them further about the eccentric caddy whose ragged overcoat trailed along the ground and with whom Loopy conferred before every shot.

All Joe could tell them as they scrabbled desperately for something that would steal a headline from the other sporting events of that Easter bank-holiday weekend was that young Loopy Lynch was the best golfing prospect he had ever seen. Disappointed not to have gleaned something more newsworthy, they slipped away to the practice ground, where Loopy was having his picture taken with Leo Martin's arm draped around his shoulder in front of a giant sign that read ALLIED BANKS OF IRELAND SERVING THE COMMUNITY!

Leo was wearing his best suit and a wall-to-wall smile. As for Loopy, he was keen to get something to eat before retiring to the practice ground and working on those low wind-cheaters under Weeshy's watchful eye. By now he knew who his opponent would be for the afternoon match: Sean O'Donnell. He was a junior International on a scholarship to Wake Forest University, an American college more noted for its golfers than its academics. He had won his match after two extra sudden-death holes, having started ten minutes after Loopy. Since Loopy's contest had taken just thirteen holes to complete, he had all the time in the world between the morning and afternoon rounds, while O'Donnell had barely time to grab a hurried hamburger before going out on the course again.

They shook hands on the first tee and played as well as could be expected in the gale that was blowing harder than ever. The turning point came at the fifteenth, when they were all square after a heroic tussle that had the lead changing regularly and neither of them yielding an inch. They were followed by a large crowd, swollen by a group of vocal supporters who had just arrived in a dilapidated bus and were racing from hole to hole across the sacred turf of Ballykissane. The bus journey had been like no other. Some of the supporters had brought tea and sandwiches to sustain them over what promised to be a long afternoon. The majority, however, had brought cans of stout and bottles of whiskey, most of which had been consumed long before the supporters piled out of the bus, looking for lavatories and their local hero in that order before the astonished eyes of the members of Ballykissane GC.

The fifteenth hole was a tricky par four, and the tee faced the sea and straight into the gale. A sharp dogleg to the left required the drive to finish on the elbow of the narrow fairway. Too short and the approach to the green was blocked by an enormous sand dune. Too far and the ball would end up on the seashore. Though not out of bounds, it meant playing off the beach or the pebble-strewn foreshore. It was arguable as to which was the least attractive option.

O'Donnell had the honor off the tee, having won the previous hole to square the match yet again. The atmosphere between the two contestants was markedly different from that of the morning match. Loopy did not know if he was still "in the zone" but continued to play steadily, following Weeshy's whispered instructions to the letter. Both young men chatted easily with each other as they ambled along the fairways, breaking off only to play their shots and then resume where they had left off. When one hit a really good shot, the other murmured appreciatively.

Taking a driver, O'Donnell hit an exceptionally long drive, perhaps the longest of the day at that hole. It seemed to have struck a hard patch of fairway, for it bounded forward past the elbow and through a narrow band of rough, ending up somewhere on the foreshore.

Loopy reached for the driver, but Weeshy stayed his hand. Wetting a finger with his saliva, Weeshy raised it skyward to test the wind. More to himself than anyone else he muttered quietly, "As I thought. The tide's changin'. So's the wind. It drops for a minute in the ebb tide, then gets up again so you'd hardly notice, anyways. But it drops all the same, so it does."

Moments later, the wind *did* drop, and Weeshy handed his charge a three iron, growling, "Go for the corner," before shuffling to the back of the tee.

Those around Weeshy, seeing the club he had handed his charge, assumed that he was either drunk or insane. They believed, as did Loopy, that it was willful suicide to play an iron into the teeth of such a wind. No iron shot had a snowball's chance in hell of reaching the elbow, it just *had* to fall short, leaving a blind second shot over an impossibly high dune.

Then the wind dropped as if someone had flicked a switch. The iron shot flew low but much farther than anyone could have expected. It pitched onto the center of the fairway, checked, and then rolled along the turf until it came to a halt right on the crook of the elbow. Just then, the wind, as Weeshy had said it would, picked up again, but now it was blowing harder than ever.

O'Donnell's ball was lying amid pebbles worn smooth from the winter storms. Some in the crowd wondered aloud if he might be allowed to drop away from what was clearly an impossible lie. The contingent from Trabane, though vociferous in support of their man, kept their counsel, even though this might be the deciding factor in this closest of contests.

The referee, the same tweed-clad gentleman as had supervised Loopy's morning encounter, remained impassive. He would only hand down his judgment if asked for a ruling by either player.

Weeshy commented as he shuffled alongside Loopy on the long walk down the narrow path that led to the fairway from the elevated tee, "We have him now, so we have. Don't let him off the hook anyways, whatever you do."

O'Donnell elected to play the ball as it lay without consulting the referee. Hitting a golf ball off loose pebbles is the most inexact of sciences. The player never quite knows what will happen between club-face and ball. The intervention of even the smallest pebble between club and ball can have the most unexpected result. When O'Donnell's recovery shot finished on the fairway but only halfway to the green, it was about as good as could be expected and drew a smattering of sympathetic applause from the onlookers.

As Loopy shaped up his approach shot, Weeshy whispered, "Come in low from the right."

Loopy could hardly hear what his caddy said with the raucous shouts of "Come on, Trabane" and "Aha, ya boy ya, Loopy Lynch!" ringing in his ears.

The older Ballykissane members understandably frowned on such partisan displays. Their idea of a suitable expression of appreciation was to murmur "Shot" or, in exceptional circumstances, give the merest hint of applause. The conduct of these dreadful people who had poured out of a bus so dilapidated that it would not have been out of place in the third world was quite intolerable. The problem was that nobody was brave enough to tell them so.

O'Hara reveled in the discomfiture of the old guard and did everything in his power to encourage Loopy's supporters to even greater displays of partisanship. Having missed the earlier morning triumph of their man, those who had endured the bumpy journey in Corkery's bus were determined to show their appreciation, even though most of them had never been on a golf course before and only had the sketchiest idea of how the game was played. As interpreter of all matters relating to golf, O'Hara now played a most valued role. His impromptu press conference between the first- and second-round matches had allowed him to recharge his batteries with Black Bush. Now in the intervals between explaining the finer points of the game to his fellow townspeople, he could be heard whooping "Come on, Loopy, ya boy ya!" with the best of them.

With the green at Loopy's mercy, it seemed that a one-hole lead at this critical juncture was well within his grasp. To get his nose ahead at this late stage in the game was vital if he was to win. Then fate took a hand. The low shot that he played just as Weeshy had told him to was running straight and true for the green. Then it struck an unseen bump on the fairway, kicked sharply to the right, and rolled into a deep pot bunker. Taking heart from his opponent's unexpected reverse, O'Donnell struck a brave pitching wedge to the hard green. It checked and rolled past the pin, ending up about fifteen feet above the hole. Should he hole the difficult downhill putt, O'Donnell could still salvage his par.

Loopy, on the other hand, was now faced with an extremely difficult up and down to save what had earlier looked like a cast-iron four. For a moment, as he viewed his ball lying in the middle of the greenside bunker, he felt like a dog that had just had its bone stolen from him. Now, instead of going one up, if he wasn't careful, he could be playing the sixteenth one down.

He took several practice swings before he climbed down into the deep hole. The flag was about twenty feet away from the lip of the bunker, but the vertical face was cut into a mound at the side of the green and presented a formidable obstacle in itself. The shot Loopy now had to execute was almost identical to the one Al Neumann had failed so dramatically to pull off at Eternity. This time it was Loopy's turn to feel the pressure. Except that he didn't. The hairs on the back of his neck began their now familiar prickling, and a feeling of utter detachment enveloped him like a protective cloak. First he eyed the small white ball lying innocently in the sand, then the sheer cliff over which it had to soar before landing ever so softly on the green.

Suddenly it seemed the easiest thing in the world to lay the blade of the sand wedge wide-open, aim well to the left of the pin, and take the club back in a slicing, wide arc. The club paused at the top of a lazy, looping backswing for what seemed like a very long time indeed before the clubhead cut through the soft sand with a slicing action as though it were trying to cut the head off a daisy. Aiming several inches behind the ball, both sand and ball exploded violently skyward, then the ball dropped like a stone from the cloud of sand onto the green. He heard the wild applause before he could clamber back out of the bunker. His only sensation was relief that the difficult shot had come off, and for a crazy moment, all he really wanted to do was to return to the safety of the womblike bunker and never emerge again.

His ball lay two feet from the pin. O'Donnell never even came near with his difficult downhill putt. In his eagerness to hole it, he had given no thought to the putt back. His brave putt had sailed past the cup, stopping a good six feet below the hole. He missed the one back and conceded the hole to Loopy. The remaining holes were halved.

The Trabane contingent went wild when the referee announced on the final green, "The match goes to Laurence Lynch, who wins by one hole."

CHAPTER FOURTEEN

The weather grew progressively worse as The Atlantic drew to a close. After Loopy's win over O'Donnell, the sun did not appear until the final day. In the interim Loopy found that the battle against the elements was as tough as that against a series of gritty opponents. It began to dawn on him that those long wintry afternoons spent on the hurling pitch in wind and rain when he was expected to put the ball over the bar and between the posts from far out had not been all in vain.

Then as now, the key to success was to be mentally prepared for the worst the elements could serve up. On the hurling field, many stopped trying to score when the wind really blew and sleet showers screamed in off the ocean, pricking the face like a million steel knitting needles. Loopy was at his best then, and it stood him in good stead as he and Weeshy, surrounded by busloads of supporters, tried to keep their balance in a howling wind. Balance was the key. He stood with his legs far apart like a sailor on a heaving deck. This gave him, as Weeshy had said it would, a firmer stance and a better platform from which to strike the ball. He also put longer studs on the soles of his golf shoes to get a better grip on the slippery turf.

Unlike his opponents, he did not wear waterproof outer garments to protect him from the elements. For one, he didn't own any, but even if he had, he would not likely have worn them. The only concession Loopy made to the foul weather was to don a second sweater and stay under an umbrella when it rained really hard. Not wearing any rain gear kept his swing free and loose. The wind, he discovered, dried off any wet clothes within minutes. A cheerful Californian, one of ABI's honored guests who specialized in reinsurance and was a valued client of the bank's, that Loopy met in the semifinals had been two up and looked to be coasting to a comfortable victory until a sudden rainstorm lashed the golf course. One moment the sky had been blue, the seagulls swooping, and the waves gently breaking on the foreshore. Next moment the skies had darkened as storm clouds gathered in an angry mass overhead. Rain lashed down mercilessly and wind blew so hard that it was nearly impossible for either player to take his stance on the tee. The Californian took some time in climbing into rain gear so elaborate it looked like a space suit.

Weeshy handed his charge a second sweater out of a pocket in the golf bag, commenting, "That's him finished for today, anyways. God himself couldn't hit a decent ball in that getup!"

And Weeshy was right. From then on, whether it was the weather or the extra clothing, the American's game deteriorated rapidly, and Loopy ran out a comfortable, if very wet, winner with two holes to spare.

Later on the practice ground as Loopy practiced "wind-cheaters"— the low-trajectory shots that stayed beneath the gales that blew over and around the enormous sand dunes of Ballykissane—Weeshy dug deep into a pocket and produced a small, grimy bottle. "Here, take a slug of this. It'll help keep out the cold and the wet. Better than any hot shower, I'll swear."

Loopy knew full well that he was being offered a drop of "the hard stuff." Though illegal, poitin was still made in the remoter areas, but nowadays the bootleg whiskey was used more as an embrocation than

a drink. He tried desperately to think of some way he could decline
the offer, but failed. He put the bottle to his lips and pretended to take
a big swallow. Keeping his tongue firmly against the top of the bottle,
he managed to take on board as little as possible of the fiery spirit
while managing not to offend his prickly caddy.

"Best medicine in the world!" Weeshy remarked as he drained
what was left in the bottle with one gulp. "Now let's see you hit a *really*
low drive into the wind. It's going to blow like bloody hell tomorrow,
much worse than today, and if you're up against who I think you are,
you'll need to be at your very best."

After his victory in the first round, ever more busloads of supporters had arrived from Trabane to cheer him on. That, as much as
Weeshie's whispered instructions, had helped him survive the early
rounds. However, what had started out as one busload had by the final
day turned into no fewer than six. To these were added many more
who had traveled by car and minibus. While it was Loopy's unexpected
march to the final that attracted most of them, for some there was another reason, too.

For weeks rumors had been flying around Trabane that their bank
was to be closed. It was bad enough that jobs were being lost at the
Maltings, but the news of the bank closure was simply the last straw.
The Lisbeg branch, a suboffice of the Trabane branch that had oper-
ated just two days a week, had closed after Christmas. On that occasion, Leo Martin had explained that the Trabane "outlet" had been
upgraded in preparation for the relocation of both staff and customers from Lisbeg. He had not explained how old-age pensioners,
the blind, and the lame would make the journey from Lisbeg to their
larger neighbor. The local paper carried an advertisement that told
of the closure, claiming that it would improve the service to the
bank's customers overall and that was that. There had been no warning to, no consultation with, those customers whose service was to be
"improved."

Now that it looked as if Trabane was to suffer the same fate, some of the townspeople had resolved to take a last stand on the issue. SAVE OUR BANK notices had begun to appear in some shop windows. Through all of this, Leo Martin kept as low a profile as possible. When asked if his branch was really going to close, he would testily explain that banking was a modern industry, one that continually evolved and reinvented itself, and that people should look at "the bigger picture."

What he did not say was that if this meant transforming Trabane from an already struggling seaside resort without any tourists, and a dilapidated Maltings plant shedding more and more jobs, into a soulless dormitory town lacking essential services such as banking, then so be it. That was the price of progress, as Leo and his bosses saw it. Amid mounting protests, the local paper lent its support to the anticlosure campaign. O'Hara had been a regular, if anonymous, contributor, the owner-cum-editor being a particular friend of his. Because schoolteachers were also civil servants, O'Hara's freelancing had to be kept secret from his superiors. Now that he had retired, the current editorial showed clear signs of his authorship:

> Should the rumor that Trabane is to lose its only bank so soon after our next-door neighbors in Lisbeg prove to be true, then lifelong customers must surely ask why thousands of pounds are spent by Allied Banks of Ireland in promoting golf tournaments for the wealthy while closing down branches in rural areas as a cost-saving exercise at one and the same time. The fact that one of Trabane's native sons is competing in one such tournament only serves to highlight this contradiction. It is to be hoped that those who flock to Ballykissane to help our local hero, Larry Lynch, bring back the coveted Atlantic Trophy will not fail to remind the sponsors, Allied Banks of Ireland, that their lifelong customers will not take this mortal blow to Trabane lying down.

In the carpark of Ballykissane Golf Club, some of the buses had banners draped along their sides that read in bold lettering:

SOB—Save Our Bank

If this weren't enough, someone had edited with spray paint the large billboard poster under which Loopy had so recently posed with Leo under the legend:

Allied Banks of Ireland serving the community!

The word *serving* had been altered to *screwing*. In this charged atmosphere, the last stages of the Atlantic Trophy were to be played out, with the old guard at Ballykissane becoming increasingly unhappy with the way their tournament was proceeding. Months earlier there had been a clash with the sponsors over the number of advertising billboards the bank wished to place at strategic points around the course. Now the biggest billboard under which the official photographs would be taken at the end of the tournament had cruelly been defaced.

An even less welcome development was the arrival of hordes of supporters for the lad from Trabane who had fought his way into the finals, aided and abetted by his disreputable caddy. Weeshy had been reported many times by disgruntled golfers for bad behavior on the course. They complained of his spitting, grunting, and ill-concealed profanities. He had even been known to stalk off the course in disgust, leaving his player to carry his own bag for the remainder of the round. His worst offense to date, however, had been to walk out on Sir Andrew at a critical stage in last year's final. As neither party was prepared to discuss the matter afterward and no complaint had been lodged by his lordship, no action had been taken.

Now Weeshy was to be seen on the practice ground coaching his latest charge on how to tackle the elements. Some of the older members felt that a caddy's duties ended on the last green and that Weeshy had no business giving this young whippersnapper the benefit of his knowledge, especially when it might be used against one of their most distinguished members, Sir Andrew Villiers-Stewart.

However, a more immediate cause for their concern was the possibility that their fairways might be swamped by protesters. It had not passed unnoticed among club members and Loopy's supporters alike that Sir Andrew Villiers-Stewart was not merely a peer of the realm and the other finalist in The Atlantic, but that he was also a director on the board of Allied Banks of Ireland. What was not so widely known was that he sat on the board of the big British distillery that owned the Maltings—Trabane's biggest employer and currently in the middle of a downsizing. He was regarded in both commercial and golfing circles as a man for all seasons. The worse the balance sheet, the broader the smile on Sir Andrew's aquiline features as he reassured shareholders of one of the many companies whose directorships he retained that the disastrous set of accounts just revealed were but a mere hiccup in the onward and upward progress of their company. He could soothe the angriest shareholders baying for blood. He reminded them that the darkest hour was always before the dawn, that every cloud had a silver lining, and employed any other platitudes he thought necessary to reassure the doubters. He had found down through the years that often the best way out of a difficult situation was to call for a viability study. That way, one could always pass the blame for bad news on to whoever had conducted the study while the good news could be claimed for oneself. The exercise had served him well in the past, and he had no reason to believe it would not do likewise in the forthcoming Annual General Meeting of ABI, or the distillery.

Admittedly, there had been some unrest recently in the rural areas where the bank had embarked on a policy of slash and burn worthy of Cromwell. Outlets in the smaller towns were being closed at short notice. It was left to the likes of Sir Andrew, ably abetted by a hardworking PR team, to soothe those opposed to the elderly being forced to take buses over long distances to cash their pensions. Small businesses going to the wall for want of financial services meant village life being further degraded by such closures. Fifty or so "outlets" had already been closed in recent times throughout Ireland, many of them being, like Lisbeg, part-time facilities in small communities. Trabane was different in that it had at one time been a thriving seaside resort that had but one bank. No rival bank would be left to take up the slack if and when Leo moved to Dublin and the promised sinecure in one of the better-class suburbs. When Leo had broken the news to his wife, her reaction had left him dumbfounded.

In words that let no possible room for misunderstanding, Rosa had told him that she was staying on in Trabane. She liked the place, had put down strong roots, and had no intention of abandoning her friends there in exchange for the hell of traffic and pollution that was dear old dirty Dublin. She failed to add that she had even less intention of breaking off the satisfactory affair she had been having for more than a year with Joe Delany.

In golf, as in commerce, Sir Andrew was rightly regarded as a safe pair of hands. An Oxford blue and frequent competitor in the British Amateur, no one knew the vagaries of links golf better than he. As for Ballykissane, he knew every hump and hollow of its greens and fairways like the back of his sinewy hand. Even though he played there only in summer, his home course being the even more testing Royal County Down, he was a three-time winner of The Atlantic. Despite his last victory having been seven years ago, he had been seeded number two after Neumann. Now, with the young American beaten, Sir Andrew had been installed as a clear favorite to add Loopy's scalp to his belt.

Sir Andrew disapproved of the inroads that space-age technology was making in his beloved game of golf. He preferred steel-shafted wooden clubs, irons that were twenty years old, and a putter that had belonged to his late father. He heartily disliked the current fashion of brightly colored clothes for golfers. Corduroy slacks, a check flannel shirt, and an old pullover were *his* preference. That the name of a university—however renowned—should be emblazoned on a golf bag, peaked cap, and shirt was an abomination. Indeed, he privately attributed last year's defeat by young Neumann as much to HARVARD catching his eye everywhere he looked as to the unseasonably fine weather.

As he strode to the first tee in the teeth of a howling gale, he found this year's conditions more to his liking. The young man standing between him and his fourth victory seemed pleasant enough. He was dressed properly, too, without any logos or peaked cap. His caddy was the only blot on an otherwise promising landscape. Weeshy and his lordship were not soul mates, and neither party made any secret of the fact. This year his lordship chose to carry his own bag, a slim leather affair that held less than the fourteen clubs permitted.

Dominick, the headwaiter at The Royal Hotel, had informed him that his opponent was called Larry Lynch and that he had recently been recruited from the game of hurling. It seemed, if Dominick was to be believed, not to have been all that smooth a transition, for the young man was said to have a marked loop at the top of his backswing, which had earned him the rather unimaginative nickname Loopy. Some humorists had already likened the young man's golf swing to an octopus falling out of a tree.

Dominick had thought it more tactful not to inform his lordship about Weeshy caddying for his opponent. There had been a falling out last year between his lordship and Weeshy, rumored to have been over the size of a tip. The matter was supposed to have ended with the caddy flinging the coin at his lordship's feet, muttering, "Ye can keep yer f*cking queen's shilling." He then added insult to injury by inviting his lordship to stuff the coin in a place where the sun did not shine.

CHAPTER FIFTEEN

G̲ood afternoon, Sir Andrew, may I introduce you to your opponent today, Laurence Lynch."

They shook hands as his lordship glanced over Loopy's shoulder
and murmured, "Ah, Weeshy, old fellow, so we meet yet again on the
field of battle, eh?"

The response, something between a grunt and a snort, was far from
friendly. Stewards with yellow armbands were already having difficulty
restraining the crowd trying to encroach on the first tee to get a better
view of the opening drives. The slender ropes they carried to hold
back the crowd seemed wholly inadequate as they pleaded yet again
with the spectators, "Keep behind the rope, please!"

Stewarding had never been required before this. However, because of the numbers arriving to support Loopy and to protest the closure of their bank, a meeting of the Tournament Committee had
hurriedly been arranged the previous evening. It had been decided
with some reluctance that stewarding would be necessary for the
thirty-six holes of play on the final day. Placards of any sort would be
forbidden, and one brave soul who tried to smuggle one under his coat
had his SOB sign confiscated on the spot. The wind had become ever

more frenzied as the match referee introduced the finalists and addressed the crowd.

"Thirty-six holes of match play, ladies and gentlemen. I would make a special plea to all spectators to obey the stewards. That way everyone will get to see the match properly. Thank you and good luck to you both, gentlemen."

Sir Andrew was first to hit. In a gale that threatened to blow him off his feet, he rifled his ball less than ten feet from the ground, arrow straight down the first fairway. Loopy played a two iron and sent an almost identical shot twenty yards past his opponent's. It, too, came to rest on the fairway. With the elevated green well out of reach, his lordship played a low fairway wood that bisected the large dunes on either side of the fairway and came to rest at the bottom of the slope leading to the first green.

Loopy got his first surprise of the day when Weeshy handed him the driver for his second shot. "White stone to the left of the path. Don't be afraid to hit it, anyways!" Weeshy's old driver probably had a bit more loft than a modern metal fairway "wood," but it was still a high-risk shot to try so early on in a thirty-six-hole match.

Weeshy wet his finger and put it in the air. "Gimme back the driver. You won't need it, not yet anyways. The wind's softenin' a bit. The spoon'll do you this time."

Loopy exchanged the driver for the three wood and made a few experimental swishes with it. The wind seemed to have become stronger again as he took the club back with exaggerated slowness. He had widened his stance even more than previously to maintain his balance in the wind. In doing so, he had restricted his backswing before, with his trademark loop, he started the downswing.

He drew a bead on the white stone high up in the dunes and concentrated totally on keeping his head and body steady as he visualized the ball soaring toward the distant target. After the shot he was almost afraid to lift his head to see where the ball had actually gone. A deafening roar told him what he needed to know without looking up.

"Aha, ya bhoyo!" and "Good man yourself, Lynch!" greeted the shot as it flew through the air. He looked up just in time to catch sight of his ball losing its forward momentum and drifting gracefully to the right before dropping out of the sky in line with the distant flagstick. It was impossible to say whether the ball was on the putting surface or buried deep in the dune grass at the back of the green.

Marching down the fairway, Sir Andrew turned to Loopy. "That was a brave shot, young man. Do you think you made the green?"

Loopy was uncertain how to reply. Was this some form of gamesmanship? Or was it nothing more than a polite gesture between two sportsmen out for a game on a wet and windy morning? Only the crowds following them, barely constrained by the nylon rope, gave lie to the idea that this was an ordinary round of golf.

Loopy was uncertain how to address a peer of the realm. No way was he going to concede the psychological advantage of addressing his opponent as "your lordship." Nor could he call someone more than twice his age Andy. He solved the problem by calling him nothing at all.

"Dunno really. Must admit it felt good though."

"Do you mind if I take a look at that driver you were thinking of playing before Weeshy changed his mind?"

Loopy passed the club to him. Weeshy, barely inches away, was snuffling and snarling loud enough to be heard above the gale. His lordship examined the club closely, paying particular attention to the head, which he turned over and examined minutely, as if reading the label of a claret about which he was uncertain.

"Hmmmm, interesting, *very* interesting," he murmured as he shot Loopy a questioning look, then stared hard at Weeshy for a long moment before handing the club back without further comment.

As they parted company to allow his lordship to execute a tricky pitch shot up the steep slope and onto a green that was all but invisible save for the top of the flagstick, Weeshy tugged at Loopy's elbow. "Don't be *talkin'* to that bastard, anyways. Keep your mind on your game. We'll need all our the wits about us to win this one, and that's not one word of a lie!"

Loopy was about to protest that the conversation had been started by his opponent, then thought better of it. He, too, had heard tales of Weeshy walking off the course when upset, leaving the golfer to carry his own bag for the rest of the round.

On their reaching the green, two balls were within ten feet of the hole. It was Loopy's turn to putt and he marked his ball, as did his opponent. Within seconds of Sir Andrew replacing his ball on the green, a gust of wind blew it downhill to within inches of the cup. As he had not been near his ball when this happened, he merely shrugged his shoulders, looked quizzically at the match referee, and drawled casually, "Replace, without penalty, I presume?"

The referee nodded and the ball was replaced. Loopy was on the green in two, his opponent in one more as Loopy knelt behind the ball, looking along the line to the hole. Weeshy was directly behind him, stooping over his charge and eyeing the line of the putt intently. Taking the pin out of the hole, he said to Loopy as he headed for the side of the green, "Two inches to the left and barely touch it."

Standing over the ball, Loopy placed the putter behind the ball before making the delicate stroke that would trickle it ever so gently down the slope to the hole. As he did so, he was rocked by another powerful gust. It almost blew him off-balance. More significantly, it moved his ball several inches *away* from the hole. Without consulting Weeshy he walked over to the referee and said in a calm voice, "I'm calling a one-shot penalty on myself. The ball moved as I was about to putt. Okay?"

The referee nodded but said nothing.

Once again Loopy stood over the ball, aimed for where Weeshy had said, and stroked the putt as gently as if it were a tiny kitten. It took off at an alarming rate, gathering speed as it accelerated downward, spurred on by the wind. It struck the back of the cup, did an almost perfect horseshoe lap of honor around the rim of the hole, then dropped, exhausted, into the hole. Three shots plus the penalty called down on himself made for a par four. The opposition still had a tricky downhill putt to halve the hole. This putt struck the hole also but ran around the lip and stayed out.

The referee announced in a voice loud enough to reach the farthest extremities of the crowd, "Laurence Lynch wins the hole by one shot."

As they made their way across the plateau to the next tee, Loopy felt another tug at his sleeve. Thinking it was Weeshy about to abuse him for calling the penalty shot on himself even though justice was done in that he had won the hole anyway, he was surprised to discover that it was his opponent trying to get his attention.

"Very sporting, young man. They still teach good manners in Trabane, it seems. Don't see much of that nowadays. Won't stop me from trying my level best to beat you, though!"

Loopy thought he saw a twinkle in his opponent's eye—or maybe he was just squinting against the wind. It was Loopy's honor to hit first off the elevated tee—and one he could have done without because the par three, always difficult in the calmest of weather, was now verging on the impossible. Any shot from the elevated tee that was caught in the maw of the howling crosswind was almost certain to be blown out of bounds onto the road on the left. Unless, of course, one had the luck of the devil like Neumann when his ball struck the boundary fence—and bounced back into play. However, miracles like that were rarities in golf.

On this occasion even Weeshy seemed unsure of himself. He shuffled around the tee looking this way and that, snorting and muttering unintelligibly to himself. He seemed to be looking everywhere except toward the distant green that lay far below them, snuggled up against the out-of-bounds fence. Conditions were much the same as those prevailing when Loopy had played Neumann in the opening round. The wind was from the same direction—only much, much stronger.

Loopy remembered how Weeshy had handed him a six iron on that occasion. He was expecting something similar now, given that the ball would have to travel all of two hundred yards in a viciously gusting crosswind. To his amazement, Weeshy handed him a three iron, just one club shorter than he had used off the first tee. It seemed at the very least to be two clubs too much, and he was about to protest when Weeshy whispered into his ear, "Same shot as ye hit against the Yank. Grip well down the shaft and hit it hard about thirty yards to the *right*. We want to keep it low, in the shade of Old Moll."

Loopy hit a crisp, low ball to the right that didn't drift back on the wind quite as much as he had hoped it would. Nevertheless it was safely in bounds and pin high. His opponent may have played the same iron for his shot looked identical to Loopy's in length and trajectory—except that the wind got a better grip on it so that the ball veered hard to the left at the last minute before trickling onto the front of the green. Both shots were of a high order and were rewarded with a smattering of applause from the more knowledgeable spectators standing behind them on the tee. The vast majority of the crowd had rushed ahead of play, down the hill, and were now waiting impatiently for the two players to appear. Kept well back by the stewards and their taut ropes, they still had no idea of where the two balls had come to rest.

In truth, few of them were much interested in the finer points of a well-struck low iron into a severe crosswind. Most of them had arrived from Trabane that morning, and many of them had never been on a golf course until now. If their grasp of the game was rudimentary, it did not deter them from shouting encouragement for their man, much to the consternation of the stewards.

Every so often a SAVE OUR BANK placard would appear out of nowhere, get held aloft for a brief moment to loud cheering, before vanishing from sight again under a spectator's coat. As Loopy walked down the steep path leading to the green, he could sense the carnival atmosphere already among the spectators. A small knot of sleek, smartly dressed men, part of the crowd yet separate from them, were chatting easily among themselves while keeping a close watch on the contest. These were the senior staff of the sponsors, Allied Banks of Ireland. In their midst stood Leo Martin, looking natty in a navy blue blazer that, like all the others in his group, sported the ABI logo and crest on the breast pocket. Toward them, the body of the Trabane supporters directed the occasional catcall.

Tired of the "blazers" and their talk of public relations, Leo's wife, Rosa, drifted away to become part of another group that included Joe Delany, his wife, and Pat O'Hara. Both Joe and O'Hara, as the acknowledged experts on the game, were continually being asked by supporters how the match was going. Those not familiar with golf could find it hard to understand that in a thirty-six-hole final the result could still be in doubt six or seven hours from now. Many of them were more interested in discussing that morning's rumor that the bank was going to close at the end of the month. Anyone not yet aware that Sir Andrew was a director of ABI was soon made so. The blazers continued to be the object of some adverse comment, not all of it delicately phrased.

Loopy conferred with Weeshy about the short approach shot. The ball had to steer a course between two yawning bunkers before reaching the green. Left to himself, Loopy would have pitched a high lob over the larger of the two bunkers and hoped the ball would finish somewhere adjacent to the hole. Weeshy had a different idea as he handed him the putter: "Nice firm putt, two feet to the left of that bunker. Don't be short, whatever you do!"

Doing as he was bid, Loopy putted the ball along the apron of the green. It skirted the bunker by a safe margin before rolling down the slick green to some twenty feet below the cup. In his anxiety not to leave it short, he had overhit the ball, but, he consoled himself, at least it was an uphill putt, albeit a long one. On greens dried out to a rock-hard consistency after three days of hard wind, any sort of downhill putt would have been a nightmare. No matter how hard it rained, Ballykissane dried out instantly. The thin layer of green turf allowed the heaviest downpour to seep through to the deep sand base underneath.

Sir Andrew seemed only to give his long putt a cursory glance before stroking it firmly toward the hole. It never occurred to Loopy that he might hole the putt. It was almost fifty feet long with a break to the right. Old Moll, the enormous sand dune, ensured that the green itself was an oasis of calm, sheltered from the wind by her enormous bulk. The ball seemed about to stop a foot short of the hole but found a downhill slope that dragged it the last twelve inches into the dark recesses of the cup. It was an enormous putt, the longest anyone had holed in the tournament thus far, and it drew applause from friend and foe alike. To Loopy it felt like a dagger thrust deep into his heart, but Weeshy appeared unmoved. Nor did he join in the applause. Loopy did, clapping with an enthusiasm he did not feel, yet appreciating the excellence of his opponent's play. They were now all flat, even and with everything to play for. Sixteen holes later they were still all flat as they went in to lunch.

By then the crowd had become restive. When it dawned on them that unlike at a hurling match, they were not going to have a result for many hours to come, they drifted off in search of sustenance. The clubhouse, with a dress code that insisted on jacket, collar, and tie, neither sought nor attracted their custom. Instead many walked the mile or so into the town where food and drink was available in more congenial surroundings than those prevailing at the golf club. Many of those who had made the long trip on the buses would find a seaside town like their own, albeit a far busier and prosperous one, more attractive than traipsing round a windblown golf links. They had paid their respects to Loopy, cheered him on for as long as they could manage, registered their protest with the powers that be in Allied Banks of Ireland, and by lunchtime felt it was high time for a drink.

Back at the golf club, lunch was a more formal affair. Sir Andrew, engulfed in a sea of blazers, was whisked off to a large table reserved for the sponsors in the main dining room. Loopy joined his friends and supporters in the bar. When a reporter asked Joe Delany if he had given any advice to his pupil as to how he might cope with the wily Sir Andrew, Joe explained that Loopy had long since learned everything he could teach him and had now graduated to a higher plane. His last word on the subject was "Anyway, he's in good hands right now. That caddy of his is some genius, I can tell you. Not only does he seem to know every blade of grass on the course, but he can club young Loopy to the very inch. Mind you, the other guy knows a thing or two also. Looks like we're in for a ding-dong battle this afternoon."

The same reporter got a frostier reception in the dining room. A red-faced man in a blazer told him in no uncertain terms that Sir Andrew did not give interviews during lunch—or halfway through an important golf match for that matter. Just as he was leaving empty-handed, it struck the reporter that his tormentor's face was in some way familiar.

"Excuse me, but are you Mr. Martin by any chance?"

The blazer grumpily admitted as much, though secretly flattered by the recognition. The lad *was* a journalist, after all.

"Can you give me a statement about the closing of the Trabane branch then? There are people out there with banners and . . ."

Leo's brow darkened. His face reddened as he bundled the cub reporter out of the dining room so fast that his feet barely touched the carpet. When Leo returned to the table, the bank's public relations officer eyed him quizzically and asked what was the matter. When Leo explained as best he could, the PRO exploded.

"Jaysus, Leo, you should have called me over. That's no way to handle those bastards, chucking them out on their ear. You can bet your life the little swine is already on to his editor with some cock-and-bull story about closing down Trabane. I must say, Leo, you haven't han-

dled the whole business half as well as I had hoped. I can tell you here
and now that you've been a big disappointment so far. What we want is
a nice quiet closure with no fuss or bother. Instead of which, the whole
bloody thing is being blown way out of proportion. You can see for
yourself with those fucking placards and some clown defacing the billboard that shutting down Trabane is becoming a major issue. Which,
in case you didn't know, is *exactly* what the board of directors *don't*
want. You stay here and don't say a bloody word to *anybody*, man,
woman, or child, about the bloody closure from now on. Go over and
talk to Sir Andrew while I go and see if I can find that bloody reporter
and mend a few fences."

Having found him with difficulty, the PRO spent the rest of his
lunch break pouring pints of stout into the reporter in an effort to
quell the rumor that Trabane was really going to shut its doors at the
end of the month. His task was made no easier by the rumor's being
true. Having missed out on most of what looked to have been a festive
lunch, a disgruntled PRO joined his colleagues just as the last of the
Irish coffees were being drained.

CHAPTER SIXTEEN

To the morning's wind, rain had now been added. During lunch it sidled in across the heaving ocean, announcing its arrival with a machine-gun rattle of hail on the clubhouse windows. Sir Andrew, who had lunched lightly in anticipation of the battle that was to come, inwardly welcomed it like an old friend. Some of his happiest hours on a golf course had been spent in foul weather. The pleasure of directing a well-struck ball onto a fairway in blinding rain was keener than he could possibly hope to explain to those fair-weather golfers around the table. They could not appreciate the pure joy of dispatching a crafty pitch-and-run to a bone-hard green in a howling gale and, having judged it to a nicety, watching it scurry obediently up to the flagstick. For him that was a skill far greater that the high-towering lob-wedges to water-soaked putting surfaces, a form of outdoor darts that earned such drooling admiration from excitable television commentators. Best of all, he thought to himself, was putting on an exposed green in a gale. The miracle of links golf was that greens remained hard and fast despite the heaviest rain shower. The deft stroke, the sureness of touch, required to trickle a ball into the tiny cup came only with a lifetime of experience. Or did it?

For the first time in his life he had encountered a youngster who seemed to have been born with the self-same skills that he had taken a lifetime to acquire. A lifetime of enjoyment, he reflected happily, but nonetheless a lifetime. Now, in the twilight of his golfing career, he was facing a new and not especially welcome phenomenon: a young man with a ridiculous golf swing who played the game really well. Not just well, he reminded himself, but honorably. Calling a penalty on himself at the very first hole was in the best traditions of the game. He wondered if the young man was in any way involved in the demonstrations against the bank that had continued to erupt sporadically during their match and decided not. His young opponent just didn't seem the type to indulge in that kind of gamesmanship—quite the opposite in fact. His caddy, the fractious Weeshy, seemed to have coached him well, and none was better versed in the vagaries of Ballykissane than that old reprobate.

He was amused rather than annoyed that the driver that had gone missing from his bag last year should reappear in such unusual circumstances. He had suspected all along that Weeshy had "borrowed" it from him after their bitter argument over a mere shilling. Had the scoundrel not been so short-tempered and insulting, the whole affair would have been amicably resolved long ago. But when Weeshy dragged the name of Her Royal Highness into it, it was a step too far. Still, the scoundrel had forgotten more about golf than anyone around this table, with the possible exception of himself, would ever learn in twenty lifetimes. To make matters worse, Weeshy had a festering grievance to nurse, and this afternoon might well prove the old villain's last chance to settle the score.

He was disturbed from his reverie by that idiot Martin asking if he would like an Irish coffee. How anyone in his right mind could even *contemplate* taking alcohol halfway through an important match was completely beyond him. Of course the man was a complete idiot. Public Relations had been bitching about him recently over the Trabane thing. Or things, rather. For he must not forget the delicate issue of the Maltings' plant, also. It would, of course, depend on what was in the viability report. Either way, things looked bad for Trabane. It was odd that young Lynch came from there. Coincidence, he supposed. Or fate? *Don't be bloody ridiculous,* he told himself. *You're getting too old for this game if you are to start worrying about fate.* Your fate is in your own hands—now what was that idiot's first name again? Liam? Larry—no, that was young Lynch! Leo? *Leo!* That was it! Well, if he had to talk to the blighter, might as well learn something of his opponent's family background. Might just come in useful before the day was out.

"Tell me all about young Lynch, Leo."

The flustered manager did not need to be asked twice. He embarked on a rambling account of Loopy's family circumstances, his progress as a golfer, and that his family kept an account in his bank. It was disappointing to learn of the family circumstances. The bank recruited from a well-defined family and educational profile, and Loopy's background did not even come close to matching either of these. It was an open secret that ABI employed gifted amateurs in sports such as sailing, tennis, rugby, and golf. They were given a job title that enabled them to maintain their amateur status while drawing a handsome salary from the bank. They were expected to do little more than entertain clients and continue to feature prominently in their chosen sport. Sir Andrew had rather hoped Loopy might qualify for one of these sinecures, but Leo Martin had seemed to make it quite clear that young Lynch's family circumstances were such as to put that out of the question.

He ignored Leo's well-meaning suggestion that his opponent, though a golfer of some promise, would not seriously challenge him that afternoon. Even an idiot like Martin must surely have realized holding a three-time winner of The Atlantic to all-square after eighteen holes could reasonably be construed as a serious challenge.

Sensing that his observations on the probable outcome of the final had not been as well received as he had hoped, Leo fell silent. He could hardly have been expected to regale his lordship with the story of how Loopy had seen him cheating and the subsequent rearrangement of Brona Lynch's bank loan.

Just as they stood up from the table, a braver soul than Leo asked what his lordship thought of his chances. After a long silence, he replied, "I don't really mind whether I win or lose this one. Maybe it's that I'm getting old, but it's been a long time since I've enjoyed a round as much as the one this morning. I can only thank God that good manners and sportsmanship still survive in the modern game. For once I don't feel like an Old Testament prophet crying in the wilderness. That young man is just the sort we need to keep in amateur golf."

As they left the table, Sir Andrew realized that he had forgotten to interrogate Leo on the closure of his branch. To Sir Andrew it had been, until now, just another item on a crowded agenda. Having seen the placards and heard the occasional catcall, he hoped that there would be no repeat of the unruly scenes that had occurred during the morning round. It was all very well to make the game of golf available to the masses; indeed, he had been advocating this for many years; but if the masses insisted on behaving like football hooligans rather than decent, respectable golf fans, then that was a different kettle of fish.

The club captain, in apologizing to him both as a competitor and a board director of the sponsors, had been confident that the stewards were well on top of the situation. Furthermore, it seemed that many of the later recruits to what one reporter was already describing as "Loopy's Legion" had tired of the contest after an hour or two and headed for the attractions of Ballykissane village. As these consisted of three pubs and four fast-food outlets, he feared for their mood if they should return to the golf course before the match had ended.

Young Lynch was already waiting on the first tee. After a quick handshake and another exchange of *Good lucks*, they were once more

on their way. The rain had turned to hail, and the wind had, if anything increased in velocity. All in all, conditions were just about
playable. Again the first hole was not without incident. Again Loopy
registered a par four—which his lordship equaled by holing out a difficult chip. If the ball had not struck the flagstick and gone in, it would
have rolled off the green and back down a steep slope. But it didn't.
They were still all square, and Sir Andrew noted that Loopy joined in
the general applause for what was a lucky break. At the second, both
played low irons conservatively to the right, and even so, Loopy
thought for a heart-stopping moment that his ball was going to be
blown over the out-of-bounds fence.

Weeshy had no such qualms and called it while still in midair:
"Don't worry. Front of green, to the left. Easy chip."

The hole was halved in par threes and the match was still level; after twenty holes.

At Eternity, Loopy had his one and only lucky break of the round.
In his heart he knew that its length, almost six hundred yards, had to
be to his advantage over the older man. Sir Andrew had yet to score
better than a par five at Eternity. Ballykissane was a traditional layout
with tough opening holes of par four, three, and five. Now they were
teeing off on the third of these, the twenty-first hole, and all square in
the match as Weeshy handed Loopy the driver. The wind was fiercer
than ever, gusting from left to right and waiting to blow anything but a
perfectly struck shot out of bounds onto the road.

The instructions bellowed in his ear were barely audible above the
near hurricane: "Well left, low and hard!"

Standing up to drive the ball, he felt the old sensation return for a
fleeting moment or two. The hairs on his neck prickled and a deathly
calm enveloped him in a cocoon that silenced the screaming wind and
the excited chatter of the spectators. He drew back the club so slowly
he felt as if his arms were frozen into a series of jerky frames rather
than following a fluid, flowing motion. Still in an oasis of calmness, he

watched with trancelike detachment as the ball flew far to the left, low and hard, just as Weeshy had instructed. It flew over the thickest of dune grasses, where, had it dropped back to earth, it would never be found again. For what seemed like an age, it flew in a perfect parabola, borne on the wind to the safety of the fairway, rolling to a halt less than a yard from an evil pot bunker. As if that were not luck enough, it found a gentle uphill lie.

"Same shot again," Weeshy barked at him through the wind and rain, handing over the driver, whose leather grip he had just dried with a towel marked BALLYKISSANE GC, which he had almost certainly appropriated during the break for lunch. The rain was now bucketing down harder than ever, and some foolhardy spectators put up umbrellas only to have them blown inside out by the gale. His opponent was also on the fairway, some thirty yards nearer to the green, but had played two safe shots to get there.

As he took a wide stance to brace himself against the gale, Loopy felt that this could be the turning point in what had so far been the closest of contests. He did his best not to think of the last time he had tried to hit a driver off the ground. He was wearing the sweater Amy had given him that day, but it was the sensation of O'Hara's elderly driver shattering to pieces that was at the forefront of his mind as he took his stance. If he could only get the ball airborne with Weeshy's driver, a difficult enough exercise in itself that few golfers attempted even in friendly games, and yet keep it low and on the fairway, he should have an excellent chance of going one up and taking the lead. All of a sudden, he knew, he just *knew*, with a chilling certainty that if he could just get his nose ahead at Eternity, victory would be his.

Yet hitting the driver off the fairway was a calculated risk. A perfectly executed shot would almost certainly win the hole. Against that, the slightest hint of a slice or even hitting the ball too high in the wind must inevitably send it careering out of bounds and onto the road in this vicious crosswind. The instant the driver made contact with the ball, the feedback from the clubhead back up the shaft to his hands told him that it was a cracker, similar in shape and length to his drive off the tee. The ball made a friend of the wind and used it to steal extra yards of roll as it bounded along a fairway still hard as a rock despite the flurries of rain and hail. After two mighty blows on a hole measuring almost six hundred yards, his ball lay in a valley in front of the green, less than seventy yards from the pin.

His opponent was well short of the green in three with a testing pitch over a greenside bunker. Normally Sir Andrew would play a bump and run to the green. He could almost play the shot in his sleep, and anyone who regularly played links courses had to master it. In conditions such as today's, it was ideal because the wind did not affect its low trajectory. This time, however, a yawning bunker intervened between his ball and the green, ruling out any chance of playing his favorite shot. He had no choice but to execute a high lob into the wind and make it land on the putting surface. From where he was, to pull it off would require both a delicate touch and the luck of the devil.

To his credit, he nearly succeeded. Cut upward with an elegant swing, smooth as silk, the ball obediently climbed high into the sky. Then the wind grabbed it at the top of its arc, stopped it in midair for a split second, and flung it back into the bowels of the bunker. Because it was still raining, the sand had become sodden wet, making an already difficult escape even more so.

Loopy was next to play. With a clear run to the pin, he played the low bump and run through the valley and up the slope. The ball scuttled along the ground like a rabbit, coming to a stop within ten feet of the flagstick. This left him with a putt for a birdie four.

His opponent had already played that many shots and was still lying at the bottom of a deep, wet bunker. Hands on hips, Sir Andrew surveyed his situation with obvious distaste. He looked at the shot he would have to make out of the bunker from every angle, assessing his chances of leaving his ball close enough to the flag to get down in one putt for a six. Then he glanced briefly at Loopy's ball on the green. Whether he did not want to risk the embarrassment of failing to get the ball out of the bunker, or he did not want to gift Loopy the psychological boost of making a birdie at the longest hole on the course in appalling conditions, no one would ever know. With a wry smile, he walked over to Loopy's ball, picked it up, and handed it to him.

"Well played, young man. I concede the hole."

The referee intoned solemnly, "Mr. Lynch goes one up with fifteen holes to go."

This was greeted by whoops of delight from those hardy souls who had deserted the village bars to brave the worst the elements could throw at them. The referee again appealed for order, "Quiet *please!*" as they moved to the next tee.

The Linhursts appeared out of the crowd to congratulate Loopy. Edward said, "Keep at it. You have him on the run now!" while Amy whispered, "You look fantastic in that sweater!" As she walked away, she turned and blew a kiss in his direction—which made him feel even better about going one up in the most important match of his life.

Reporters who were present for the final day of The Atlantic were in agreement on at least two issues. It was the worst weather in living memory, and the battle was won and lost on the twenty-first hole. Ironically they had come to a similar conclusion about the previous year's final when Al Neumann had destroyed his lordship's chances— and canceled out his lead—by hitting the third green in two. But that feat had been achieved in perfect conditions. Today the reporters were all of one mind that Loopy's play with the driver off the fairway into the teeth of a crosswind was a match-winner.

What finally won the day for Loopy and his caddy was the long par three. Two hundred and eighteen yards off an elevated tee to a green surrounded by a moonscape of dunes thickly coated with grass and weeds. The narrow, two-tiered green was necklaced with deep bunkers. Right beside the seashore, it was today playing almost directly into the wind, with no place to hide. Any shot, high or low, was going to feel the full blast of the gale, and landing anywhere but on the green was a lottery. One might be lucky enough to find a reasonably good lie on dune grass that had been trampled down by the spectators, or just as easily find the ball so deep in the grass that hacking it out regardless of where it might end up was the only option.

They had halved the preceding holes, and Loopy still retained his slender one-hole lead as he sized up the tee shot to the distant green. The flag fluttered stiff in the gale as he pondered which club to play. Nothing less than a driver or a fairway wood had any chance of reaching the putting surface. At the back of his mind was the comforting thought that his opponent might not be able to reach the green with any club in his bag.

"What do you think?"

Weeshy shrugged his shoulders, grimaced, spat on the ground, and handed him the driver before whispering into his ear, "Whole duck or no dinner, we might as well be hanged for a sheep as a lamb! Bring it in from the left, anyways. Take your time, though, I think the tide's changing."

From the mixed metaphors Loopy gathered that his caddy was in favor of playing the brave shot and taking the game to his opponent rather than playing safe. For once Weeshy had not indicated how far left Loopy should lay off into the wind, and the reason for this quickly became apparent when the wind suddenly dropped noticeably. As Loopy stooped to tee up his ball, he decided to wait for another moment or two to see if the wind would drop even more. He remembered how changing from a driver to a three iron at the fifteenth had won him the match against O'Donnell. That, too, had been a turning point, when Weeshy predicted that the wind would drop for a brief moment as the tide turned.

The par-three fourteenth he was standing on was the hole before that, and just as exposed to the elements. If he could hit the driver while the wind was at its lowest ebb, then his chances of hitting the green simply had to improve. As he took a few practice swings more than usual, he sensed that the wind was strengthening again, so without further ado he aimed well to the left, toward the foreshore, and hoped for the best as he smashed the ball off the tee. Like a kite on a string it soared out toward the breakers crashing on the beach, then caught the wind and drifted lazily onto the back of the green. The shot was greeted by the loudest applause yet and, despite the pleas of the referee, a cacophony of wild whoops from the Trabane contingent. Their ranks were now swollen by several visibly tipsy supporters who sensed that a famous victory was within their grasp.

"Good man yourself, Lynch!"

"Come on, Trabane, c'mon, the village!"

When Sir Andrew took his stance, the wind had regained most of its earlier fury, a point not lost on Weeshy to judge by the smugness of his grin. The ball never had a chance of reaching the green. It was lucky to find a playable lie from which the best Sir Andrew could do was to hack it onto the front edge of the green, leaving a forty-foot putt up a three-tier green. As he was still farther from the hole than Loopy's first shot, he putted up to within six feet of the cup, an excellent effort in the circumstances. Loopy left his birdie put six inches short, and his lordship made his second concession of the afternoon by picking up his ball and saying, this time with no trace of a smile, "Your hole."

The referee tried to make himself heard above the excitement of the crowd. "Laurence Lynch wins the hole and goes two up with four holes to play!"

In ever-worsening conditions, the next three holes were halved in one shot over par, and the match ended on the seventeenth with the announcement "Laurence Lynch wins the match by two and one!"

There followed the most amazing scenes ever witnessed in the long history of Ballykissane and the Atlantic Trophy. Bottles of stout and noggins of whiskey appeared from nowhere. Undeterred by wind or rain, the celebrations began there and then, accompanied by snatches of song and bursts of prolonged cheering.

"C'mon, the village!" was a cry taken up by a knot of burly, excited men who heaved Loopy up on their shoulders. Despite the pleas of the referee for order and decorum, they bore him away on a lap of honor around the green as photographers jostled with each other to record the occasion.

They finally set Loopy down in front of the clubhouse, where the presentation was to take place. A roped-off area seemed awash with blazers, green for the members of Ballykissane and blue for the high command of Allied Banks of Ireland. Someone was trying desperately to get the microphone to work, as it emitted piercing whistles and ear-shattering shrieks. These were not quite loud enough, however, to blot out the chants of "Save our bank, save our Bank!" that vied with the more raucous "Good man yourself, Lynch, ya boyo!"

CHAPTER SEVENTEEN

The Irish Rover was not the sort of place that featured in any directory of Good English Pubs. It was a place where the Irish in Birmingham congregated to exchange information about jobs to be had, horses to be backed, and, at weekends, money to be spent on lukewarm English bitter beer. It was always quiet in midweek, when Sean Lynch found himself nursing a small beer and lighting a fresh cigarette from the stub of the last one. He picked up a copy of the *Irish Post* that someone had left behind. As he sought the section where news of Trabane might feature if anything of interest had happened in the village over the past week, a headline caught his eye: "Trabane Boy Wins Atlantic Trophy."

He was surprised to learn that his son had won one of the most coveted trophies in Irish amateur golf some days earlier. He ordered another glass of beer and got down to some serious thinking.

Loopy's victory also gave food for thought to the members of Trabane Golf Club. The behavior of his supporters had gladdened some of his ardent backers in the club and appalled those who had never approved of him representing Trabane Golf Club in the first place. To them, Tim Porter was the man for the job. Admittedly he had never come close to winning, but his background enabled him to mingle effortlessly in the highest circles.

At a committee meeting shortly after Loopy's win, Pat O'Hara proposed it be celebrated with a gala dinner. Tim Porter thought it was a great idea and suggested that Loopy hand over the huge chunk of silverware that was the Atlantic Trophy to the club for safekeeping until the following year. The suggestion would have met with Brona's approval for she had already told her son, "You're not keeping that thing here in this house. I wouldn't get a wink of sleep worrying that it might be stolen. All that silver must be worth a fortune, but who's going to polish it every week? Not me, that's for sure!"

The meeting agreed to a gala dinner and that Leo Martin would do the honors on behalf of the sponsor, ABI. Loopy would then make a brief acceptance speech and present the cup to the club. In his heart of hearts Leo hated the whole idea. He feared the dinner would provide a platform for further protest at the imminent closure of his bank. He had heard on the grapevine that the announcement, though delayed for some reason, would be made any day now. In the meantime he remained tight-lipped. When pressed, all he would reveal was "The matter is now out of my hands!"

This was nearer the truth than Leo could have imagined. Sir Andrew had been reviewing the case for closing the Trabane branch since the protests at the Atlantic Trophy and a conversation he'd had about it with Loopy. Privately he had rather enjoyed the discomfiture of some of his fellow directors with whom he sat on the board of ABI. The protesters, while noisy, had, on the whole, been well-behaved. He was adamant that they had not affected his play in the least and had insisted that his defeat at the hands of the younger man was fair and square.

The more he looked into the underlying reasons for the closure, the less convinced he became. The Trabane branch, though poorly managed, was perfectly viable. Plans to shut it down were for cosmetic reasons only, it seemed to Sir Andrew. It was no secret that the ABI share price had been falling of late. This was in sharp contrast to the shares of their competitors, which were increasing in value, a source of some embarrassment to the directors. With the Annual General Meeting of the bank less than a month away, the board could expect some heat from the shareholders unless they were seen to be doing something to add value to the shares.

Something had to be done—and quickly. The PR people recommended a ruthless cost-cutting exercise in every department—save their own. A key plank of their "slash and burn" policy was the pruning of smaller branches, an exercise calculated to soothe the big institutional stakeholders. The bank staff affected by the closures would either be relocated on promotion like Leo Martin or handsomely pensioned off. Tactics such as these, employed on a grander scale, should boost the share price, it was claimed. This should please everyone—except those long-suffering clients who would have to go elsewhere for their banking needs.

"All well and good," Sir Andrew announced gravely to his fellow directors as he tapped the Trabane file, "just so long as one did not overdo it!" Almost fifty closures over two years, he murmured, was definitely overdoing it. The press coverage, while as yet mercifully just local, was but a straw in the wind. One need look no further, he reminded them with a wintry smile, than the recent protests on the sacred turf of Ballykissane. Sir Andrew strived to keep a straight face as he reminded them of the abuse that had been aimed at the bank directors and staff during the presentation ceremony. It looked, he stressed, as if fences needed mending—and quickly.

They should begin, he suggested, by abandoning the plans to close the Trabane outlet. There would be no loss of face, he was quick to point out, because it had never publicly been announced that the damn place was to be shut. It had merely been *leaked* by some incompetent idiot, quite possibly that local manager fellow whose name he could never remember. Not, he conceded, that it was all the manager's fault, since he may well have been acting on the instructions of the PR department.

That department, Sir Andrew observed sternly, had not come out of this at all well. However, there was still time for them to make amends, by devising an exit strategy for the bank in which all would emerge without too much egg on their faces. Naturally there must be no hint of a climbdown. No suggestion that ABI were reacting to pressure from the public or any of that kind of nonsense. A discreet word dropped in the right place at the right time to the effect that the rumors about the closure were just that—*rumors* should do the trick. Much stress, of course, would be laid on the importance of places like Trabane to the Irish tourist industry. A tongue-in-cheek emphasis that the very suggestion that Trabane might be left without the services provided by ABI was just *too* absurd to be taken seriously.

Even if they succeeded in this salvage operation, the PR department was overdue for a major shake-up. They had, Sir Andrew decided, become too arrogant and self-satisfied for their own good, and new blood would have to be introduced as soon as possible. For instance, the young lady who had devised the "turnaround" strategy for the Trabane Maltings might be enticed away from her consultancy work to help revitalize the bank's lackluster PR team. As might—he gasped in admiration at his own brain wave—the current holder of the Atlantic Trophy. He had listened with interest to that young man as he'd spoken of the tough times his hometown was experiencing as they'd both waited for the presentation ceremony to begin.

Well, Sir Andrew sighed with satisfaction as he closed the folder, that the bank was now remaining open and the Maltings were about to start rehiring might yet be the makings of Trabane. Until recently Sir Andrew had never given a second thought to the place, but the spirit of the protesters at Ballykissane and the gutsiness of their young golfer had suggested to him that it was a place that might well be worth fighting for.

It came as something of a surprise, therefore, when the group opposed to the gala dinner learned that their most ardent supporter, Leo Martin, had suddenly changed sides. In so doing he had taken from them the strongest plank of their argument—namely the cost to the club. Leo informed the committee that because of his strenuous efforts on their behalf, he could now reveal that ABI had agreed to sponsor the event. All club members were to be the guests of the bank.

The bombshell reduced Pat O'Hara, who could be relied on for an acid observation or two where Leo and his bank were concerned, to a stunned silence. Even he joined in the applause that greeted the news, though he managed to restrain himself from joining in the backslapping to which Leo was subjected. Turning to Joe Delany, O'Hara growled under his breath, "There's more to this than meets the eye, you mark my words. I wouldn't trust Leo or the crowd he works for as far as I could piss into a high wind!"

Joe would have none of it. It was just what the young lad deserved, he insisted, and if the bank wanted to pay for the celebration, then so much the better. It was Loopy's night off, so he didn't hear the news until the following morning. Even then, it barely registered because of the night before.

A week earlier on his way back from the Irish Rover to his digs, Sean Lynch had literally fallen over an old man lying in the gutter—someone with an accent like his own.

"Give us a hand up out of here like a decent man, will you?"

Sean looked down on the spread-eagled figure. Soaked from the rain and the splashes of passing cars, the man was a pitiful sight, but his eyes grabbed Sean's attention. They were old eyes, tired eyes, the eyes of a loser. They were uncannily like those same eyes that stared back at him every morning from the cracked mirror as he shaved in the dingy room that he now called home.

The bundle of rags struggled to his feet with Sean's help and, recognizing a familiar accent, snarled, "What are you doing over here? Why aren't you back where you belong? I left it too long."

Sean tried to give the old man a few coins but he pushed them away. "Keep it yourself. There's someone back home has a better right to it than me."

He shuffled off, pausing a moment to call back over his shoulder, "Just don't leave it too long like me."

That, as much as reading of his son's victory, was why he found himself back in Trabane.

Now as he peered through the window, he was taken aback. He saw what he had feared most—the recurring nightmare that had haunted him since he'd left. It would wake him up with a start, sweating with terror. It was always the same nightmare, the one in which his family were only too glad to see the back of him. That, he told himself over and over, would be the last straw.

The dangerous cocktail of emotions deep inside him was fueled by the sight of his wife, well-dressed with her hair perfectly groomed. She hadn't looked like that since the day they'd married. Could she possibly have taken up with someone else? The panic ratcheted up his emotions another notch or two. His daughters, too, were a picture of contentment, their tongues clenched in concentration as they poured over their homework. As for Larry, his son had changed out of recognition. He had grown, filled out around the chest and shoulders. No longer a boy, he was now a man, and for some reason that he could not fathom, Sean resented this most of all.

It looked to him as if the family he had abandoned were doing better than ever without him. Should he slink away, unseen, back into the night and the hell that was the back streets of Birmingham? *No*, he told himself, *this is* my *home and I have as much right to be here as any of them.* With that, he lifted the latch of the door and walked into the kitchen.

The family froze when they saw him framed in the doorway. His eyes raked their faces, hungry for some flicker of welcome. There was none, just as he had feared. His nightmare had come to life and the old anger flared up inside him. Suddenly he felt wronged that he should have come all this way with the best of intentions only to be met with coldness, even hostility.

The harshness of his first words shocked even himself: "Am I not welcome in my own house, is that it?"

The question hung in the air for what seemed like a lifetime. It was no sooner out of his mouth than he wished he could have swallowed it back. Too late, for his son had leapt to his feet, fists clenched.

"Take it easy, will you! It's just that we weren't expecting you to walk in the door, that's all! Isn't that it, Mam?"

"Of course, Larry, of course. That's it, *exactly*! Here, Sean, take a chair for yourself and sit down. I'll get you something to eat. Then you can tell us all about London—"

"It wasn't London, it was bloody Birmingham, in case you didn't know!"

Brona would have let it pass, but not Loopy.

"How *could* she know? You never wrote, did you?"

The accusation reduced them both to silence, but they glared at each other furiously until Brona came back with a plate of bacon and cabbage.

"There, Sean, get that inside you first, then you can tell us all about your travels."

"No travels . . ." It was as if some inner demon had taken control and was determined to argue with everything anyone said to him. He pushed away the plate untouched. "It was bloody *Birmingham* from start to finish. One filthy room between seven of us—"

Loopy cut him short. "Why didn't you write—or phone? Mam was worried sick about you."

"None of your business, and don't use that tone of voice with me. Why can't you show a bit of respect for your father? Didn't they teach you that much at school?"

Brona was distraught as she tried to make peace between them. Her world, which had been so good before Sean had walked through the door, now looked to be disintegrating before her eyes.

"Ah, go on, Sean, can't you eat what's set before you? Aren't you hungry or what? I thought you'd be starving after that long trip."

"I got something to eat on my way here."

"Oh, I see," Brona bridled at the rejection. "Well, you won't be needing this so."

Surprising even herself, the usually timid Brona swept the plate of food off the table and emptied it into the rubbish bin.

"The bus was late so I had a bite in town before I came out here. That's all. There's no call to take offense at me for that, surely, is it?"

Another silence, then: "Did you sell my hay?"

"*Your* hay?" Loopy could hardly believe his ears. "*Your* hay? We sold the hay sure enough. Got a good price for it, too, didn't we, Mam?"

Brona nodded. She sensed what was coming and felt powerless to avert it. A part of her actually *welcomed* the inevitable confrontation between father and son. Suddenly it dawned on her just how much her son had grown up since Sean had left. Not just physically but in other ways, too. It did not show itself in an empty bravado, as it had with his father, but rather in a quiet self-confidence that seemed to grow day by day.

"We did indeed."

Sean turned to his son. "Well?"

"Well *what?*"

Sean was beginning to lose his temper. "You know damn well what I'm asking. What did it make?"

Loopy was being as unhelpful as he could. What right did his father have to burst in on them like this and threaten to ruin everything? Suddenly he hated his father more than ever. He hated him for being a gambler. He hated him for frittering away every last penny the family had ever had, and most of all, he hated him for the wrong he had done to them all by vanishing and then, just as unexpectedly, reappearing.

Up to this it had been a lukewarm hate that simmered deep inside, but now it was about to erupt, like lava trapped inside a volcano. In-candescent with rage, Loopy could not bear to share the same table, the same room, or even the same house with this ill-tempered stranger. Loopy tried manfully to control his emotions by being as un-helpful as possible, but he knew that this could not last forever. Only one more wrong word would bring it to a head. If his father thought he was dealing with the self-effacing, shy teenager he had left behind, he was in for the surprise of his life.

Letting his temper get the better of him, Sean bellowed, "C'mon, tell me out straight! What did it make? The hay. *My* hay!"

There was a lull, then Loopy said in a steady voice that betrayed no hint of what he was feeling, "Mam, I think you'd better send the girls to bed. Then we can talk better."

"Since when are you giving the orders round here?"

Sean was getting angrier by the second, but Loopy surprised even himself with menace of his cool reply. "Since you shagged off to En-gland, that's when. Now why don't you say good-night to your daughters, then we'll talk all you want about *your* hay when they're gone to bed."

Something in his son's voice made Sean agree. He gave each of the girls a brief hug, muttering, "Off to bed with you now."

When the girls were safely out of earshot, Loopy again asked the question that had plagued him for months on end. "Why didn't you write? We didn't want money from you or anything. All we wanted was to know whether you were alive or dead. What stopped you from writ-ing or telephoning?"

In the silence that followed the girls' departure, Loopy's question remained unanswered. No way was Sean going to admit to his son that it was a matter of pride. If he hadn't any money to send with the letter, there would be no letter from him and that was that.

As for Brona, she was tired of trying to make the peace. Even though she hated confrontation and would normally go to any lengths to avoid it, she realized that the dilemma of Sean's return was going to be resolved here and now. In truth, little by little, she had learned to live without him. Now, just when she was coming to terms with his absence, he'd come back uninvited and expected everything to be just as before. Not good enough, she told herself as she sat back in her chair and waited for her husband to answer.

"Like I told you already, it's none of your bloody business."

"But it *is* my business now. Since you left, things have never been better, isn't that so, Mam?"

Brona, though no longer as timid as before, was still reluctant to admit that this was so in front of her husband. After all, he *was* her husband, but then her son was the best godsend any mother had ever had. He had sold the hay, cleared the bank debt, and made a better life for them all. Even that awful Leo Martin was now bidding her the time of day whenever they passed on the street. The girls were happy and well fed. Was all this going to end because Sean chose to walk through the door uninvited? No, by God, it damn well was not.

Her voice took on a harder edge as she replied, "Sean, there's no two ways about it—Larry is right. Things are a whole lot better since you left."

"There you are so, Da, *that's* your answer! You weren't there when we needed you, so why are you back here now, all of a sudden?"

"For my share of that hay you sold to your fancy friend."

"*Your* share? Are you out of your mind? Whatever you might have heard in town before you got here, *your* share is gone to pay off *your* debts. You ran out of here owing everyone except the cat. Now it's all paid off and you have the nerve to walk in here out of the blue, looking for money. If you were any good, you'd have sent *home* some bloody money to feed your children instead of losing it to the bookmakers or pissing it down the gutters of Birmingham."

Loopy had got to his feet as he was saying this. Now his father pushed back his chair from the table and did likewise.

"I don't have to take that kind of shit from anyone, least of all my own son. Just because you won some bloody golf thing doesn't entitle you to answer me back like that. 'Twas far you were reared from golf, that's for sure. If those snobs up at the Golf Club have made you forget your manners since I left, then it's high time I taught you some."

Loopy was shaking with rage as his mother tried to keep them apart.

"Sean, for God's sake, don't start a fight the minute you walk in the door. There must be some way we can settle all this."

"I'll settle it quick enough, don't you worry, Brona. But first I have to put some manners on this lad."

Father and son glared at each other, their faces inches apart. Loopy felt the hairs rise on the back of his neck as he growled, "Anything you have to teach me can be done out in the yard. That way we won't wake the girls. No, Mam"—raising a hand to stifle her protests, he continued—"this has to be done and done *now*. There's no way of getting around it. It's been coming a long, long time. No way is *he* going to walk in here and ruin all our lives all over again. I'd kill him first."

Turning to his father, Loopy nodded toward the door and said in a voice he barely recognized as his own, "C'mon outside and teach me that lesson you're talking about."

Before they had even squared up to each other, Brona was already ringing the police station. By the time Sergeant Keane arrived, Sean was more than glad to see him. Sean had had the occasional punch-up in Birmingham, but no one had ever come at him with anything like the murderous ferocity of his own son. Loopy had hit him before he was ready, then followed up his advantage with a vicious knee to the groin. After that it was all downhill. Every time Sean struggled to his feet, Loopy knocked him down again. Shortly before the police car arrived, it had dawned on Sean that he was going to suffer less pain if he remained lying down. Brona had been watching from the doorway, praying that no one would be killed.

Sergeant Keane was an old friend of the family's who knew all about Sean and his hasty departure. "Ah, Sean," he addressed the prostrate figure in the friendliest manner, "is that yourself? Aren't you a stupid man to go and fall in your own backyard. Is that blood on your face? And there's your son helping you up to your feet. Just like a good son should. And he *is* a good son, make no mistake. Not a bit like his father. Steady on there, Sean, now don't be exciting yourself till you hear me out. Did you know, by any chance, that there's a bit of a warrant out for you? That's right, a bench warrant for your arrest. That's right. Some bookmaker or other took you to court while you were away in England, so he did. I didn't want to bother your missus, especially since the postman tells me she hasn't heard from you since you left. Can't you calm down now, Sean, like a good man and listen to me carefully, because I'm only going to say this the one time. If you get into the back of the car with me this minute, I'll give you a lift to the railway station. Then you can get on a train that'll take you to the next boat back to England. That way it'll make things easier on yourself and everyone else. Now, of course, if that doesn't suit you and you'd prefer to stay on 'round here, then, of course, that's entirely up to yourself. But I have to warn you that if you don't get on that train like I'm suggesting, I'll have to lock you up in the barracks till the next court day. It's ten to one that you'll go to jail after that. A betting man like yourself should know that those are bad odds—even for a gambler like Sean Lynch. Now, *you* wouldn't like me to have to lock you up, would you? No, I thought not. Well, there it is all explained clear as day for you. Hop in the car and go back where you came from or stay at home and go to jail."

Sean got in the car and waited wordlessly for Sergeant Keane to finish speaking to Brona, standing by the open door with Loopy's arm draped around her shoulders.

"That's it so, missus. It'll be like nothing ever happened at all. You never saw me—or Sean, for that matter. You see if word got out that Sean was back here, I'd be in terrible trouble altogether for not serving him with that bench warrant. Tell you what, though, missus, if you'll take my advice, you'll swear out a barring order against him one of these days. Then if he *does* show up again uninvited, all you have to do is phone me at the barracks. That way there'll be no need for young Larry here to run the risk of ruining that golf swing of his by hurting his hand the way he did just now."

Sergeant Keane gave mother and son a knowing wink and was gone with his passenger before they had closed the door behind them.

"Do you think he'll be back?"

"Not if you get the barring order like the sergeant says you should." Brona thought for a moment. "I'll apply for it first thing tomorrow."

Next morning they drove into town together, Brona to see a lawyer and Loopy the doctor. The lawyer helped her to fill out the court application for a barring order against "one Sean Lynch." She smiled through her tears as she expressed the hope that there wasn't more than one of him, but the solicitor didn't quite see the black humor of it, so she let it pass. Loopy's having his knuckles bandaged by the doctor required the telling of lies. He tried to remember to tell the same lie to Tim Porter when he met him outside the surgery door.

"Great bloody win, Larry!"

"Lucky, Tim, lucky."

"Luck my arse! Everyone tells me you played out of your bloody skin. What happened to the hand?"

"I slipped and fell in the yard at home. You okay yet?"

"Dunno till the sawbones takes a peek at me. That's why I'm here. Tell you something though. Don't ever fool around with your kidneys, *absolute* bloody agony! Only thing they let me drink is bloody water, bloody great *gallons* of the stuff. Now tell me about the speech you're going to make."

"What speech? You know I'm no good at speeches, Tim."

"Well, you're going to have to make one at the bloody dinner, you know."

"What dinner is that?"

"The *Gala* Dinner. For chrissakes!"

"Gala Dinner? What are you *talking* about?"

Tim gulped. Realizing that he had let the cat out of the bag, he could only blurt out, "I thought they'd told you! Christ, I hope it wasn't meant to be a *surprise* or anything."

CHAPTER EIGHTEEN

Loopy found Joe Delany giving a lesson and waited for him to finish. While Loopy waited, a group of youngsters on a summer training program asked for his autograph. He tried to look as if he were accustomed to doing this every day of the week, when, in fact, this was his first time ever. He signed golf balls, old scorecards, even a school copybook. When he signed *Larry* Lynch, they insisted that he sign himself as *Loopy* Lynch. That was what everyone was calling him now, and it looked as if the name was going to stick.

Joe appeared, grinning broadly. "Now how's the game with you?"

"Dunno really, haven't caught a golf club since I got back. Too many things happening."

Joe nodded, looking at the injured hand. "Yeah, I know. Not least your Gala Dinner. That should be a bit of fun anyway. Everyone determined to get pissed as newts at Leo's expense. Pat says it's just a softening-up exercise before they close down the bloody bank. Still and all, if they're throwing a party in your honor, the least you can do is to go and enjoy yourself at it."

"Oh, yeah? Tim Porter tells me I have to make a speech."

"Of course you do. Didn't you make a grand one after The Atlantic?"

"That was in the heat of the moment. I didn't know where I was with all the excitement going on around me."

"Just as well you remembered to thank Weeshy. He'd never have forgiven you if you forgot him. You wouldn't want that old divil as an enemy, that's for sure."

Loopy agreed. He didn't tell Joe what had happened to the driver. He had almost forgotten the incident until Joe's mention of the caddy jogged his memory. Suddenly he was back standing in the carpark of Ballykissane. The presentation of the Atlantic Trophy was long over, the crowds had gone home, and Weeshy was putting the golf clubs into the back of O'Hara's car. He stopped to remove the old driver from Loopy's bag, muttering, "I'll mind it till the next time."

Loopy thanked him for letting him use it, then asked him what he owed him.

"Your friend looked after all that before he left with his daughter, anyways. A grand girl she is, too. Keen on yourself, I'd say. Well, she could do worse, I suppose. A decent man that Linhurst fella, if ever there was one. He gave me enough to keep me drunk for a week. Oh, he did indeed. Not like that mean shagger comin' towards us, anyways—sure he wouldn't give you the time of day!"

Weeshy turned his back on the approaching figure of Sir Andrew, who was striding toward them, golf bag slung over his shoulders and a pair of spiked brogues clasped in one hand. He had the air of someone just finishing a friendly round rather than that of the defeated finalist at a premier event. Ignoring Weeshy's back, he made for Loopy with an outstretched hand.

"I know we had that chat about Trabane and all that before the presentation, but I never got the chance to properly congratulate you after the match. Your fans whisked you away before I could shake your hand. You're a good golfer and have the makings of a great one." Addressing Weeshy, who had turned round to see what was going on, Sir Andrew asked innocently but with a mischievous smile, looking the caddy straight in the eye, "Isn't that so, Weeshy, old boy?"

When Weeshy made no reply save for a grunt, Sir Andrew turned back to Loopy.

"Y'know, they say that time and tide wait for no man. I think Weeshy knows different. That tactical delay of yours on the fourteenth tee when you waited for the wind to drop as the tide changed was a stroke of genius." He chuckled as he pointed toward Weeshy. "I'll bet my last penny that old reprobate put you up to it. Anyway, well done. You deserved to win. So refreshing to see the game is still sometimes played as it was meant to be—fair and square and with no quarter asked or given."

With that Sir Andrew turned on his heel and made for his car, an impressive-looking Bentley. He stopped in midstride as if something had suddenly occurred to him.

"I say, Weeshy, old chap, would you mind awfully if I had another look at that driver of yours. It's awfully like one I used to have until quite recently."

Weeshy handed it over without a word, not even a grunt. Sir Andrew examined it carefully, even going so far as to give it a loving swish of a practice swing. No one said a word. The carpark was silent as a grave.

Eventually Sir Andrew broke the silence, looking straight at Weeshy as he declared, "Interesting club that. Very like one I had myself. Not many of them around nowadays, eh, Weeshy?"

When this elicited nothing more than a grunt from the caddy, Sir Andrew turned to Loopy. "Young man, you certainly used it to good effect. I hope our mutual friend"—Sir Andrew nodded toward Weeshy—"will see fit to loan it to you whenever you feel you may need it. As I said earlier, it was a pleasure to compete against you today, and no doubt about it, the best man won." He extended his hand and took Loopy's in a firm clasp. "I take it you can be reached at Trabane Golf Club should the occasion arise."

With that Sir Andrew handed the club back to Weeshy without comment and strode briskly to his car. Moments later Weeshy, the driver tucked inside his coat, stalked off toward the village with the familiar rolling gait that made him seem to glide over the ground.

It was over, an anticlimax if ever there was one to the greatest day of Loopy's life. Slowly, all the energy drained out of him, Loopy plodded back toward Pat O'Hara, who was waiting impatiently to be driven back to Trabane.

Suddenly now, Joe Delany's voice cut through Loopy's woolgathering.

"Sorry, Joe, I didn't quite catch that. I was miles away there for a moment."

"I was asking you, would you feel like a four-ball this afternoon? I've Mr. Linhurst booked for a round at two o'clock. If you could organize Pat O'Hara, we'd make up a four. Much more fun than a twosome. Bit of laugh, no serious golf for a change, though you might like to try out a few drivers. If your hand hurts, you can pack it in early. What do you think?"

"Nothing I'd like more. Don't worry about the hand, it's only a bruise and a few gashed knuckles. I'll phone Mam to say I'll be late. Then I'll see if Mr. O'Hara is available."

Joe gave a hollow laugh. "Oh, he's available all right, don't you worry. He was in the bar at ten o'clock this morning curing himself with coffee, if you don't mind. He'll kill himself with the drink if he doesn't watch it. What was he like in Ballykissane?"

"Not bad at all. Staying with the sister, he hadn't much chance to party."

"I hear she's a right old bitch, is that right?"

Loopy tried to be diplomatic. "Well, she's no barrel of laughs, that's for sure. I'll go and ask him if he'll play at two o'clock."

As Joe had said, Pat O'Hara was in the bar. Loopy was relieved to see that he still had nothing more than a sandwich and coffee in front of him.

"Ah, home the conquering hero comes!" The schoolteacher had a subdued, quirky air that Loopy had not sensed before. "Did they tell you Leo is throwing a party for you? Pulling the wool over people's eyes, if you ask me. Bread and circuses for the populace before they close down the bloody bank, that's what friend Leo is up to, mark my word!"

Ignoring this, Loopy asked instead, "Can you make up a four-ball?"

"When?"

"Two o'clock."

The schoolteacher consulted his watch. "Jaysus, that's in less than half an hour. Yeah, of course I can. I'll have another coffee so. Will you join me?"

"Yes, but I've got to phone home first!"

"Right, you go and do that. Want anything to eat?"

"A club sandwich maybe."

"Right you are. Who are the other two?"

"In the four-ball, you mean?"

"Yes, that's what I mean."

"Joe and Mr. Linhurst."

O'Hara clapped his hands in glee. "Right, my boy. We'll pluck those two pigeons clean and no mistake." Suddenly the elation in his voice disappeared to be replaced by a more somber, confidential tone. "Do you know what I saw last night?"

"What?"

"Rats, my boy, rats as big as dogs. There they were, two of them sitting down at the end of my bed, staring at me with eyes like burning coals. Damn near scared me to death, I can tell you!"

"Then you woke up, right?"

"Not on your life! Easy known you know damn all about the d.t.'s."

"D.t.'s? What are they?"

"Ah, the sweet innocence of youth! Delirium tremens, that's what they are. Anyone who drinks as much whiskey as I do is an odds-on bet to get them sooner or later."

He sounded almost complacent, as if he had been anticipating their arrival for quite a while, which prompted Loopy to ask, "Had them before?"

"No, oddly enough, this was the first time—and the last." Then, more forcefully: "Once was more than enough. Take my word for it."

There was a long silence as both considered the implications of that last remark.

"So what are you going to do about it? *Them*, I mean."

If Loopy expected a flippant reply, he was to be disappointed. The older man unleashed a sigh that seemed to come from the soles of his feet before asserting in a voice that brooked no argument, "I've given up the drink, that's what I'm going to do about it!"

Another even longer silence greeted this.

O'Hara seemed to feel some further explanation was required. "It wasn't *just* the rats. I didn't tell anyone this before now, but the last time I was in hospital the doctors warned me that I'd be dead inside the year if I didn't quit."

"That didn't stop you drinking the minute you got out of there, did it?"

"True for you, but I didn't have much to live for then. Now things are beginning to look up, what with yourself winning The Atlantic for starters. So I changed my mind—or rather, those bloody big rats changed it for me."

Joe had left a message on Edward Linhurst's answering machine saying that their game had been switched to a four-ball. As the four golfers strolled down the fairway, they chatted easily among themselves. Linhurst first spoke of Loopy's big win and then of his daughter Amy's new career as a business consultant. He was obviously unaware of how much Loopy knew about her by now or of their plans to see so much more of each other from now on. O'Hara, for his part, speculated on how far Leo Martin would push out the ABI boat at the Gala Dinner but did not refer to his going on the wagon. Joe teased Loopy

about the speech he would have to make, having brought along a selection of drivers for Loopy to try out. Since The Atlantic, Loopy had
been seeking a replacement. It was not so long ago, O'Hara remi-
nisced, when all Loopy would have had to do was go to the nearest golf
professional and have a club, made to his specifications. Although both
Sir Andrew and Loopy had used drivers with wooden heads, the days
of the traditional club-maker were dead and gone and nothing was going to change that. The testing of the various drivers, with O'Hara
making pithy observations on the appearance and price of each, made
for a lighthearted round of golf. Nor was any reference made to the injured hand.

Soon talk turned to what Loopy was going to do next. His handicap
would be plus two by the end of the month, which, Joe explained,
would allow him to play in all the big amateur events. There was, however, the matter of money. As Loopy had seen for himself, playing in
such tournaments was expensive. Right now he simply could not afford to join the amateur circuit. If he were very, very lucky, he might
be offered a job with some institution like a bank or an insurance company. That would enable him to play in some of the big events, but
that was a chance in a million. As Edward Linhurst drily observed,
banks nowadays were answerable to shareholders, and hiring staff on
their golfing prowess alone was simply not on. Pat O'Hara insisted yet
again that Loopy should graduate before finally deciding what he
would do. This did not appeal to Loopy, but he spared O'Hara's feelings by remaining silent.

Joe Delany was even more circumspect. His view was that Loopy had
indeed won The Atlantic, but that was just *one* event. It might have been
a fluke or it could mean that he had a special talent for the game. The
only way to find out, Joe insisted, was for Loopy to pit himself against the
best. When he asked how this might be done, Joe snapped, "Q school!"

"*What?* You can't be serious. You mean qualifying school, the one
for the pros?" Loopy couldn't believe his ears. "Are you trying to tell
me that I should turn *pro*? Is *that* it?"

The thought had never occurred to him—not in his wildest dreams. It was one thing to make a living from the golf club, tending bar and the driving range. To earn his living actually playing *competitively* had never crossed his mind.

Pat O'Hara, as usual, disagreed with the others. "You know damn well that I never approved of you leaving school early. You did because you had to, I suppose, what with your father going off to England and all that. I wanted you to finish your education so that you could make something of yourself in the world. Everyone needs some sort of qualification to get ahead. If you're not careful, all you'll have to show for the most important years of your life is a good golf game. I'm no judge, but you seemed to have something special going for you when you won at Ballykissane. As Joe says, you're as good as the rest of amateurs now with your plus-two handicap, but you can't afford to play with them. We both saw what it costs to play just one tournament, and that was only up the road, so just imagine what it would set you back with travel, caddies, hotels, and the like. What you need is a proper job that allows you to play the amateur circuit, and you're not going to get a job like that unless you are properly qualified for something or other. The first step along that road, my lad, is to bloody *graduate*, and don't mind what the rest of them may tell you!"

The talk drifted to other topics for a while, then Joe steered it back to Loopy's future once more, saying, "Maybe Pat's right for once." O'Hara grunted but did not interrupt. "The Q school is probably out of the question. First there's the expense. It's well over a thousand pounds to enter. Another drawback is that it's over six rounds, not the usual four. Guys I know who've played in all the big tournaments say every one of those one hundred and eight holes is tougher than playing the first hole of The Open."

Edward Linhurst was able to confirm this. "A friend of mine who played in the Walker Cup before turning pro swears that playing for your country is a cakewalk compared to the Q school."

The discussion had brought them to a halt, but with people waiting behind them, it was time to move on.

As they hurried toward the green, O'Hara questioned this. "Why the extra pressure, Joe? I thought The Atlantic was about as tough as it gets, pressure-wise."

Joe shook his head with a hollow laugh. "Don't get me wrong. What Loopy did was fantastic. I'm proud as hell of him and there's nothing I'd like better than to see him do well in the pro game. But you'd better believe me that Q school is a killer. Two hundred hungry golfers fighting it out with each other like animals for a player's card to get a crack at the tour."

"How many get a card?" Loopy forced out the question though his throat was dry. He was uncomfortable at having his future discussed so openly in front of him. He was also a bit surprised that Amy had not told her father how close they had become. Perhaps she had gone off the whole thing—which to Loopy was far more disturbing than this talk of his future, especially the Q school.

"Thirty-five eventually. After four rounds, seventy-five get to play the final two rounds. Then the thirty-five lowest scores get their card—for the year."

"For the *year*?" Loopy was incredulous. "Just a *year*? What happens after that?"

Joe couldn't help but smile at the look of dismay on Loopy's face. He explained gently, "Well, last year forty-four got cards. That was the lowest thirty-five plus those tying on the last qualifying score. Of those forty-four, only eleven managed to win enough to stay on the tour."

"Jaysus, Joe . . ." O'Hara looked genuinely shocked. Being off the drink had made him edgy, but this genuinely caught him unawares. "I didn't realize it was *that* bad. Are you *sure* those figures are right?"

"Positive. I checked them out this very morning. Three-quarters of those who *did* get their card had to go back and do it all over again the following year. Only some of them didn't bother. Couldn't face the torture all over again, I expect. Only sixteen of them came back for a second dose of the medicine."

"What happened to the others?" Loopy had to know.

Joe shrugged. "Who knows? Some of 'em gave up golf altogether, I expect. Others probably went back to being teaching pros, just like me."

"Were you ever tempted to give it a go?" Loopy just *had* to ask that question.

"Of course, but I was never good enough. Couldn't afford to anyway, even if my game was up to it. Married early, commitments, that kind of thing . . ." Joe's voice trailed off, then became stronger as it took on a wistful note. "And believe me, it was a damn sight easier to get a card then—and hold on to it—than it is today."

There followed a long silence, eventually broken by Edward Linhurst asking Loopy, "Well, what do you think?"

"Doesn't really matter, does it? The thought of turning pro never even crossed my mind until just now. Anyway, it's out of the question."

When no one pressed him on this, he felt he owed them an explanation. "Look, I've something to tell you all, only please don't let it go any further."

O'Hara cut in quickly, "If it's about your father, the whole village knows by now that he was back. For a short visit, I'm told. Shorter than he intended by all accounts. Is that what happened to your knuckles?"

Loopy nodded ruefully. He turned away, not wanting them to see him blinking back the tears. When he had recovered some of his composure, he answered O'Hara, "Yeah, that's what happened. So you can see why I can't suddenly take myself off to some foreign country to try to qualify as a pro. With my father gone again, probably for good this time, someone has to replace him—and I'm the eldest. The sooner I get a proper job the better, and golf will have to take a backseat for the time being."

They lapsed into silence for a while, each left with his own thoughts. Then they spoke idly of other things—their play, the condition of the course—the sort of things golfers discuss during a friendly and sociable round of golf. They arrived at the last hole without mentioning Loopy's future again, each still lost in his own thoughts. In a strange way each felt cheated in some way.

Joe Delany, without quite realizing it, hoped that through Loopy he could yet live out his earlier ambition to become a touring pro. Fate had unexpectedly handed him an uncut gemstone in the form of Loopy that he had hoped to shape and hone into a glittering diamond. Now the stone had shattered at the first cut. The future held nothing more for Joe than the dreary business of giving lessons, selling golf gear, and making sporadic love to bored wives.

Pat O'Hara, too, had a sense of loss, though he found it hard to put a finger on exactly why this should be. It wasn't the drink, though being off it just a few hours was already making him irritable. He told himself that life had something better to offer than a whiskey-soaked future and had hoped that he could have guided this young man in his post–Atlantic Trophy future. Now it looked as if this amazing golf talent was about to join the stampede of youngsters desperately seeking a run-of-the-mill job rather than following his star, however distant it might appear. O'Hara's salvation, too, might have depended on the unique talent he had stumbled across that afternoon Loopy had driven the thirteenth green. In all his years teaching, he had never found anyone who had lived up to, much less exceeded, his expectations for him. Now, like an exhausted miner on his last dig, he had unearthed a nugget of purest gold when he'd least expected it. He might have passed his twilight days in following his pupil's progress on and off the golf course and, in doing so, worked out some kind of salvation for himself.

Now all that remained was the challenge of staying on the wagon and baiting the banks, especially in the person of Leo. What O'Hara had told Loopy about his earlier experiences was absolutely true. In O'Hara's hometown all those years ago, the three big buildings were the church, the police station, and the bank. He realized he was probably cutting off his nose to spite his face where his hatred of banks was concerned, but he was, he told himself bitterly, too old to change. About the banks, of course, he corrected himself hurriedly. Not too old to swear off the drink, though, even if it meant an endless vista of cups of coffee and the regulars in Foley's Bar sniggering behind their hands. He had already heard one of them that very morning muttering to a crony, "O'Hara off the drink? You must be joking. There's no way you can teach an old dog like that new tricks, just mark my words!"

Well, O'Hara told himself, he would do just that. He would mark their words and show the bastards who was right in the end. That, however, was not going to make things any easier in the meantime. He had briefly considered joining Alcoholics Anonymous but decided against it on the grounds that he wasn't quite ready to put his hand in the air and relate the story of his life to a collection of total strangers. Not just yet, anyway, he decided.

Then there was Amy. She had told her father that very morning of an offer from Allied Banks of Ireland to join their PR team. Her report on the Maltings had so impressed Sir Andrew Villiers-Stewart that, wearing his banker's cap, he had almost *begged* her to join the newly formed Public Relations Bureau at Allied Banks of Ireland. Apparently, most of the older PR types at the bank had been posted elsewhere, though why this had happened, no one had yet explained. The only thing stopping her from snapping up the offer there and then was that the job was based in Dublin. Though that was closer to Trabane than her present job in London, it was still too far away from Loopy now that she realized how much she loved him.

Even Edward Linhurst himself, the man who supposedly had everything, felt a vague sense of loss. He couldn't explain it, but as he walked off the last green, he felt like a dog that had lost its bone. With the work on his house completed, time was already weighing heavily on his hands. The long walks along the beach suddenly seemed less invigorating than before, and his golf game was not improving quite as much as he had hoped. He realized with a start that he had been unwittingly linking his future with that of Loopy. With directorships in the city and friends in many of the better golf clubs in England, he could have secured invitations for his young protégé to play in tournaments that would otherwise have been closed to him. Without realizing it, he had been casting himself in the role of Loopy's manager and mentor, a dual role that might go some way toward dispelling the dark cloud of boredom that was threatening to engulf him.

LAST CHAPTER

. . . And to those of our critics who claim that we are getting too big for our boots, I can only say . . ."

With every fiber of his being, Pat O'Hara wanted to bellow the word *bollocks*, but his being sober caused a loss of nerve. Instead he contented himself with a deep sigh and put a hand over his mouth to hide his utter disgust.

". . . that Allied Banks of Ireland has grown from within. Not by taking over our competitors who are left free to compete, as indeed they should be, in a free market . . ."

O'Hara wanted to shriek, *What about Lisbeg?* but restrained himself. Could he be getting mellow, he asked himself, or was his still being on the wagon what sparked this unusual display of self-control? He couldn't help but notice that the rest of the crowded marquee were drinking in Leo's honeyed words. They had wined and dined at the expense of ABI and were loath to see their hosts in anything but the best of light. Even O'Hara could not have accused those who'd sponsored the Gala Dinner of stinting in any way. Drink flowed all evening and Linda had excelled with an array of lobster and cold cuts that had the buffet table groaning under their weight.

Loopy and Brona sat in the place of honor at the top table, on a podium that looked out on two hundred or more merrymakers. They were flanked on one side by Leo and Rosa, Joe and Linda, and on the other by Edward and Amy, who sat next to Sam and Tim Porter. The PR man for the bank and O'Hara were side by side at another table on the lower level, facing the stage and not twenty feet away from Leo.

Sir Andrew Villiers-Stewart had sent his regrets, but the PRO who had given Leo such a hard time during The Atlantic was sent in his place to keep an eye on things.

". . . It is therefore my pleasant duty to welcome you all here on behalf of Allied Banks of Ireland. As you all know, this dinner was organized at very short notice, and I would like to congratulate Linda on the wonderful job . . ."

Leo's praise was swamped by a wave of applause. As soon as it died down, he resumed, "Her husband, Joe, who has coached our hero of the hour . . ."

Even louder applause, accompanied by the stamping of feet and shrieks of "Good man yourself, Lynch!" When quiet returned, Leo intoned, "Young Larry Lynch . . ."

More applause, louder than ever, followed this. It was a full minute before Leo could make himself heard: "In whose honor we are all gathered here tonight."

Another staccato burst of hand-clapping, scattered calls for quiet, and O'Hara wished they would let Leo get on with it, otherwise he looked like keeping them there all night.

"I do not propose to keep you much longer"—*Good!* thought O'Hara, now getting edgier and more impatient with every word that passed from Leo's lips— "however, I must tell you the program for the rest of the evening. In a moment we are going to have the raffle. Hopefully by now you will have all bought tickets for the sweater with the Loopy crest on it that our guest of honor wore with such distinction when winning the Atlantic Trophy . . ."

Leo's words were lost yet again in another outbreak of cheering, foot-stamping and clapping but he pressed on regardless.

"I now ask Tim Porter, himself a golfer of great talent who has represented our club with distinction on so many occasions, to say a few words before he makes the draw."

Tim made his way to the microphone, where Leo stood close to him, unwilling to relinquish any of the limelight.

"Ladies and gentlemen, it is a very great pleasure for me to draw the winning ticket for the raffle. As my good friend Leo said, Larry Lynch wore that sweater with honor right through the week. Let me be the very first to say that he accomplished something I myself never managed to do, he *won* the damn thing!"

This was greeted with the loudest applause yet.

"So without further ado, I will pick a ticket out of the hat. It is number . . . let me see . . . number one hundred and thirty! And the name on it is . . . oh, it's so hard to read this handwriting after all the hospitality, but I'll do my best . . . the name is Miss Amy *Linhurst*. There she is, ladies and gentlemen, seated at the table over there. Stand up, Amy, and let the people see how gorgeous you are."

More cheering and hooting as a blushing Amy reluctantly rose to her feet and then, spurred by some unseen prompting, called back to Tim, "I'm giving it back to the club!"

Tim was in his element. "What a wonderful gesture, ladies and gentlemen. Doubly so, if I may say so, since it was Amy who gave that very sweater to our hero of the hour just a few weeks ago. Now she is giving it back to the club, who will, no doubt, put it on display. The money raised from the raffle goes to the Simon Community to help them look after those less fortunate than ourselves. Now I hand you back to our master of the revels, our good friend Leo Martin!"

Leo took the microphone in a grip of steel and bawled into it, "Thank you, Tim, and thank you, Amy, for being so sporting as to donate the sweater to the club. Allied Banks of Ireland, as I have said, is delighted to play host to you all tonight. Now that I mentioned the bank, I have something to tell you."

O'Hara was by now at the end of his tether. He wanted to scream in a voice loud enough to be heard at the back of the marquee, *You're closing it down, that's what you're going to shagging tell us!* Instead, he rose to his feet, made his excuses to the PR man seated next to him, and made his way through the tables to exit. He had almost made it to the back of the marquee before Loopy or anyone else at the top table quite realized what was happening. Leo was still droning on, oblivious to having one less listener.

"Ladies and gentlemen, you may have heard, as I did, the ridiculous rumors flying around that our bank is going to close. Well, I am here to give you my solemn assurance that the Trabane branch of Allied Banks of Ireland is to remain open. Not only that, but it will shortly undergo a major refurbishment to cater for the extra business we so confidently predict will come from a thriving seaside community like ours."

A burst of applause greeted Leo's words, even though some in the audience might not agree that Trabane was thriving. Even if the bank *was* staying open, the Maltings continued to leak jobs like a sieve. Still, as they came to grips with what Leo was saying, his listeners gabbled excitedly to each other. A dutiful smattering of applause came from those at the top table, while cries of "C'mon, the village!" drifted up from the back of the marquee. Sensing that it was now or never, the PRO leapt to his feet, clapping wildly and shouting "Bravo!" at the top of his voice. Others followed his example and got to their feet, cheering and clapping. O'Hara's early exit was already forgotten by the few who had noticed it. The standing ovation, contrived though it was, obviously heartened Leo, for he picked up where he had left off in even better voice.

"So now that you have heard it from the horse's mouth"—here he paused for a laugh that did not come—"I hope we will hear no more nonsense about closures. Allied Banks of Ireland is a fixture in Trabane and, like the town itself, will go from strength to strength.

"And now, ladies and gentlemen, the moment you all have been waiting for. Without further ado"—Leo particularly liked the ring of that phrase and was determined to make it his own—"as I say, without further ado, it is my very great pleasure to introduce you to our guest of honor, whose thrilling victory in the Atlantic Trophy we are all here to celebrate. He warned me earlier that he will only say a few, a *very* few, words. Fair enough, I told him, just continue to let your golf clubs do the talking for you. So now I'll ask you one and all to put your hands together for"—a dramatic pause before he bellowed—"Loopy *Lynch*!"

The noise threatened to bring the marquee down as Loopy took hold of the microphone. He almost let it slip from his grasp for his hands were lathered in sweat. His left leg was twitching uncontrollably, and he badly wanted a sip of water to ease the dryness in his throat. In the circumstances he did well to make himself heard in a voice little more than a croak.

"Thank you, ladies and gentlemen. I'm not going to thank anyone in particular because so many of you all have helped me in one way or another. The only person I'm going to single out is my mother. Stand up, Mam, and let them get a good look at you."

With a whispered "I'll kill him for this when I get him home," Brona rose to thunderous applause, smiled, and bowed her head. Then, having experienced her fifteen seconds of fame, she sank back into her seat, grateful that the ordeal was over as her son continued:

"The only other thing I want to do is to thank the people of Trabane who have supported me up on the hurling field, the golf course, and in other ways I won't even talk about. I'll never forget you, and I just want to say a great big thanks to each and every one of you for giving me the night of my life."

As Loopy took his seat to ever more cheering, he saw out of the corner of his eye someone running up to Sergeant Keane, who was seated at the same table Pat O'Hara had so suddenly vacated. Whatever was being whispered into his ear, it caused the sergeant to stiffen and his jaw to drop in horror. He left his seat and hurried out the exit at the back of the marquee, closely followed by Father Spillane. Their sudden departure sparked off a buzz of speculation that quickly turned to consternation when news of the accident filtered up to where Loopy was sitting. Linda rushed up to him, her eyes brimming with tears.

"There's been a crash, a terrible . . ."

She buried her head in her hands, weeping uncontrollably. Then, regaining some of her composure, she sobbed, "Pat O'Hara crashed into a wall. Someone who saw it said he was swerving to avoid a dog, a young spaniel. He lost control of the car. It sounds bad. *Very* bad. We're going there right now. You'd better stay. You *are* the guest of honor, after all."

"Guest of honor be damned. I'm going with you."

T he church was packed to overflowing as Father Spillane read the mass for the dead. Pat O'Hara would have appreciated the irony of *De profundis clamavi*—"from the depths I cry." It was the traditional prayer for the dead and one of the few remaining traces of Latin to survive in the Roman faith. Its mournful, meaningless phrases rolled around the parish church like summer thunder breaking over the bowed heads of the congregation, many of whom had been pupils of the deceased.

Loopy remembered O'Hara's love of Latin and his disgust at its neglect by a succession of popes. It would have cost O'Hara his job to openly criticize in the classroom the changes wrought by the Vatican, but the Golf Club bar was another matter.

"It wasn't enough for the eejits to remove it from the school curriculum. No way. They had to go and translate all those grand prayers that no one understood back into English. Did you ever hear the like? *Orate fratres* sounds a damn sight better when you don't have a clue what it means. Now we have some big lump of a farmer's son in a dog collar roaring, 'Let us pray, brothers!' and it's not the same thing at all, at all. No mystery, y'see, that's the trouble. Apart altogether from it getting up the noses of every woman from here to Rome who wants to know why there's no shagging mention of the sisters!"

When Loopy would ask O'Hara what possible use a dead language could be to anyone, he would just sigh and roll his eyes to heaven. Now incense hung in the air, blending with his beloved Latin to make a powerful cocktail of sorrow as candles flickered on the altar where the soul of Pat O'Hara was being commended to God with all the pomp and ceremony that Father Spillane could produce.

Loopy and Margaret, the only surviving relative, were sitting in the front row, flanked by Brona and the children. Margaret had invited them to join her, otherwise she would have had to sit there by herself all through the mass, an ordeal in itself.

"Poor Pat always spoke highly of you and your family, so it's only right that you should keep me company as I mourn his passing."

The school choir sang "Amazing Grace," their shrill young voices a reminder that for three decades or more their teacher had prepared the youth of Trabane for the life that he had just departed. As the mass ended, Father Spillane sprinkled holy water over the wooden coffin that held the mortal remains of Pat O'Hara. Then it was time for his final journey.

The road from the church to the cemetery ran through the town. All the shops along the route had closed their doors for the procession's passing. Foley's pub had already disgorged its customers onto the pavement. Caps in hand, they bared their heads, and some went so far as to drop to their knees in silent tribute to a departed friend and, until recently, fellow drinker. Some of them went so far as to suggest that had O'Hara still been drinking, he would never have seen the dog, much less killed himself trying to avoid it. That way, the Linhurst girl might be missing a dog, but O'Hara would still have been to the good.

Loopy, walking behind the hearse, his arm linked with Margaret's, fought back the tears and wondered bitterly if the Irish had more respect for the dead than the living. *Here's someone who gave all his life to teaching the kids of this town,* he told himself, *and what did he get in the end? A lousy funeral with three bloody wreaths and a dozen mass cards. Some thanks for a lifetime's work! I hope to God there'll be a better turnout for my funeral when the time comes.*

The wreaths had been sent by the GAA, the Golf Club, and his sister-in-law, Margaret. Seamus Norbert had sent a mass card on behalf of the Trabane Gaels—this despite O'Hara's proud boast that he had never attended a GAA match in his entire life. Another card, placed on the lid of the coffin by Leo Martin in person, promised that a solemn, requiem mass would be offered for the soul of the recently departed. The irony of this would not have been lost on the deceased, for it came from Allied Banks of Ireland. Loopy sent a mass card, as did Brona and the girls. Whom the rest were from he didn't even bother to look.

The night before, Pat O'Hara had lain in state in his own small house. A long queue snaked down the street, waiting to pay their respects. Margaret, dressed in black, stood next to the open coffin, accepting the sympathy of those who filed past. She said the same thing to Loopy as she had to everyone else: "Sure God took him in His own good time."

Loopy couldn't bear to look at the corpse as he offered Margaret his condolences. He preferred to remember his friend as the jubilant figure he was at the Atlantic Trophy, leaping up and down and screeching with excitement, "Attaboy, Lynch, good man yourself! We'll show 'em what you're made of!"

Loopy was just beginning to realize how much he was going to miss his friend, cantankerous and difficult though he might have been. O'Hara had warned him sternly that drawing strength from the old fort was all well and good, but from now on whatever strength Loopy needed would have to come from within.

"You'll find there'll be no forts where you're going, my lad. What'll you do then? You'll have to look inside *yourself*, that's what! From now on, *that's* where you'll have to get your strength, and never forget it!"

A week later O'Hara was dead. Loopy was glad O'Hara had had those magic days at the golf tournament. He seemed to have found a new vigor in walking every inch of every hole that Loopy had played. He led the cheering as the crowds grew larger the closer Loopy got to the final victory. O'Hara would turn to complete strangers during a lull in play and proclaim loudly, "Played his first round of golf with me, y'know. Right from the start I could see that he was something special!"

Loopy remembered O'Hara's bear-hug moments after Loopy had received the huge silver cup. How often had he heard him say that a lifetime's teaching would be worth it all if he could produce one, just one, pupil who had done well because of him. Loopy hoped more than anything else in heaven or earth that those few days at The Atlantic had made the schoolteacher's empty life seem a bit more worthwhile.

Almost without Loopy's realizing it, they were at the graveside. An angry mound of fresh earth, glistening in the rain, was heaped beside the dark rectangle into which the coffin would be lowered. But first came the prayers for the dead, doleful mantras promising life eternal far beyond the grave. These were followed by a decade of the rosary given out by Father Spillane, with Margaret at his shoulder mouthing the responses in a dull monotone. Ten Hail Marys and one *Pater Noster* . . . "Our Father, who art in heaven . . . hallowed be Thy name . . . Thy kingdom come . . ."

For Loopy, his gaze shifting from the coffin to the waiting grave, it seemed to take forever. Suddenly the droning stopped, even if the rain still pounded mercilessly on the forest of umbrellas surrounding the open grave. The polished timber and silver handles of the coffin were flecked with raindrops reflecting the last rays of a weak, watery sun trying desperately to break through the dull, gray overcast. Then it was time to step forward and help lower his old friend into the earth. As he did so, he renewed the vow he had made minutes earlier.

I'll be the one. I'll show them that you did *make a difference for at least one of your pupils, so rest easy, old friend.*

. . .

The Golf Club had laid on a meal for those who had attended the funeral. Loopy, without even meaning to, found himself behind the counter, helping Linda. She needed him as the crowd was growing bigger by the minute. It was better that he had something to do rather than sitting grief-stricken between his mother and Margaret, who was still receiving the condolences of everyone who passed by:

"Ah, sure, wasn't he the lovely man, God rest his soul." Followed by Margaret's unchanging reply: "God took him in His own good time!"

Loopy was so busy bringing plates of sandwiches and trays of drinks to the tables that he barely noticed the arrival of Joe Delany and Edward Linhurst. They were waiting at the door for Amy. When she joined them, Loopy saw that she was wearing a long, black leather coat. Suitably funereal and yet very smart, he thought as he directed them to a table not far from where his mother and Margaret were sitting.

"Hello, Amy." He gave her a big hug. "Good to see you. You're looking great. Now what will you have? The usual?"

Linhurst threw a quizzical look at his daughter. "The usual" suggested a degree of intimacy of which he was not aware.

Joe was in first. "A pint of stout and a ham sandwich for me."

"Same for me," Linhurst intoned, adding, "and the usual for Amy, whatever that may be."

After Loopy had gone to bring their order, noticing the look of surprise on her father's face, she explained quietly, "Loopy and I have been seeing quite a bit of each other. Enough for him to know what I eat and drink anyway."

"Nobody tells me anything round here."

"Well, you never asked, did you? We met on the beach the morning after I ate the head off him for bringing you home pissed."

Linhurst made as if to say something, but she cut him short with an impatient wave of her hand. "I apologized and told him I was wrong."

Well, that's a first, for sure! Linhurst left the thought unspoken.

"He accepted my apology and then we got to talking about this and that. I mentioned that I was doing a viability check on the Maltings and he set me right about a few things. So much so that I more or less changed my mind and recommended that instead of shutting the place down, they should expand the operation instead. Looks as though that's exactly what they are going to do."

"About Loopy and me—as you know, I've been away most of the time since then, but we've kept in touch by phone." After a pause she added, as much to herself as anyone else, "He's a really nice guy, once you get to know him. He's coming back now, so talk about something else."

"Two pints of stout, a plate of sandwiches, and a gin and tonic with lemon but no ice for the lady."

"Sit down here for God's sake," Joe insisted. "I'd better go and help Linda behind the bar for a while."

He left and Loopy took his seat next to Edward Linhurst, who muttered in his ear, "Didn't realize you two were friendly. Friendly enough to know what she drinks anyway."

Amy cut in, "Don't let him drag anything out you, Larry. He's awfully curious behind that calm exterior, is my dear father. Simply must know everything about anything, that's him."

Suddenly Joe was back. He said to Loopy, "Linda has just reminded me that there's a registered letter in the shop for you. In all the excitement over the funeral, I forgot about it. I'll get it for you now."

As Joe left, Edward Linhurst turned to Loopy. "I've been wanting to ask you this. Have you decided yet what are you going to do with yourself now?"

Loopy played for time, not quite sure what Linhurst meant. "How do you mean?"

"I mean, are you going to look for a job or something? You could always stay here and help in the bar while living at home with your mother, I suppose, but there's not much of a future in it, is there?"

Loopy nodded glumly. "I suppose you're right. I hadn't really enough time to think about it properly these past few days but—"

Just then Joe Delany rejoined them with the letter. "Arrived here yesterday."

It was addressed to Laurence Lynch, Esq., c/o Trabane Golf Club.

Loopy examined it before opening it. "What does *Esq.* mean?"

" 'Esquire.' It's almost never used nowadays, except by a certain class of person . . ." Linhurst might have elaborated further had not his daughter again cut him short, her eyes firmly fixed on Loopy.

"English upper class actually. It's just another of those silly hangovers from Daddy's generation." Amy held Loopy's gaze, glad that the ordeal of the funeral was done with and that his eyes were no longer reddened from grief. Usually they were nice eyes, she reminded herself, big brown ones. The sort of eyes she could gaze into for a long, long time.

Joe Delany, however, was more interested in the contents rather than the form of address of the letter. "Can't you open it for God's sake and see what's in it?"

"I wonder who this is from?" Loopy muttered.

Joe was becoming agitated. "Well, you're not going to find out till you open the bloody thing, are you!"

Wordlessly Loopy ripped open the envelope and straightened out the folds of the heavy vellum notepaper, whose heading was Allied Banks of Ireland in embossed print.

Dear Mr. Lynch,

I was greatly taken by the manner in which you comported yourself during our match. Nothing I have learned since then has caused me to alter that view. I have no idea what you intend doing with the rest of your life, but in case you are undecided about what career to pursue, I would suggest that you read the attached form carefully. As you will see, it is an application for the post of junior executive in our Public Relations Bureau, where I anticipate there will be some vacancies in the very near future.

Usually there is an educational requirement, but I feel the Board of Directors would look favorably on your application if you were to indicate that you were prepared to study for graduation while in our employ. As for the job itself, it requires a young person of pleasant personality with as broad a range as possible of sporting expertise. I am reliably informed that your prowess with the hurley almost matches that with your golf clubs.

Should you wish to apply for this position, a letter of reference is required. You should have no problem in obtaining one. I would ask you one favor in return. As the interviewing panel will almost certainly include myself, please do not indicate that we are already acquainted, as this may give the wrong impression to the other members of the interviewing board.

Yours faithfully,
Andrew Villiers-Stewart, Bart.

Joe Delany spluttered a profanity. Amy clapped her hands in delight and bent across the table to kiss Loopy full on the lips— something that did not escape his mother's notice a few tables distant.

Edward Linhurst gave a low whistle and said, "Looks like he's practically offering you the job. I advise you to grab it while it's there. It'll allow you to play all the golf you want and get paid for doing it without losing your amateur status. You can have that reference from me, if you want. I still put quite a bit of business their way, which may be of some help."

Suddenly it all became too much for Loopy. He almost broke down, blinking back the tears. Amy put her arm around his heaving shoulders. It was her turn to whisper into his ear occasionally, but most of the time she just sat there with her arm around his shoulders, a comforting presence.

Out of the corner of her eye Brona saw everything, but chose to stay where she was. Her son seemed to be in good hands, and anyway, Margaret was halfway through describing her last visit to Rome and how she'd nearly met the pope. Joe Delany and Edward Linhurst sat in silence, averting their gaze from the young couple by drinking their pints and working their way through the plate of sandwiches.

When Loopy regained his composure, he muttered to no one in particular, "I *know* it's him. He's up there already, smiling to himself and pulling strings. I *know* it!"

The others nodded wordlessly and raised their glasses skyward.